I0629074

DEAD GUILTY

(Previously published as AN ACT OF REPARATION)

By

Susan Godenzi

Copyright © 2013 Susan Godenzi

The right of Susan Godenzi to be identified as the Author
of the Work has been asserted by her.

All characters in this publication are fictitious and any
resemblance to real persons, living or dead, is purely
coincidental.

Cover designed by Susan Godenzi

Photo supplied by Shutterstock

Dedication

For my husband Neale, Mr Wonderful, who is helping me make all of my dreams come true. For my mother Adelaide, who taught me to dream. And my son Lewis.

To my lovely friends who helped me in the beginning with loads of encouragement and coffee dates. Especially Julie, who did the first read through.

CHAPTER ONE

She knew she was far too excited to listen to music while she ran, so she left her iPod on the kitchen bench. Pulling her recently dyed blonde hair into a high ponytail, Lexie Reed put on her running shoes, grabbed her keys, and let herself out of the house.

Running down Meredith Street, Lexie noted every second car was either a BMW or an Audi, her Elwood neighbours had been moving up the social-ladder in her absence. She ran to Marine Parade, turned left and headed toward Brighton. Late morning, and mid-week, there weren't too many people about. A few mothers jogging, pushing prams that looked as though as they might require their own trailers. Running alone along the bike/pedestrian track felt luxurious after the running tracks in New York, which were getting as congested as the roads and city streets.

Lexie felt that Melbourne had a sense of peace and calm that had been missing in New York. She was back in her hometown now, only a matter of weeks, after living the previous five years in New York. And she was ready to start the next stage of her life.

She ran past the Life Saving Club, where a primary school was on an excursion. There were screams and squeals of delight coming from a bunch of ten year olds as they splashed each other in the shallows of Port Phillip Bay. The sounds pricked her eyes with tears.

At twenty minutes she turned around and headed for home. She had her pitch ready for Megan Kestler, editor-in-charge of *Contemporary Woman*, whom she was meeting at one o'clock. Lexie let herself back into the house, kicked off her runners and headed straight to the bathroom.

While the water heated for the shower, she undid her hair and scratched her scalp, itchy from sweating, then ran her fingers through her hair. She inspected her face in the mirror. The last few years of disappointments were starting to show; there was an obvious sadness in her brown eyes, which she tried to disguise with heavy eye make-up. Lexie was sensible enough to know she was attractive, but that didn't mean she always felt it. When the shower screen steamed up, she stepped under the water.

Checking herself in her bedroom's full-length mirror, Lexie didn't so much approve of the outfit but she knew that Megan would. She was aiming for Modern Woman. Lexie remembered a statement Megan had made many years ago, which meant today Lexie had to wear those high-heels. She looked at her runners with fondness.

Lexie screamed when she checked the time. Ten minutes before one o'clock! She'd lost all track of time trying different outfits on. She would just make it - if she was lucky and found a car park straight up. She snatched up her bag and ran, as best she could in the heels, down the path to her car. When she got to it, she realised that the keys were still on the kitchen bench, along with her mobile phone.

She couldn't get into her car, or her house, or use the phone to let Megan know that she'd be late. Panic niggled in Lexie's fingers. She shook her hands to get rid of the sensation. She'd been organised, had the timing all worked out: how long to run, when to shower.

'No, no, just start walking, you don't have time to get in a flap,' she said out loud. 'You won't be all that late.'

She took off walking toward St Kilda, careful not to twist an ankle. No sooner had Lexie crossed the street separating her suburb of Elwood and St Kilda, than cars started to slow down as they approached her. When the first car slowed and lowered its window, Lexie was expecting to be asked directions. She'd not been prepared for, 'How much? And can you leave the heels on?'

She ignored the kerb crawlers that followed, concentrating on the footpath in front of her, trying to convince herself that Megan wouldn't be too angry when

Lexie arrived fifteen minutes late for their meeting, and then proceeded to beg for a job.

Lexie didn't cry when she noticed the large, round, raindrops hitting the concrete footpath. She realised that crying wasn't going to help. Her makeup was probably going to run anyway, due to the sweat that was forming on her forehead, and the rain that was getting heavier by the second. Tears would only add to the carnage that had already begun.

The start of Acland Street was in her sights; she was almost there. Megan Kestler was scary at the best of times, and today Lexie thought, was going to be a real test of their relationship. She started to swagger. She had two blocks to build the pretensions of confidence. Grabbing her hair, she squeezed as much rainwater out as she could, then tossed her head back, pushed her shoulders back and started to laugh, hoping that the bluster would save her.

Lexie made sure to keep a smile plastered on her face as she entered the café. She spotted Megan immediately, even though it had to be close to six years since she'd last seen her. The woman had an aura of sophistication and authority about her. Lexie imagined she could see a little black cloud hovering over Megan's head, threatening to break at any moment. She had an empty cup in front of her and Lexie could see that she was probably very close to leaving.

She continued her swagger all the way to Megan's table, laughing as she approached. 'Megan, my God, you won't believe what a puddle of trouble I've got myself into,' Lexie said as she looked about for the Ladies' Room. 'I'll just go freshen up, as the American's say. I won't be a tick.'

Lexie washed away the make up that had turned into a ghoulish mess. Grabbing several paper towels, she dried off what she could, and strutted back to Megan's table.

The bravado crumbled when saw the look of concern on her prospective employer's face. She dropped down on the seat opposite.

'Megan, I'm so, so sorry. I locked myself out of my car, and my house, and my mobile was inside, so I couldn't ring you, or anyone. I've never done that before, ever! I tried to get here as fast as...well, these stupid shoes, I couldn't even walk fast, let alone run...'

'Take a breath, girl! I had a latte and I had,' Megan tipped her head towards the counter and smiled, 'something very nice to look at while I waited.' Holding up two fingers, she indicated for two more coffees for the table.

Lexie's eyes followed Megan's directions, taking in the very attractive dark-skinned man at the cash register. 'Umm, I see what you mean.'

'I know it's been a long time, but I do remember that punctuality was always one of your strong points. So, I figured that something had to have happened to delay you, and you wouldn't be too far off. Anyway, I love to watch Marco. I know I can't have him; he belongs to Danielle over there. But, I can still look. So, are you ready to give me your pitch, Lex? I'm all ears!'

Lexie took a deep breath and began her well-practised speech. 'Domestic Violence, or Intimate Partner Violence,' Lexie made inverted commas in the air. 'Which is the latest term for a practice that's been around since Adam first took a swing at Eve.'

Megan looked troubled and leaned in closely and asked, 'And why that particular topic, Lexie?'

'When Doug and I first moved to New York, I became friends with a woman in our building: Ava. We got on almost instantly. However, whenever I tried to get close to her, or if I suggested couples activities, Ava would put distance between us. She would avoid me for weeks at a time, and then make attempts to resume our friendship, without explanations. I found it very confusing, but I also felt at the time that it was something I shouldn't push. I was worried that she was suffering from depression,' Lexie lower her head in an attempt to conceal her shame. 'It was only after her husband killed her that I found out that he'd been abusing Ava for years! I was devastated that I could be so near to something like that and not see it. I believed I had been the worst kind of friend. I had totally let her down with my ignorance.'

Lexie looked at Megan before she continued. She had her full attention.

'I wanted to make amends. Last year I did a workshop at NYU on reporting of Intimate Partner Violence; my plan is to go into women's crisis shelters, interview women and their children if I'm allowed. There are several shelters willing to allow me in their doors and I've got several experts to include in my story for resources—mental health professionals, GPs. I have a professor at a Melbourne university, an expert in Women's Studies.' Lexie stopped and took a breath.

'This is good, Lex, very good. And topical; now is the perfect time for something like this. The magazine could do with a shot of decent commentary. How long do you think it would take? How much time for the research alone? Though you sound as though you've already made a start on that,' Megan sounded charged. 'Are you looking at one article, or a series?'

'Megan, I'm not sure if you're aware, but I've come back to Australia alone, because, well, I...Doug and I got divorced. I'm in a position now where I need money to start coming in sooner rather than later. That brought me to the idea of your magazine, and a regular monthly feature for as long as I have the material. There are so many different angles for this,' Lexie sat back and drank her latte, panic taking over. What if Megan didn't go for it, what then?

'I had heard about you and Doug, and I'm sorry, darling. That prick never deserved a woman of your calibre. Now, I can't make a decision like this on my own. I've got to get the gang together, brainstorm, the lawyers and accountants, blah, blah, blah. Contracts, etc, etc...But, Lexie, let me just say, that I'm very excited.'

*

Four days later, Lexie sat in her car, parked in the garage. Her mobile phone lay in her lap. She was expected at her mother's house in half an hour for pre-dinner drinks. Visits to her mother's were never going to be any different. They would always start with time spent trying to think of excuses for not going, and they would always end with Lexie feeling that she had disappointed her mother, yet again, and always. She hadn't heard from Megan Kestler, so she couldn't tell her mother that at least she'd got a job.

She'd been sitting in her little white Peugeot for ten minutes, trying to think of an excuse. *Some writer you are*, she berated herself, *where's your imagination*? She stared at the phone.

She jumped as it started to ring and almost dropped it as she snapped out of her stupor. 'Hello?' she said, not taking notice of the caller ID.

'Lex, love, it's Megan Kestler, your new boss! Welcome to the team. Ten o'clock tomorrow morning, my office, we'll go through our proposal with you. I think you're going to love it.' Megan didn't attempt to suppress her excitement.

'Fantastic! I'll be there,' Lexie said. She put her phone in her bag, started the car and reversed out. With the earlier sense of dread now gone, she headed toward her mother's house, the sudden autumn downpour not standing a chance of dampening her elation and relief.

*

'Oh, Alexis, you're soaked. Wait there while I grab you some towels. No, don't walk on the tiles! Stay right where you are.' Erica Reed was the only person to call Lexie by her full name. Lexie felt it was just one more sign of the lack of affection from her mother. She loved her mother, but they didn't share a friendship. When she crossed the threshold to her Erica's house, she was eternally fourteen years old.

'Here, you can change into these. Your sister left them here after her last visit with the boys. Probably more appropriate than what you're wearing anyway.' Erica left

Lexie at the front door, and went to see to the dinner preparations.

In her old bedroom, Lexie lectured herself: 'Don't let it get to you. You are thirty-nine years old, for God's sake! Her words have no bearing on your life. Have a drink, eat dinner, and give her the good—no the *great* news—and leave. It's simple, suck it up, girl.' She smiled when she saw her reflection in the mirror. Her sister Dana was at least two sizes larger and liked her clothes baggy, so the effect was comical on Lexie's slight frame.

'I'm in the living room, Alexis. What will you drink, a Manhattan? That seems appropriate,' Erica called out.

'Sounds great, Mum, thanks,' said Lexie, knowing that her mother was now trying to make up for her earlier barbed comment. 'How's Dad's golf tour going? Got a date for his return yet?' She took her drink and sat on the sofa.

'He's still got two more weeks away. He loves these seniors' tours; catches up with the old crowd.' Erica had been a golf widow for many years. Lexie believed that her mother was more than happy with the role.

'I received some fantastic news just before I left home,' said Lexie. 'I have been commissioned to write an on-going series for *Contemporary Woman* magazine. So I'll be earning a living, finally.'

'Is that the one with that dreadful Megan Kestler? I've never liked that woman!' Erica responded as expected.

'Yes, that's the one. Megan is the editor-in-charge,' Lexie shrugged off the comment. 'I'll be writing about domestic violence in Australia.'

'And what do you know about domestic violence, Alexis? You're not going to tell me that Douglas hit you, and now you're going to tell the world about it? Is that why you got divorced?'

'No, Mother, Doug never laid a finger on me,' Lexie stifled a groan. 'I know a lot about domestic violence because, as a journalist, I do research. That's my job—it's what I do. Anyway, I'm very excited about the future. So now, what's for dinner?'

It would be a waste of time explaining any of it to her mother. She would more than likely be of the opinion that it would only be a problem for the lower classes of society. So it was best to stick to safer subjects, such as the weather, and meals, and what her dad was up to.

'Have you heard from Douglas since you arrived back in Melbourne?' Erica asked.

'No, I haven't. And I don't expect to either. We are divorced, after all. The last I heard, from mutual friends, was that he'd met someone, and they're getting married in October.' Saying it aloud hurt Lexie just that bit more.

'All that time together, and for what?' Erica said. 'I just don't understand.'

'Mother, I'd rather not talk about any of this, OK? Can we just eat? I've got an early start tomorrow, so I won't be able to stay late.' Lexie really wanted to leave now.

'Right then, vegetable lasagne and salad. No need to cook meat with your father away. Will you have a wine?' Erica busied herself dishing up their meal.

'No, thanks, that Manhattan was enough. Dinner looks lovely,' Lexie was tired of the same conversational seesawing.

CHAPTER TWO

Detective Senior Sergeant Wil Saddington was aware of his mobile phone vibrating in his pocket. It had been going off every couple of minutes for the past half hour, but he continued to ignore it.

'Monica, please! This isn't necessary,' Wil pleaded.

'Just because you keep saying it, Wil, doesn't make it so,' Monica said to Wil while looking at the mediator, as if seeking assistance. This was their third visit, and they were no closer to a settlement than when they first walked into the office three weeks before.

'Wil, as I've stated to you before, your wife has made it very clear that there will not be any reconciliation,' the mediator intercepted. 'The divorce will be happening. This is your chance to allow it to be more private, less traumatic for both of you. By all means, get yourself a solicitor, go through the courts, if you feel the three of us can't work things out in here.'

'Why can't you believe that I've changed, Mon? I'll prove it. We can go to couples counselling! I've already booked an appointment with that Relationships Australia,' Wil said, not looking Monica in the eye.

'Oh, let me guess—you drove past their office, saw the sign and thought, *Yeah, that'll do, that's what she wants*. Well, it's not what I want anymore. That might have helped three or four years ago, but not now. Now, all I want is out,' Monica rose from her chair. 'Thank you, Mr Pinson, but I don't think this is working for me. I'll go ahead with my solicitor for the divorce. I presume they will contact you for any relevant information you can give them. Thank you for your time and patience.'

Turning to Wil, she said, 'Wil, from now on, everything goes through the solicitors, so go get yourself one, OK? Goodbye, gentlemen.'

Wil watched his wife walk out of the office. He felt drained of all energy. Reality was hard to swallow and a huge wad of sorrow stuck in his chest.

'Wil, I'm sorry things haven't worked out. Can I get you anything—water, coffee?'

'No, no thanks. What I want has just walked out. And I guess I'd better get out of your way too.' Wil shook the man's hand without enthusiasm, and walked out onto busy Bell Street.

In the white glare of mid-morning, he stood, stunned. The sun clawed at his eyes. For the first time in his life, he didn't know what he was supposed to do next. Then his pocket vibrated again.

'Shit!'

He read the last text message sent from Senior Sergeant Terry Hanly: *66 Salisbury Street, Coburg East. Whenever you're ready, princess. Guy's not going to get any deader, I guess!*

Wil got into his unmarked police car and pushed his way into the eastbound traffic. He was only about two kilometres away from Salisbury Street. Despite the short distance, the heavy traffic meant the trip was going to take longer than he wanted, adding to his frustration.

In Salisbury Street, Wil was busy smacking the steering wheel after two failed attempts to park the Commodore, when he saw a police cruiser further up the street take off. He sped up the block, happy to finally catch a break. His first victory for the day.

It was obvious which house was the crime scene— blue and white checked tapes were strung up from fence posts and trees, flapping in the breeze. Wil was fishing out his ID ready for the first officer, but got waved through, the tape lifted for him to duck under. Curious neighbours hung around in clusters. Wil noted the uncut lawn and untended garden. An old dirty doll lay abandoned under a tree near the front window. Wil could see Terry inside the house, holding court, clipboard in hand. As soon as he saw Wil, Terry made a note on his attendance sheet.

'Jesus! Who found the poor bastard?' Wil said as he entered the house, taking in the crime scene. The body,

18

dead for many hours, was still on the living room floor. The blood, now black and glutinous, had left the head in a gush and reached the far ends of the rug. While the arms and legs, splayed out from the torso, appeared normal, the head had been neatly separated into left and right hemispheres. Wil put on the booties Terry handed him.

'Hey, Sads, nice of you to join us. Watch your step now,' Terry indicated a patch of vomit the detective was about to step in.

'What do we have, a delicate axe murderer? Doesn't look like the crime of a hurler.'

Wil wasn't in the mood for any of this, he just wanted to go home and throw himself into his own misery, not that of the poor bastard on the floor.

'No, that'll be from our own man. First On Scene— first scene ever, in fact. Only out of the academy a month, poor prick. Thought we'd need an ambulance for him for a minute there. The neighbour who found the vic and called it in, well, she's been a great comfort to young Constable Davis,' Terry raised his eyebrows and smirked.

Wil peered out the window. He hadn't taken much notice of them when he'd entered the property. He could just make out a woman in a short denim skirt and tight T-shirt, rubbing the back of a young man in a police uniform who was sitting on the low brick fence.

'Is he taking a statement, or asking her out? What the hell's going on, Terry?' Wil's mood was deteriorating fast.

'Julie Asling, neighbour to our victim here, Sean Laidlaw. She states Sean's wife and kids up and left four weeks ago. Ms Julie out there has been doing her civic duty, and paying the occasional house call on young Sean here, in the hope of whatever. Your guess is as good as mine. Anyway, she said she was on her way over to *visit*, and, as she approached the house, she saw the door open. She assumed Sean had left it open for her, so she waltzed on in. Wishes now that she hadn't been so bold.' Terry followed Wil's gaze to the sexy redhead. She was still rubbing the constable's back.

Terry shook his head, 'I think she's found Sean's replacement!'

'So she stumbles across her wannabe boyfriend, his head severed in two, and *she's* comforting our latest to the ranks of blue. Tough cookie,' Wil tried to lighten his voice, reining in his emotions. 'She touch anything?'

'Says she didn't. Just turned right around and ran straight back to her house to call us. By the way, what took you so long to get here? Your partner's starting to froth, as he tends to on occasion.'

'None of your damn business, Terry,' Wil cut him off. 'Where is Marty?'

20

'Fine, Boss, be like that. He's sniffing around the bedroom. Back through the hall there, last door on the right. The techs have been through there, but your partner wasn't satisfied. Time to break up the love fest.' Terry headed out to deal with Constable Davis.

'Marty, sorry about the delay, and don't ask, OK?' Wil said as he entered the bedroom. Wil had partnered Detective Senior Sergeant Martin Hanratty for the past five years. While Wil could see how Marty's previous partners couldn't stand working with him, Wil had found that he liked the way Marty worked. Marty was a good detective—it was just that he had lousy people skills. He was all too prone to saying what he thought before thinking about the consequences. He'd rubbed a lot of staff up the wrong way over the years. Wil knew he'd be relying on Marty now more than ever, the way his personal life was looking. 'So, what's your take on this one?'

'Maybe she's come back to talk, things got ugly.' Marty headed out of the bedroom, brushing past Wil. 'He's threatened her, but comes off the bad end of the situation. It looks real personal to me, not some sort of home invasion gone wrong. We'll have to see if there was a lover involved, for either of them. We've got a KALOF out on the wife. Photos of her and the girls are being copied and circulated as well.'

Marty nodded confirmation to the waiting technicians—they could now remove the body.

By three that afternoon the investigation was in full motion. The Major Incident Room was established: photographs of Sean Laidlaw, 'before' shots plus the gruesome 'after' shots, were displayed at the far left side of the Incident Board—the case would build from this point on throughout the investigation.

Before death, Laidlaw appeared to be a confident, good-looking man. Short, wavy brown hair, with brown eyes. His clothing was neat and uninteresting. In death, he was hideous and sinister. All of the officers shuddered when they first saw the pictures.

Enlarged photographs of Jillian Laidlaw, for now their prime suspect, portrayed a different image. Not a hint of confidence in her picture. Shoulder length white-blonde hair, falling forward to shield her face; forlorn and distant pale blue eyes. Photos of the Laidlaws' two daughters, Charlotte and Bonnie, had been placed on the board also, but off to the right of the board—miniature replicas of their Nordic looking mother.

Busy technicians were still setting up desks and computers. Phones were ringing, some going unanswered, others being handled by uniformed officers. The noise level was rising as the room filled. Wil tried to lose himself in his own thoughts, but couldn't put one together with another.

'OK, I think it's time for a meeting. Get what you've got together, and I'll go around the room. Who's ready to start now?'

'I am, Boss,' Constable Davis stood, red-faced. 'Sean Laidlaw doesn't have any convictions, but there've been two incidents where police have been called to the Laidlaw residence. Once in August last year: a neighbour called Fawkner Police Station, concerned about screams coming from 66 Salisbury Street. When officers got to the house, the wife refused any help, said it was just an argument and all was sorted. As she wasn't pressing charges, no action was required. The second incident was only two months ago, 14 January, same thing: neighbour calls, police respond, no charges, no action required.' Davis resumed his seat.

'Good. We've got a place to start,' Wil nodded to the young officer, hoping it conveyed encouragement. He knew that earlier Terry had given the young man a pretty strong verbal spray. 'Looks like our victim was an abuser, and his wife was possibly too scared of him to take out an intervention order. Not that they carry much weight anyway. How many men who breach orders actually end up in jail? It's got to be under fifteen per cent.' Wil was showing empathy, when all he wanted to do was go home and sulk.

'I've got the victim's parents' names and address. Will you and Marty be doing the death notification? Or did you want me to?' Terry said from his desk.

'We'll take it, Terry. Soon as this is wrapped up and things are moving. Thanks.' Wil took the details from the senior sergeant.

Taking her time to arrange her notes, her hands shaking, Constable Melissa Trengrove stood and took a slow deep breath.

'Boss, nothing in our system on Jillian Laidlaw, apart from the incidents Davis mentioned. I'll go online: Google, Facebook, Twitter—maybe she'll pop up somewhere.' She sighed as she sat back down, visibly relieved to have finished.

'Thanks, Mel.' Wil noticed the blotchy red patches on her neck from her nervousness. *Great*, he thought, *I've got to work with a baby, a neurotic and Marty!*

Terry referred to his clipboard. 'I have officers doorknocking the neighbourhood. Techs are going through the vic's computer. Forensics is back already on the fingermarks. Quite a few different marks found throughout the house, no signs of anything being wiped, or even attempts at wiping. The best they've got to work on is a decent mark taken off a photo frame. No hits in the system, but it's something to hang onto for down the track.'

'All right, we've made a start I guess. It's about fifteen hours since the murder occurred. That's a long time, as you're all aware. Marty and I will go inform the vic's parents. As oon as there's any hint of a final autopsy report, I want to know. I'm sure we all know the cause of death: head split in half. But once it's confirmed, and any idea of the weapon, I want that info too. Where is Marty, by the way?' Wil suddenly noticed his partner was missing from the meeting.

Wil checked the men's room, then the canteen. No sign of Marty. While he was in the canteen, Wil realised he'd missed lunch, and was now starving, so he grabbed a salad roll and an iced tea. Half an hour later, he found Marty in their office, on the computer.

'What are you doing in here? Why didn't you just use one of the computers in the MIR?' Wil asked. 'Were you there for any of the meeting?'

'Yeah, yeah, some of it. I had an idea, but there was too much going on in there. It was disrupting my thoughts. The bit the neighbour said, that she didn't think Jillian Laidlaw had any family, that got me thinking—if she didn't have family to turn to, you wouldn't think that she'd go running to his parents when their son was abusing her.' Marty clicked away at the keyboard then sat back, looking pleased with himself.

'I bet I'm right on this. Check this out,' he said. On the screen was a list of women and children's shelters within a ten-kilometre radius of the Laidlaw home. 'I'll bet my entire Judas Priest collection that Mrs Laidlaw and the junior Laidlaws are holed up in one of these places.'

'I'm liking it, I'm liking it a whole lot, Marty. But you can keep your crap collection. Before you go charging into any shelters, though, I'll see if the Laidlaws know where their daughter-in-law and granddaughters are. You get the new connie and Mel to help you sort out a plan for approaching these shelters. I'll go see the parents and be the bearer of bad news.' Wil grabbed his keys off his desk.

*

Back in the unmarked, Wil was happy to be alone for the half hour drive to see the Laidlaws, and not having to argue with Marty about whose turn it was to pick the music. He put in his favourite CD—Miles Davis's *Kind of Blue*—and left the station car park. He drove through familiar back streets heading to the freeway, letting the music wash over him. Once on the freeway, he took several deep therapeutic breaths, then felt his body relax. The late afternoon sun washed the city in a warm egg yolk hue, autumn colours were starting to show themselves here and there. *Everything is changing,* he thought.

Exiting the freeway, the going was slow. The first traffic light he came to turned red. Wil watched with envy when a runner jogged past.

The peak hour traffic inched along. The half hour trip turned into fifty minutes. Wil was feeling sadder the closer he came to his destination. Sadness for himself as well now, as the realisation hit him that he would be alone from now on. He wasn't going to be sharing anything with Monica.

Parking, he checked that the number on the letterbox was the same as in his notes. It was a neat house, precision cut edges to the lawns. Wil walked to the front door, head lowered. He pressed the doorbell, and heard it chime inside the house. Stepping back onto the drive, Wil could see a woman, early sixties, walking toward him from the far end of the garden.

'I thought I heard the doorbell,' she said removing a pair of gardening gloves. 'Can I help you?'

'Mrs Laidlaw?' said Wil.

'Yes, Christine Laidlaw,' she said with a warm smile.

'I'm Detective Senior Sergeant Wil Saddington, with the Moreland Major Incident Unit. I need to speak to you and your husband. Is he here, Mrs Laidlaw?' Wil watched as the woman's smile disappeared.

'Yes, he's inside. My guess is he's nodded off in front of the telly. Come in. Should I be worried?' Christine held the front door open for Wil to enter. She concentrated on slipping off her muddy shoes, then followed Wil inside. 'Wait here a minute I'll just wash my hands, then we'll go and find Ralph,' she said as she left him in the entrance.

'Ralph, wake up dear, there's a policeman here, wants to talk to us,' Christine rubbed her husband's arm.

'Huh? What do you want, you stupid wo...' Ralph Laidlaw sat up straight, looking embarrassed when he spotted Wil.

'Mr Laidlaw, my name is Wil Saddington, I'm a detective with the Moreland Major Incident Unit.' Wil walked up to Ralph and offered his hand, then showed the couple his ID badge.

Christine sat on the end of the couch and indicated to Wil to sit in the remaining armchair.

Wil returned his ID to his pocket and sat down. 'I am sorry to have disturbed you, but I have bad news for you,' Wil paused. 'I have to inform you that your son, Sean, has been killed. A neighbour found Sean's body this morning. His death is suspicious, and we are conducting a murder investigation. I am sorry for your loss.' Wil repeated same old routine words—for a situation that was anything but.

Christine gasped; Wil saw the colour draining from her face. Ralph got up from his armchair, and stood, staring down at Wil. He looked as though he was going to ask Wil something. Wil waited for the man to speak. Instead, he went and sat by his wife's side on the couch. Ralph put an arm around Christine as she sobbed into his chest, neither of them said a word. The husband continued to stare at Wil.

'Do you have other children, Mr Laidlaw?' Wil ventured, unsure what to say at this point, but he had to keep going.

'No, Sean is our only...was our only...' Ralph choked on his words.

'Can I call anyone for you? Do you have any family here in Melbourne?' Wil got his mobile out, ready.

'No, no! It doesn't make any sense.' Ralph gave his handkerchief to his wife. 'Why?'

'We only have limited information. He had been assaulted,' Wil said.

'Who by... How?'

'I can't give you many details at this stage of the investigation. But I can tell you that it was quite violent. Are you aware of any enemies that Sean may have had?' Wil had so many questions, but wasn't sure how far, or how fast, he could go with questioning the devastated couple.

'Oh God! Jillian and the girls, are they all right? Where are they?' Christine screeched, sitting bolt upright.

'I was hoping that you might know their whereabouts. The neighbour, the one who found Sean, told us that Jillian had left with the girls about a month ago. Sean was in the house on his own.'

CHAPTER THREE

Lexie headed north toward Essendon. She was expecting forty minutes for the trip, allowing an extra ten minutes for the leftover morning peak traffic. The traffic along Mt Alexander Road was heavy but flowing. It began to thin the closer Lexie got to the turnoff. Not much had changed on the road since she had last called Melbourne home. The large oak trees were putting on their usual autumn show. Trams clattered along, making the traffic aware of who was boss of the road. Block after block were filled with one- and two-bedroom apartment buildings, occasionally separated with a small park.

Many turns, and four roundabouts later, she turned into McHale court. Lexie found McHale Shelter at the end, tucked into the left hand corner of the cul-de-sac. There wasn't enough room to park, so she turned the car around and drove back to the corner, looking left and right for somewhere to leave her car.

Directly in front of her was a huge red brick church. Lexie turned left out of the court, and then into the car park belonging to St Agnes Cathedral. There weren't any other cars. An old man, busy sweeping the front stairs to the church, turned to Lexie and nodded as she locked the Peugeot. She took that as confirmation she was right to leave the car, and headed off to the shelter, full of a sense of purpose.

The shelter was a large old Edwardian mansion; only it didn't appear so regal now. Broken mould-covered tiles left gaping holes in the roof. An overgrown garden filled with big trees looked spooky, but offered many dark places perfect for hide-and-seek. There was little sign of life, apart from smoke billowing from a neighbour's chimney, a plume of which drifted down across the shelter, giving it an almost haunted look.

Lexie opened the front gate and let herself in, noting that it looked as though it could be anybody's home. There weren't any signs announcing the type of accommodation provided within—it gave no impression that refuge could be sought behind these walls. Lexie figured that was the point, to remain anonymous, unobvious, part-hidden. She couldn't resist the urge to walk the side garden path. She followed it along the north side of the house. It led to a small play area; remnants of children's play lay abandoned, a blue shell sandpit and buckets and spades. There, a cubby-house had been erected against the neighbouring fence. A small table with two little chairs inside, cups of imaginary tea laid out on the table. A missing fence paling gave the little house a broken look. Private children's chatter could be spied on through that gap, Lexie thought.

The playground made Lexie think about children playing here, oblivious, while their mothers were inside the shelter, their lives in tatters and their futures uncertain. She crouched down to pick up a small hair-clip, the sparkle from pink and purple diamantes catching her eye.

'What are you doing?' A man's voice startled Lexie. Losing her balance, she fell forward onto her hands and knees. Embarrassed to have been caught snooping, she jumped up. Still clutching the hair clip in one hand, she brushed the dirt off her knees with the other.

'Sorry, I'm Lexie Reed, I have an appointment with Sonja De Bruin.' Lexie looked up into the man's face. His dark gaze intense as he eyed her up and down. His security guard's uniform did not give Lexie any sense of safety. She could see his muscular arms, and the impressions of his tattoos showed through the stretched white material of his shirt. He looked more thug than protector. He towered over her so that she had to tilt her head back to look up to his face. She shivered.

'Ms De Bruin is *inside*, waiting for you. Please come with me.' He turned and walked back toward the front of the shelter, his authority exerted.

Lexie slipped the hair clip into her coat pocket absent-mindedly. She had to recover herself, and quickly. She didn't want the shelter's director to think she was incompetent. Lexie knew how lucky she was to be allowed to enter the shelter as a journalist. She knew some of her colleagues didn't always instil confidence in the general public, especially those in vulnerable situations.

As she counted her steps up to the front door, she felt her confidence returning. Lexie took a quick look about the entrance hall, noting a poster of a sad and battered woman being given a comforting hug by a Salvation Army officer. Another poster warned of the dangers of using alcohol to *block things out*. The security guard led her to an office in one of the front rooms, and motioned for her to enter. He then walked off further into the house.

A woman, about Lexie's height and size, got up from her chair behind a large antique desk as Lexie entered the room.

'Ms Reed, I'm Sonja De Bruin, Director of McHale Shelter. Come in, sit down.' Her strong accent gave away her country of origin.

'South African, is it I can hear? How long have you been in Australia?' Lexie shook the woman's hand, but didn't feel any friendliness or welcome in it, only the tips of her fingers being offered. She could never understand why women bothered to shake hands if they didn't intend to do it properly. The woman gave a half smile, which appeared to take some effort.

'I came to Melbourne seven years ago. I'd been living and working in Johannesburg, where I was the director of a women and children's crisis centre for many years. The violence toward women in South Africa is a far greater problem than it is in Australia, as I am sure you can imagine. I came to Australia for a change but somehow ended up working in the same field.' As Sonja spoke, her eyes never left Lexie's.

She continued, her next words not so hospitable. 'You being here is not something that I approve of. I have been told by the powers-that-be that I am to give you my full support. They are under the misguided impression that you will be helpful to the cause. Personally, all I can see is trouble.'

'I am sorry you feel that way, Ms De Bruin. I can only give you my word that I have no interest in causing trouble for you, or anyone. I am a professional, and respectful of you and your position. My credentials and background have been checked and approved. My editor, and yes, your department superiors, *do* believe that these articles that I intend to write will help women affected by domestic violence. I can assure you that I am qualified, and that I do care. And I will be appreciative of your support.' Lexie maintained the eye contact.

'You can start tomorrow morning. There are two women here at the moment. I will speak to each of them tonight, and inform them of your intentions. It will be

35

entirely up to them whether they wish to speak to you or not.' Sonja started to get up, but sat back when Lexie responded.

'That seems very unusual. Everything I've heard and read about these places is that they are overrun, and have huge turn-aways. Especially as here you take in homeless women as well. It just seems incredible to me that you'd have such a low number of residents.'

'I can't speak for other shelters, but as far as McHale Shelter goes, we are efficient and effective in finding permanent housing for the women that come to us.' Sonja rose from her chair. 'I will get Eddie to see you out.'

'That won't be necessary, thank you, I'll manage.' Lexie picked up her bag and walked out.

As she left the shelter, Lexie decided that she could understand Sonja's distrust of her occupation. She would just make sure that she proved Sonja wrong. As far as Eddie, well, he was only doing his job—he wasn't there to make friends. But only two women in residence at a women and children's crisis shelter, in inner-Melbourne - that sparked her interest immensely.

CHAPTER FOUR

Wil arrived early at the station on the third day of the investigation. He'd been having trouble sleeping and had been eager to leave his empty apartment. A last look in the bathroom mirror before he'd headed out showed his eyes, as expected, bloodshot and bright blue. With plenty of sleep, Wil's eyes were naturally green but as soon as he started to tire, they began to change colour. It was always a giveaway to those closest to him.

Ignoring the few officers who remained from the nightshift, he went and stared at the photos on the Incident Board, hoping that they would speak to him. The phone suddenly disturbed his contemplation.

'Yes?' Wil barked into the receiver.

'Sads, it's Norm. You sound happy. Not getting any since that gorgeous wife of yours saw the light and left your sorry arse, hey?' Forensic Pathologist and Chief Medical Examiner, Norman Steinberg had been working with Wil for his entire career. 'I've got your forensics report completed—pulled an all-nighter. You want to come down and get it, or will I fax you?'

'Fax me, Norm, baby. I need a good fax,' Wil said, his mood lightened.

'Just for you, Sads, no one else,' Norm laughed as he ended the call.

The fax came through within minutes. The cause of death was no surprise—death was caused by massive head trauma caused by a sharp, heavy implement. What Wil was waiting on was the weapon. Norm was concise with his findings: *One heavy blow to the back of the head. The skull fracture extended in two directions—one to the base of the skull and the other to the top of the skull. Major laceration to the scalp with severe bleeding and spillage of the brain. The laceration was linear, initial impact marked and measured on skull, leading to finding weapon consistent to splitting maul. Suggested weapon used from a height vantage.*

Wil now added the description of the weapon to the Incident Board. He put up the picture that had accompanied the autopsy report, and wrote beside it the description: Splitting maul, also known as a blockbuster, a block splitter, or by its very fitting nickname, the 'Go-devil'.

'Morning, Boss.' Constable Davis was the first of the team to arrive, freshly showered and in neat, pressed uniform.

'Davis, come over here. I've just received the autopsy report. We have a weapon description. Now, what about you, have your formed a theory yet? Got a feeling?'

Wil didn't really care about Davis' theory; even if he did, Wil was fairly confident it'd be wrong. New graduate's first case theories – was a near certainty to be wrong. The asking was meant to be a confidence booster for the young man, to make him feel included.

'I believe it to be a random act of violence, Boss. I think a psychiatric patient, or a person high on drugs, followed Mr Laidlaw and then pushed his way into the house as he arrived home that night. I would like to look for any similar cases,' Davis said, back at his desk, sitting up straight. He turned his computer on ready for the go ahead.

'Yes, yes, good, Davis. Get to it then,' said Wil as he headed to the canteen. It was time for more coffee. He figured Davis couldn't get into any trouble for the moment.

*

Sitting at a table at the far end of the canteen, coffee, egg and bacon roll in front of him, Wil stared at a photo he carried in his wallet—a photo of Monica holding Lucas, a giggling two year old. Wil was back in the moment when he took the picture. Monica was tickling Lucas and laughing, begging Wil to hurry up and take the photo, before she peed her pants. She'd had trouble since giving birth. It had been a very difficult delivery, a series of complications, leading to a hysterectomy.

The devastation of the news that they wouldn't be able to have any more children shut something down inside of Wil. Now, as he thought about that awful time in their history, he recognised it was probably when he first started the slow distancing of himself from Monica.

They both poured all their love into their son, and Wil found that he didn't have a great deal left to give to his wife. He could see that now, but at the time he was too busy burying himself in his work. He now sat with his memories and regrets.

'Sads, you awake, man? You look all trance-like,' Marty put his tray down, not waiting for an invitation. 'You know that shit'll kill you. How can you eat pig for breakfast? How can you eat pig, full-stop?'

'Don't start all that vegan crap of yours, Marty. You tell me one more time that an egg is a chicken's menstrual period and I will shoot you. Eat your porridge and shut up,' Wil laughed, grateful for the distraction.

The canteen was slowly filling; most were single men who had no one at home to share their breakfast with.

The two detectives finished eating breakfast in silence.

*

Excitement was building in the Major Incident Room as the team learned of the weapon they were now looking for. 'Go-devil' could be heard spilling out from several conversations that were going on. Wil hated buzz words, and feared the press getting hold of this one. It was perfect for them. Sensationalism would run riot.

'People, settle down, I want to get this meeting started. OK, so we now know the murder weapon, but I want that to stay within this room, I do not want the press knowing just yet. So keep your mouths shut. Only myself or DSS Hanratty will be making any statements. We have a fingerprint, but no hits so far on any databases. Forensics has found DNA on the picture frame where the print was lifted, but they are having some issues with it. There was mixed DNA from more than one person, and while they can't separate the DNA, they can compare it to a reference sample. It might take some time for them to sort out the individual family members' DNA, which would then leave the perpetrator's. Davis, what have you got?' Wil sat as the constable stood.

'Boss, I have a full description of the victim's wife and children. I went and re-interviewed Ms Asling, the neighbour who discovered the body.' Davis went bright red when the room erupted with whoops, howls and wolf-whistles. Yelling over the top of the noise, he battled on: 'I've printed the description and photos. And I am looking for similar crimes.' He returned to his seat, hating being the new kid, the new connie.

'Didn't we get a description on day one, Connie?' Wil knew he was being just a bit cruel, but still enjoyed asking.

'Yes, Boss, we did. But I thought she might have forgotten something; it was a very stressful time for her,' the still-red constable didn't look up.

'Thank you for your diligence, Davis; keep up the hard work.' Wil could hear a muffled chuckle or two around the room.

'Following what I believe is our best bet, we have four crisis shelters to visit today,' Marty looked at Wil. 'You want in on that? The women that run those places are sure to be man-haters, so I think I'll need back up.'

'You've probably only ever dealt with your own angry mother, I bet, Marty,' Terry laughed.

'Leave my mother out of it, Terry,' Marty wasn't laughing.

'OK, boys, settle down. Yes, I'll be coming with you,' said Wil. 'Mel, any contact with the sister in Canada that the neighbour remembered?' Wil put on his jacket.

'A couple of leads to follow up on today. It's been hard with the time difference, but I feel confident, Boss,' Melissa spoke with a growing sense of assurance.

'Good,' Wil said. 'The rest of you get onto the weapon. Get onto suppliers. Search the neighbourhood again, go through the neighbour statements. Follow up whatever you think might be worthy.'

Wil and Marty got ready to leave, their usual routine started.

'There is no way in hell we are listening to your shit today. I've barely slept; you want cranky, I'll give you cranky. Play that head-banging bullshit music, and you won't recognise me,' Wil looked Marty square on, daring him. 'I swear to God, Marty.'

'All right, keep your cool, man; you're embarrassing yourself here. Compromise, hey? We'll just have a little classic Zeppelin, to calm your nerves.' Marty got into the passenger seat of the unmarked car they'd been assigned for the day.

'Your understanding of compromise is a little off track, Marty.' Wil sat in the driver's seat. 'Right, where to first, navigator slash detective slash head-case?' Wil shook his head as Marty produced a Led Zeppelin CD and slipped it into the car's stereo.

'Turn right at the crematorium, stay on Boundary Road til you pass Northern Golf Club, then it's the first on the right, Barak Court—Barak Shelter. It'll only take five minutes to get there. I think they name the shelters after whichever court they are located in. I don't know what sort of reception we'll get, hostile most likely.' Marty sat back and sang along quietly.

*

'So you think she was telling the truth?' Marty was his usual self: suspicious first, maybe trusting later. The first shelter had resulted in nothing.

'Yes, and next one, Marty, let me do the talking. We've got to learn to be more sensitive with people. These people aren't harbouring criminals; they are protecting victims. So tone it down a bit. Now, where to next?' Wil wondered just how many times he'd had this very same conversation with Marty over the years.

'It's on the other side of Essendon Airport. Trevalyan Shelter, Trevalyan Court. And I am very happy for you to do the talking. Have you been talking to that boy of your's lately? You haven't mentioned Lucas in a while.' Marty said.

'No, I haven't spoken to him for going on three weeks. He Skyped then, and hinted at a big operation coming up, but of course couldn't say. He looked and sounded fine. Of course we're always scrutinizing every word he says, every expression, looking for signs of depression, or whatever. He seems to be handling it all better than his parents are. Mon checks her phone constantly, fearing she'll miss a call or text from him. I'm more anxious when I receive calls from unknown

44

numbers. They're the ones I don't want to hear from.' Wil found it a relief to talk about Lucas, but could see Marty's discomfort as he fidgeted and squirmed in the passenger seat. Marty could handle only so much personal talk.

'He's a smart kid, Wil, he'll be fine,' Marty looked down at his phone's GPS. 'Take the Western Ring Road, left onto the Tulla Freeway.'

Three Led Zeppelin songs later, they pulled up at the front of Trevalyan Shelter, another sad-looking building, and more suspicious and defensive shelter staff. As soon as Marty exited the car, Wil was quick to eject the disc and slip it under the seat. He wasn't going to take another second of Robert Plant's screaming.

Wil introduced himself and Marty as they showed their IDs to the young woman barring them from entering the building.

'Oh, sorry, I should have guessed you was cops. Not too many irate husbands travel in pairs. Heather Merzel, she's the resident advocate; you can wait in here, I'll go and get her, she is just settling a new guest in.' The woman left them alone in an office that would have once been a bedroom.

'Why do all the women who work in places like this all look the same? Is it like a cult thing or something?' Marty liked to use stereotypes.

'Jesus, Marty, be quiet.' Wil flicked through a brochure: *The Survivor's Handbook.* He knew he should be feeling more sympathetic. It wasn't that he didn't care what happened to these women, he was just so damned tired. With all his personal baggage to deal with, he was pushing himself just to turn up for work.

'Good morning, gentlemen, how can I help you?' The woman offered her hand.

'We're looking for a woman and her two little girls. It is possible that the woman would have been seeking refuge from her abusive husband. We are making our inquiries at shelters within ten kilometres from the woman's address. I understand your reluctance to give up the location of women seeking a safe house, but we are conducting a murder investigation, and need to find this woman.'

Wil showed the woman Jillian's photograph, and that of the two daughters. 'Have you seen them, have they presented here at any time?'

'What a very dejected looking woman. No, detective, they haven't landed on our doorstep.' Heather returned the photos to Wil.

'Who was that other woman, the one who let us in, the one with the nose ring?' Marty asked, making it sound like a judgement.

'That's Billie. She's our Jane-of-all-trades around here, crisis-line operator, office-assistant, house-mum, whatever is needed, really. We have several "Billies" working here, they take turns doing different shifts, on call a lot of the time. Sometimes we are inundated with women, other times it will be a little more on the quiet side. The girls are fantastic, flexible, above and beyond. I'm sorry I can't help you.' Heather led the detectives out after accepting Wil's card.

'What a waste of a morning.' Wil's lack of sleep was starting to make him less tolerant.

'I don't feel that way at all. You're forgetting the basics of the benefits of elimination. We'll eventually get to the good stuff—shit always rises to the top. You have to be patient.' Marty went to hit the play button. 'Hey where's my CD? You bastard, what've you done with it? Jesus, Wil, all you had to do was say you didn't want to listen to it anymore.'

'Anymore! Anymore! Are you fucking kidding me? I thought I'd made myself pretty damn clear when we first got in the car that I wasn't going to be too supportive today. So here we are.' Wil loosened his grip on the steering wheel. 'You need to learn to keep your obsessions at home, Marty. Have you been seeing that doctor? Maybe you need to go back on those meds again. I have enough shit in my life at the present moment, without having to deal with yours as well!'

'You can save the whole parent bullshit thing for Lucas, OK, Wil? My mother and sisters are sufficient at bullying me in that department.' Marty stared down at the file in his lap. 'Head to the Calder Highway, then exit left at Bonfield Street. Tiffany Shelter, Tiffany Court, Keilor.' He sat back, arms crossed, the conversation over.

In silence, the two detectives approached the shelter. Again, the house was not unlike the neighbouring ones, though this one was larger than the previous shelter. From inside the house they could hear children laughing and American actor's voices. Wil assumed they were watching a DVD. Marty pounded on the front door.

The door was opened a few centimetres. 'Yes?' The woman spoke, her voice quiet.

Both showed their IDs as Wil spoke. 'We're Detectives Saddington and Hanratty from the Moreland Major Incident Unit. Could we speak to the resident advocate please.'

'Yes, come in. We have to be a little cautious around here, as you can imagine.' She closed the door to what looked like a lounge room, where four small children sat cross-legged on the floor, engrossed in a colourful cartoon. 'Shrek,' the woman smiled up at the detectives.

'Come in here, it's sort of an office. It's private anyway.' Clearing folders and magazines off a couple of chairs, the woman indicated to the officers to sit. 'I'm

48

Anna Sellens, I am the resident advocate for Tiffany Shelter.'

'Ms Sellens, we are trying to locate a woman and her two small daughters.' Wil showed Anna the photos. 'The woman's name is Jillian Laidlaw.'

'Straight up, I can tell you that they haven't been at this shelter. They are not here now, nor have been in the recent past. The women that come through these shelters are here only on a temporary basis. We help them to find appropriate accommodation, and quite often they will return home to their husbands. That happens a lot, and most of the time against sound advice. What sort of time frame are you talking about? Do you want me to check back in the files that were before my time here? Which is about eight months,' Anna asked.

'It would have been around a month ago, possibly six weeks,' Marty spoke, cutting in before Wil got the next question in. 'We don't know if a shelter is where they went, but a neighbour stated that they had left the family home. Mrs Laidlaw doesn't have family in Melbourne, so we are just really following a hunch at this stage.' Marty seemed to liked this woman.

'No, they haven't been here. Paige, she's a housemother at this shelter, but she also helps at other shelters when they are desperate for staff, she might know something. The girls also get to occasionally hear names, as they are operators for the crisis line. I'll go get her. Can I get either of you a tea or coffee?' Anna asked as she was leaving the room.

'Yes, thanks, that would be great. Black coffee for me.' Marty jumped in before Wil could decline for both of them.

'If it isn't any trouble, same for me, thanks,' Wil said, then glared at Marty when Anna had left the room.

'It isn't all about you, Wil,' Marty smirked.

Anna returned with Paige, each carrying a mug of steaming coffee. Wil saw how the facial jewellery of the second woman wasn't going unnoticed by Marty, as Marty thanked her for the coffee with a slight disapproving shake of his head. Wil was amazed at times at Marty's conservativeness, and then there were occasions where he was the polar opposite—a conservative head-banger.

Looking at the photos of the Laidlaws, recognition registered on Paige's face. 'Yes, this is Jillian and her daughters, Charlotte and Bonnie. I can't remember their surname though. It wasn't here, they were at another shelter. Give me a sec, I've got my diary in my bag, I'll just go and have look. I've been at three different shelters in the past two months. Hang on.' Paige raced out of the office.

'Paige is one of our best,' Anna said. Marty's expression hadn't been missed after all. 'She has a degree in Social Sciences. She has helped hundreds of women. She could be earning a decent salary elsewhere but she is happier here helping where she is desperately needed. She is a consummate advocate for women,' she smiled at Marty, whose eyebrows were raised.

Paige charged back into the room. 'Yes, yes, it was at McHale in Essendon. Some families you can't help but remember; others will be forgotten as soon as they've gone. The little girls were so, so sweet. Charlotte, the older one, did all the speaking, while Bonnie just stuck to her side. In fact, I'm not all that sure if I ever heard Bonnie speak. They will require extensive counselling.' Paige was very animated talking about the Laidlaws. 'Oh God! Nothing's happened to them, has it?'

'When was it that you were at McHale Shelter, do you have the dates?' asked Wil.

'I was asked to do three night shifts—they didn't have anyone else available. I often help out. Jillian and the girls had been at the shelter since the end of March, I believe. Jillian is a very scared, timid woman. She became even more afraid when her husband, I'm not sure of his name, turned up on my last night there, the Sunday night,' Paige continued, not so animated now, concern in her voice.

'I don't know how he found them. Sometimes the women will tell a friend or family member where they are staying. Even though they've been asked to keep it quiet, it somehow gets back to the husband. Possibly they've gone up to the shops and been spotted, then followed. Anyway, that Sunday night, very late, he was out front yelling up to the house—it's a two-storey big old house. He kept it up for about an hour, calling out for Jillian. Never mentioned the daughters. McHale Shelter has a security guard, Eddie Kovacs. He's there most days, or on call. But I didn't want him to come round.'

'Why not, if it was necessary, and he was available?' Wil interrupted.

'Too confrontational, I felt. Most times we can convince the men to leave, the threat of police is often enough. But this guy wasn't budging, and I was concerned the neighbours would get involved, though they're pretty good, mostly.' Paige gave Wil a smile. 'The police, excuse me for saying, can take a lot longer to arrive than we would like, so in the end I called Eddie and he was round in a matter of minutes. Did his muscle man act and escorted the husband off the premises.'

'The husband's name was Sean Laidlaw, and we are investigating his murder,' Marty said.

'This is the third women's crisis shelter we've been to today, not one of them had any security that I noticed. Why does McHale Shelter?' Wil asked.

'Um, well, it's not really my place to say. You would have to ask the resident advocate.' Paige's discomfort was apparent. 'That role is held by Sonja De Bruin. She is also the director, which means that she runs several shelters. She employed Eddie, I believe. So you would be best to ask her any questions relating to security at that shelter.'

'Were Jillian and the girls still at McHale Shelter when you were there last?' Wil questioned further. 'Did Sean return on your third night-shift?'

'No, he never came back. Eddie can be very convincing. Sometimes we'll move a family to another location. But that didn't seem necessary when he didn't show again. I spent a lot of time on the Friday evening talking to Jillian. She is a very traumatised woman; she's been scared for most of her life, and now she's terrified of the future. When someone has had a tormented life, such as Jillian has, it is very hard to instil even a glimmer of optimism in them.'

Wil could see Paige's mind start to race to a place where she clearly didn't want to go.

'I don't believe that Jillian would have gone back to her husband. You'll find Eddie Kovacs working, if Sonja De Bruin is on duty. Most weekdays Sonja is there. I'm pretty certain that she'll be at the shelter now. Would you like me to ring and check?'

'Thanks, but we'll just head on over there. You've been very helpful,' Wil shook both women's hands. 'I'll leave my card, in case you think of anything that might be useful.'

'Thanks for the coffee,' Marty nodded to both women.

Outside on the street, Wil and Marty stood beside the car. 'So is this McHale Shelter on your list?'

'Sure is, was to be the next one. See what I mean, about patience and elimination and shit rising?' Marty's said smugly.

'I do believe that some *shit* may have just joined our suspect list.' Wil was all happy now. Friends again.

CHAPTER FIVE

'Lexie, you've got to lighten up. It's only been a couple of days, and you're already getting a little depressive. I know it's your job, and you take it seriously, but, honey, you'll experience lots of emotional reactions. You've got to remember that you're reporting on those poor unfortunate women who've been traumatized, but you aren't one of them. How many have you interviewed this week?' Carla Garmendia voiced her concern. 'This coffee is rubbish, where do you keep the sugar?'

'The shelter was suspiciously quiet when I first arrived. But it didn't take long for that to change.' Lexie searched the pantry for the sugar bowl. 'I interviewed four homeless women; they were all single, no families. Not domestic violence cases. They wanted to tell me their stories—thought they'd get some money out of me. Some of the stuff they told me was verging on the unbelievable. Both women that have been there a while, allowed me to interview them. A few other domestic cases came in, but didn't want to know me.' Lexie felt drained, but knew that once she started the writing process, she would shift into another gear.

'Now, I want you to come out with me this Tuesday night. I'm not taking no for an answer,' Carla beamed, looking very excited about her plans to cheer up her friend.

'Oh no, Carla, what have you got in mind? Please, please, no blind dates. You know I'm not interested.'

'No, silly—dancing not dating—and the majority that go are women. The bonus being, so do some very dishy men. City Salsa has a first-timer's class on Tuesday nights in St Kilda. I've booked both of us in—wait for it—for the next six Tuesdays!' Carla did her best Latino dance improvisation around Lexie's tiny kitchen.

'Just think, fun, fitness, weight loss. Did you know that you could burn up to four hundred and twenty calories in one hour by dancing Salsa? I've even read that it can even reduce the risk of Alzheimer's and dementia. Now how could you possibly turn *those* benefits down? We'll be shimmying, sexy, and smart. So you'll go?' Carla hugged Lexie before tipping the contents of the cup into the sink. 'By the way, have you been paid yet?'

Lexie nodded.

'Good. Then get yourself a decent coffee machine, and some proper coffee. I'll pick you up Tuesday at eight.' Carla kissed her friend on the cheek.

'OK then, to both demands.' Lexie walked Carla to her car.

Back inside, Lexie sat at her desk and started to go over her notes of the past week. She had a lot of work to do over the weekend; she wanted to be ready for the second week at McHale Shelter. But she couldn't write, couldn't stop herself pondering Sonja De Bruin and Eddie Kovacs. Both of them gave Lexie a persistent, unsettled feeling.

Sonja had been civil to Lexie when she had returned to the shelter to start the interviews. Eddie had made his presence known, on occasion catching her off guard, appearing out of nowhere, asking her if everything was all right. She'd felt watched the entire time.

After half an hour, and no rational conclusion as to what it was that bothered her about Sonja and Eddie, Lexie berated herself. 'Snap out of it, you are becoming obsessive, along with depressive.'

She looked at her notes again, with more intent this time. The actual writing was going to be much easier than first anticipated, having followed her own set of interview steps: Give the victim control. Let them choose the location for the interview. Let them decide who can or can't sit in on the interview. Find out how they want the conversation to sound. Find out what they want to say specifically. So began 'Shedding Light on Dark', Lexie's first article.

She only realised it was getting late when she was struggling to see the laptop's keys. It was time to stop and make dinner. She put on her favourite jazz album and set about putting a meal together—an omelette and salad. Her stomach growled. While she ate standing at the kitchen counter, she started a shopping list—the fridge had been emptied.

Drinking the last glass from the bottle of Sauvignon Blanc, opened two weeks previously, *wine* ++ was added to the list. Coffee machine and coffee beans she added last, with a smiley face.

Lexie loved her little cottage, left to her by her grandmother. Her gran had known that Lexie was the sentimental one of the two sisters. Lexie knew, too, that Dana would have sold the house by now. Lexie wanted to grow old here—she felt more at home here than anywhere else she'd lived. She was grateful now that she'd rented it out when she met and married Doug, and not sold it. At the time, her mother had told her that she was silly to hang on to it. If she was committed to the relationship, she would have sold and moved on. But it was her home and she loved it. And because she hadn't lived with Doug in the house, there weren't any sad memories associated with it.

She took her wine into the bathroom, sat it on the edge of the tub and turned on the taps. Many creative thoughts came to her while she lay in a bubble bath, her favourite oils indulging her senses.

The hot bath wiped her out; she was ready for bed. Another wild Saturday night, Lexie thought, looking at the clock, the big hand on the twelve, the small one on the nine.

*

Sunday morning Lexie had woken early, refreshed and bursting with energy. She'd been for her usual run, enjoying the company of the many Sunday joggers. It had been crisp and cool, her cheeks freezing, though the rest of her stayed warm, thanks to the new woollen beanie her mother had insisted she needed.

Back at home, Lexie cooked porridge and toasted a couple of slices of sourdough, on which she heaped raspberry jam. She sat at her desk with her breakfast. Re-reading yesterday's efforts, she was satisfied with what she'd produced; just one last interview to write up.

The woman's story had touched Lexie as she had listened to the details of the tragic narrative. She'd struggled to keep herself collected. The woman, who chose to be called Beth for the article, gave details of the two incidents in which she miscarried, due directly to beatings by her partner. When Beth told Lexie that she could no longer fall pregnant due to the injuries she'd sustained from the most recent assault, Lexie had to swallow a moan that threatened to escape; her throat ached from the effort. Beth was soon to turn forty-two, and was saddened mostly by the knowledge that she would never have a family.

Now, as Lexie wrote Beth's story, she let the tears flow: tears for Beth, and tears for herself. The year before her marriage to Doug ended, Lexie and Doug had gone to see a specialist to find out why, after two years of trying, she still hadn't fallen pregnant. They'd been married for three years, both desperately wanting to have a baby. At first, she thought it was because she had been selfish in wanting to have a career first. Then the move from one side of the world to the other—that and the stress for both of them in terms of work could have been factors. Lexie had been desolate when the outcome from numerous tests and procedures indicated that Lexie was never going to get pregnant.

Doug had been distraught. He'd attempted, as best he could, to deal with the issue, but he told Lexie that he couldn't see a future with her. He wanted a family. He'd wanted more than what they were together. Lexie lost any chance of motherhood—and her marriage—in the space of twelve months.

When she finished Beth's interview, she blew her nose and washed her face. Re-reading the piece, she knew she was doing the right thing. But it was the interview with the fair-haired woman with the two little girls that cemented Lexie's resolve.

Jillian—'Hannah' for the article—spoke to Lexie of her feelings that she'd let her girls down. She knew what they were going through as children—she had seen her own mother beaten by her father. She'd always thought that when she had children she would make sure they'd have a better life than she had. And now, here they were—the cycle continued.

Jillian struck a chord in Lexie; she reminded her of Ava, and Lexie was disconcerted by the similarities in their demeanour. Lexie now recognised the signs of Battered Wife Syndrome: reserved, withdrawn, anxious, hyper-vigilant. Jillian had constantly checked the door during the interview.

But Jillian had talked freely to Lexie, saying that she finally felt she was in a safe place, and, more importantly, that someone did care. Sonja had her complete trust; she was beginning a new life. She didn't have any family in Australia, and her husband's parents were oblivious to what went on in their son's house. Her husband had made sure that she didn't keep any friends, so she had no one. Jillian's mother had died when she was fifteen. Her father then took to abusing her. When she left home and then married, the abuse continued—only the abuser had changed.

Six-thirty that evening, Lexie phoned her editor. 'Megan, hi. You're not going to believe this!' Outside was dark, and rain was lashing the windows. 'I've finished my first piece. How impressed are you?'

'You're unbelievable, girl,' said Megan. 'Email it to me, and I'll take it in to the office in the morning.'

'Sure thing, no problem. I'm back at McHale Shelter tomorrow, and I promised them I'd bring in the article and show them before it was published. I'm interviewing staff and support workers over the next couple of days. That should be interesting.'

'Yes? Why is that?' Megan asked.

'The resident advocate and her security guard weren't all that welcoming from day one. In fact, they are both on the, um, I don't know...I'm not sure what it is about them, probably nothing, just my overactive imagination.' Lexie didn't want to say too much to Megan about Sonja De Bruin. She didn't want anything to jeopardise her visits to this shelter, or any others.

'Something hinky going on between the two, do you think? Maybe a torrid love affair?' Megan chuckled.

'Megan, you're the only person I know who has torrid love affairs. No, I'm not sure. It's probably nothing. Now I'd better go and get emailing. Talk to you soon.' Lexie disconnected after they'd said their goodnights.

*

The next morning, Lexie walked up the court toward McHale Shelter, having left her car parked at St Agnes Cathedral down the road. There was a white van parked in the driveway of the shelter. She could just make out Eddie, helping two small children, possibly girls, into the back of the van. Lexie could hear them crying, and calling out. She wasn't close enough to see who they were, nor could she hear what Eddie was saying in reply.

She saw Eddie get into the driver's seat. He started the van and reversed out of the driveway. He wore a scowl and looked straight ahead as he drove past Lexie, although she felt certain he'd seen her.

That was odd! she thought, then considered scenarios as to why Eddie would be taking a child anywhere without their mother.

She climbed the stairs to the shelter, gently tapped on the front door, entered and announced herself.

'Hello, come in.' A woman with a thick dark bobbed haircut came out from Sonja's office. 'I was told to expect you. I'm Frances Spencer, nice to meet you.' She shook Lexie's hand and smiled. 'Sonja's helping with accommodation for one of the women, and asked me to help relieve her here til she can get back. Full house at the moment.'

'Nice to meet you, Frances,' Lexie returned the smile.

'Sonja said that you intended to interview her today, but that doesn't look likely at this stage. I'd be more than happy to help, but as I don't have anything to do with the business end of the shelter, I'm not going to be of any use to you, am I?' Frances sat and indicated a chair for Lexie to sit on.

'I won't bother you, then, not with you being so busy. Is there anything I can do to help?' Lexie thought it was worth taking a chance on Frances's friendliness. 'I saw Eddie drive off with a couple of children. Is their mother all right? Nothing's happened?'

'I don't know, to tell the truth. I only arrived myself half an hour ago. Sonja was leaving with one of the women, and she said that Eddie would be bringing the children later. They were probably meeting with a real estate agent, or someone like that, and didn't want the kids getting in the way,' Frances shrugged. 'Can I get you a cuppa? I'm getting myself one.'

'Yes, thanks, that'd be great.' Lexie stayed seated, a little confused. Had Sonja removed herself and Eddie from the shelter so they could avoid being interviewed?

Returning with a tray carrying tea for two and biscuits, Frances got about pouring and fussing over

Lexie. 'So which magazine is it that you work for, Ms Reed?

'Call me Lexie. *Contemporary Woman*; do you ever read it?' Lexie asked.

'I have once or twice. Personally, I haven't bought it, but I've seen it, you know, doctor's and dentist's waiting rooms. Bit highbrow for me—I'm more your *Women's Weekly* type,' Frances gave a sheepish smile. 'Another Tim Tam?'

'No, thank you, Frances, just the one will do me. So, are there any of the usual shelter staff here now, anyone I could interview?' Lexie felt unsure how to proceed from here.

'Bit of staff shuffling about at the minute, so I don't think you'll find any regulars today. Maybe for the night shift later, but you'll be long gone by then.' Frances looked at Lexie, then solemnly added, 'I used to be on the other side of things. I was once married to a man who used to take great pleasure in turning my face into pulp. I don't know if you noticed, but my left eyelid, see how it droops. I've lost the vision in that eye. Nerve damage, they said. Brain damage, I say, 'cause I returned to him even after he'd done that to me. So I can relate to the women that come through these centres. I know what they are experiencing.' Her eyes never left Lexie's face as she spoke.

'Frances, would you like to be included in the article? You can change your name. Your story is as important as anyone's,' Lexie said.

'Sure, why not, and I've already changed my name. Frances wasn't the name my parents gave me,' she gave Lexie a sad smile. 'My husband wouldn't let me get a job, you see, but then he'd withhold money from me. I wouldn't know what to do. I couldn't shop for food, and then he'd beat me for not cooking him a meal. It wasn't just me, he'd beat the dog, too. One time he wanted my attention, so he threw the cat at the wall above my head. I'm not sure how that cat survived; it got up and left that day, and we never saw it again. Now why didn't I follow that damn cat? Tabitha was her name.'

Lexie took notes without interrupting.

'Ten years and two kids later, not much had changed. I was like a zombie, you know; I was on autopilot and life was routine. Dumb and numb, that's how I felt. I didn't even daydream—how sad is that? Then he started hitting the eldest boy, he was probably about six; must have decided he was old enough.' She paused before continuing.

'I didn't do anything to stop it. If the truth be told, I was relieved. It was taking the focus off me for a change. Now, when I think about that, it just completely fractures my heart, you know. That bastard broke every item in our house, everything that I ever cherished, he smashed, every photograph he tore up, every plant in the yard he ripped out. He took my heart and stomped on that too. Then one year, we got new neighbours. I made friends with the woman, secretly of course, as I wasn't allowed friends. Regina was my guardian angel; she gave me hope, strength and courage. With her help, I got the boys and we came to a shelter exactly like this one. And I never looked back. Now I give back by volunteering as often as I can.' Frances had finished her story and started to gather their cups to put back onto the tray.

'Thank you for that, Frances. Thank you for sharing your story.' Lexie felt honoured that Frances had shared that part of her life.

Suddenly, both women were snapped back to the present by banging at the front door. 'More visitors, excuse me, Lexie.' Frances went to see who was knocking so urgently.

'Good morning, Detectives Saddington and Hanratty, Moreland Major Incident Unit.' Lexie could hear a man's voice. 'We're after the resident advocate.'

'That would be Sonja De Bruin, and I'm afraid that she's not here right now. I'm Frances Spencer, one of the volunteers. I'm not sure if I can help,' Frances responded.

'Could we come in and speak privately. We are aware of the nature of the accommodation, and wish to be respectful of the occupants,' one of the detectives said.

'Certainly, we can go into Ms De Bruin's office, I'm sure she won't mind.' Frances led the two detectives into the office.

As they entered the room, Lexie got up and collected the tray. 'I'll get out of your way, Frances. Thanks again. I'll see to the dishes.'

Lexie stepped out into the hall, tea tray in one hand—the other she used to pull the door to Sonja's office not quite closed. After she'd found the kitchen and dealt with the dishes as promised, she returned to stand outside the office. Listening, her heart racing for she feared being caught eavesdropping.

'We're hoping that you, or someone here, might be able to assist us in the whereabouts of this family,' Lexie heard one of the detectives ask.

'Well yes, they were here. They were here this morning. But as to where they are now, I've no idea,' Frances replied.

'Do you have Ms De Bruin's mobile number? It is very important that we find Mrs Laidlaw and her daughters,' the other detective said.

'Yes, hang on, let me write it down for you,' Frances said.

'I'll leave you a card. Please get Ms De Bruin to contact us if she returns to the shelter before we've reached her. And please pass on the urgency of this matter. Thank you for your time, Ms Spencer.'

Lexie could hear the men moving from their chairs, preparing to leave. She turned and retreated to the rear of the house, back toward the kitchen. There she put the kettle on. She heard the front door closing, and Frances calling out her name.

'In the kitchen, Frances,' Lexie replied. 'I thought you might need another cuppa.'

'Spot on, there! Terrible business. Those two men were detectives. They're looking for Jillian and the girls. They've only just left this morning. The two little girls are the ones you saw Eddie leave with. Did you meet them when you were here earlier, doing your interviews?' Frances sat down at the kitchen table, picking up the cup Lexie had placed on the table. She stared at the tea, looking troubled.

'Yes, I did, such a pretty family. Do you know where they've gone, Frances?' Lexie didn't want to appear too nosy, but she was starting to smell something sour. 'You looked concerned.'

'Oh, it's just…No, I don't. Usually, the less people know where the women are moved to, the safer it is for them, and us. If we get enquiries, we aren't then lying about not knowing anything; then we can't slip up, and give away their location.'

'Well, Sonja will have to let the police know where they are. Did they say what it was about, why they wanted to find them?' Lexie said.

'No, but they did say it was urgent that they speak to Jillian. Sonja will have to tell them where they've been moved to.'

'Do you mind if I hang around here for while? I promise I won't get in your way.' Lexie hoped to stay at the shelter; she wanted to be there when Sonja returned.

'I can't see why not. I hope everything is all right with Jillian. I will worry now,' Frances finished her tea and rinsed her cup, leaving it to dry on the draining board. 'I'd better get to work. Beds need to be changed, washing needs doing. You know where everything is, make yourself comfortable.'

After Frances left the room, Lexie got out her laptop, and set it up on the kitchen table. She went to Google, but didn't know what to type. All she had was Jillian's first name. Not much for a search engine to go on. She then went to the latest news stories. There had to be more to this than a case of abuse for detectives from a major incident squad to be making inquiries.

She found it right away. Wife wanted for questioning. Husband found bludgeoned to death in family home. 'No way! They've got to be kidding!'

Lexie, very quickly and quietly, notebook in hand, quietly went back into Sonja's office. On top of her desk, near the telephone, was the card the detectives had left earlier. She copied the details into her notepad, then returned to the kitchen and her laptop.

Reading the piece about the murder, Lexie learned Jillian's surname. She then Googled Jillian Laidlaw and was horrified to learn that all the newspapers were treating Jillian as the prime suspect and calling it a *domestic gone wrong*. She knew the police were similarly inclined. The two detectives she knew were Major Incident. She was not persuaded at all that the Jillian she'd met earlier in the week was a murderer. She hadn't appeared angry or confrontational; her demeanour had been that of a person who was defeated. Lexie surmised that Jillian wouldn't have raised her voice to her husband, let alone her hand.

Reading further, she learned that Jillian and the girls had left the husband in the weeks prior to the murder. The main supplier of information to the papers was that of a neighbour, Julie Asling. She'd had quite a lot to say. Her opinion of Jillian wasn't very high, it seemed. She'd been quoted: *Jillian left a loving husband, without explanation, taking his children and denying him access.*

This wasn't right; Lexie's mind was spinning. She had to talk to someone, but wasn't sure to whom she could turn. She drank her now cold tea, trying to calm herself so as to think clearly. 'Yuck!' Tipping out the tea, she boiled the kettle again.

Going through her meticulously kept notes, Lexie found the names of the women who had been working at the shelter while she'd been conducting her interviews.

Dianne and Carol had been there during the day. Linda had covered the night shift with Paige, who had been called in from another shelter to help, as they were short staffed and had a full house.

Lexie remembered Paige. She'd been impressed by her. An extremely smart, articulate young woman, with a very caring, kind heart—though the facial jewellery and garish red hair were a little in conflict with her education and background. Lexie felt they could be friends and they'd exchanged mobile numbers. She was tempted to call her now and ask if she was aware of what was going on. But was she overstepping the mark?

She heard the front door open and close, followed by what Lexie assumed was Sonja's office door closing. She closed her laptop and packed up her notes, putting

72

everything into her briefcase, and stowed the case on the floor inside the pantry.

Quietly, Lexie let herself out the back door. She walked down the garden path that led to the front of the property. There, in the driveway, was Sonja's little blue Audi convertible and Eddie's white van. Lexie returned to the kitchen. She retrieved her briefcase and headed toward Sonja's office.

As she arrived at the door, it suddenly opened, and Eddie came out of the room, stepping straight into Lexie. He grabbed her by her arms to steady them both; she felt his fingers dig into her flesh with more force than required for a simple bump. 'Sorry,' he said, staring her down.

'My fault,' Lexie replied turning away from him. 'Is Sonja in?'

Eddie blocked the doorway and pulled the door closed. 'Yes, but she's very busy just now. I wouldn't bother her if I were you. Come back tomorrow. Probably ring first.' He was almost daring her to oppose him.

'If you'll just let Sonja know I was here, thanks,' Lexie perceived the threat; she decided leaving was the sensible thing to do.

She found it hard to concentrate on the drive home, her imagination was running riot. Lexie realised, too late, that she was in the wrong lane on the freeway, ending up on the Westgate Bridge and heading towards Geelong, the opposite direction to home.

The afternoon traffic was building, as was her frustration. 'Just relax, enjoy the view,' she told herself, noticing just how much this side of the city had changed in her absence. The Docklands had expanded, with many multistorey apartment blocks and construction happening in every direction.

Taking the first exit after the bridge crossing, Lexie headed back across the bridge towards the city. The shortening days meant that evening came in more quickly; the city's lights were already coming on in many places. It wasn't as spectacular as the Manhattan skyline, but she loved it all the same.

Where are you, Jillian? Lexie wondered.

She was going to keep her eyes and ears open. She was going to do whatever she could for Jillian and her girls. She wasn't going to let her down. This time, she'd be there.

Back home, her misadventure on the freeway having added an hour to the trip, Lexie decided on an early dinner. Pouring a glass of wine, she then settled down on the sofa to eat, drink and think. She wanted to phone

Paige right away, but decided to wait until she had sorted the disordered thoughts in her head.

She had to let go of her imagination, get back to the facts and what she knew. Her aversion to Sonja and loathing for Eddie were not enough to go pointing fingers and making accusations. Lexie knew she had to speak to the two detectives investigating the murder. She was certain that Eddie and Sonja were involved somehow in their case—and she wasn't being a hysteric. She thought about the facts. The man, Sean Laidlaw, had been at the shelter. Lexie knew about it, it wasn't a secret. Paige had called Eddie to get the man to leave—and he had.

Her meal finished, the kitchen cleared, Lexie called Paige.

'Hi, Paige, it's Lexie Reed.'

'Lexie, how are you?'

'Great, thanks. Look, Paige, there's something that I'd like to talk to you about. Are you free tonight, could we meet for a drink?' Lexie asked.

'Sure, that sounds better than what's on offer on the telly. I've just been studying the TV guide and was becoming quite disheartened—a night off and I'm left with *Masterchef.* Where did you have in mind?' Paige asked.

'I thought the Soho in South Yarra, that's if it's still there. That's about half way between us. Do you know it?' Lexie said.

'Yes, I do, and yes, it's still there. In fact I was there last Friday, so now I'll be able to say that I'm a regular,' Paige laughed into the phone.

'Say seven o'clock, then?' Lexie asked.

'See you there!'

*

Lexie arrived first and found a booth. The place was quiet, being so early in the week. She was feeling a little nervous; she didn't want Paige to think what she was proposing was ridiculous. If she couldn't convince her that Eddie and Sonja were involved in the murder of Sean Laidlaw, there was no way that the police were going to take her seriously.

She saw Paige enter the bar; you would have to be virtually blind to miss the girl, Lexie thought. Smiling, Paige crossed the room, and slid into the booth opposite Lexie.

'Did you see that? The barman waved and nodded, like yeah, I'm a regular, and I'm loving it!' Paige laughed as she dexterously removed her coat without having to get out of the booth.

'Seriously, now, how could he not remember you—with that hair, nobody could forget you. I love it, by the way, only wish I had the guts to try something so radical. What would you like to drink?' Lexie grabbed her wallet.

'Let's see, I don't think you asked me here to discuss hair colours, so I'll have a grown up drink: vodka, ice and a slice of lemon, thanks, Lexie,' Paige said.

Returning from the bar with their drinks, Lexie resumed her place in the booth. She had a taste of her drink, while she formulated her first line in her head.

'OK, today I was at McHale Shelter. I was there to interview Sonja and whichever staff on duty were happy to speak to me. The thing is, as I arrived, Eddie was leaving with two little girls in his van. When I went into the shelter, Frances was there, and she told me that Sonja had left earlier with Jillian, the girl's mother. Remember them?'

Paige nodded, so Lexie resumed. 'Not long after I got there, two detectives arrived. They were looking for Jillian because her husband had been murdered, and if the news stories are true, she's their prime suspect!' Lexie waited for Paige's reaction.

'What, you've got to be kidding! I heard something on the radio earlier tonight about some axe-murder devil-thing, but didn't really listen close enough to know what they were talking about. Figured I'd read about it in the

77

paper tomorrow,' Paige took a sip of her vodka. 'There's no way Jillian Laidlaw is a murderer. I doubt she has even smacked her children. There is no violence in that woman. She has very little of anything left in her.'

'I know, I agree totally with you. But the police are looking for her, and Sonja has taken her away, and nobody knows where to.' Lexie took a mouthful of her drink and looked at Paige. 'The thing is, I was there at the shelter when Sonja and Eddie returned, after the police had left. Eddie wouldn't let me speak to Sonja. He actually blocked her office door, wouldn't let me in. He told me to leave, and to call before I wanted to return. Something is going on at that shelter, and I think we need to go to the police.'

'This is all off the record, right?' Paige asked.

'Absolutely—this has nothing whatsoever to do with the articles or the magazine. My only concern at this stage is Jillian and her two little girls. Something is amiss at that shelter, and with Sonja and Eddie. I've turned to you, well, because you know them all, you must have some idea what is going on there.'

'I have to know I can trust you. The whole journo thing causes a lot of grief on occasion. People have been caught out before, putting trust where they shouldn't.' Paige looked Lexie in the eye.

Lexie nodded that she understood where Paige was coming from.

'As you know, I haven't worked at McHale very often, only relief shifts, so I'm not on the inside, so to speak. But I can say this: no other shelter is run the way that this one is. Secrets, security—that Eddie wouldn't pass a police check, I'm positive. I've talked to the police already, Lexie. I was the one who told them about McHale and that Jillian and the girls were there.'

'So you told them about the husband turning up on the Sunday night—out on the street calling out for Jillian?' Lexie asked.

'Yes, I told them about that, and how I had to call Eddie to come and get the guy to leave. You're not thinking...' Paige finished her drink before she continued. 'Eddie convinced the guy to leave. I saw him drive off.'

'And when did Eddie leave?'

'Straight away. Oh my God! He followed him out of the court.'

CHAPTER SIX

Across the Yarra River, on the other side of the city, Wil and Marty were in the MIR, finishing up reports on the morning's interviews. Marty was pushing for Wil to acknowledge Marty's instinct in finding the location of Jillian Laidlaw.

'We haven't found her yet, Mr Hotshot detective,' said Wil. 'But I guess I will give you kudos for this one— we're on her trail at least.'

Wil placed his report in the internal-mail-tray; it would make its way to the higher ranks during the course of the evening.

'What did you make of that journalist being there?' Marty said. 'She seemed pretty pally with the volunteer lady, Frances. I didn't mind Frances, looks like she's had a hard life. She wasn't icy like some of those other women we came across. She reminded me a bit of my mum.'

'You don't know the other woman is a journalist, you're only guessing. But, and this really hurts me to say, you are right more often than not. She didn't look like she belonged there. So I won't be at all surprised if it turns out that she is a journo,' Wil shook his head. 'I can't really say that I took much notice of her though.'

'I've tried ringing the shelter a few times, but keep getting the engaged signal. You haven't had a call from that Sonja woman yet?' Marty was itching to move.

'No, I haven't heard from anyone. I say we head back over there. Hopefully it won't take long. I'm meeting Ray for dinner in the city later on. You finished here?' Wil grabbed his jacket from behind his chair.

'That time of the month already?'

'What the hell are you on about?

'Ray—dinner. Don't you two meet at that same place every month? And never with your wives! I bet the waiters think you're gay.' Marty seemed to think what he'd said was funny.

Wil ignored him. In the car, he smacked Marty's hand as he was about to slip a CD into the stereo. 'I want to listen to the news. So just sit back and relax.' Wil turned the radio on.

The axe-murderer, who the police are calling the Go-devil, is still at large. The slaying last week of Sean Laidlaw in his home has police completely at a loss. The victim's wife and two little girls are still missing, and assumptions are being made that they too could have fallen victim to foul play. This could make the Go-devil Melbourne's latest serial killer.

Wil slammed the power button with his fisted left hand, killing the radio.

'Jesus, fuck...How did they fucking get that...I'll kill 'em when I find...' He hit the steering wheel over and over. His anger had him accelerating, not concentrating on the traffic in front and the red taillights.

'BRAKE! BRAKE!' Marty screamed at Wil. He grabbed the hand brake, pulling it on, simultaneously grabbing hold of the steering wheel. Wil slammed on the brakes at the same time. The car went into a spin then came to a crashing stop, slamming sideways into cars stopped in the right lane. The car's air bags erupted, filling the car.

Wil was dazed, but managed to shake it off.

'You stupid bastard! What did you do that for? Christ's sake, Marty, you could have killed us!'

'Someone had to stop the bloody car, you weren't exactly in control,' Marty replied as he checked himself for any damage. 'Your tantrum was going to cause a crash far worse than this.'

'Jesus! Get on your phone, now. Ring Terry and tell him what's happened. I want a car brought to us, and people to deal with this mess you've made,' Wil barked while he was punching down the air bag, trying to escape the car.

Meanwhile, people were getting out of their cars, inspecting the damage. They were also on their mobiles, calling the police, Wil guessed. Others filmed the scene on their mobile phones.

'Great,' said Wil. 'The media will love this lot, eye-witness footage and all!' Half an hour later, Wil and Marty pulled up outside of McHale Shelter in another unmarked car. Wil had taken full advantage of his rank—having someone else clean up his mess.

It was getting late and the court was dark, most of the houses nearby having only a few lights on inside. They could smell the smoke coming from the neighbour's chimney. It made Wil feel nostalgic for home.

Both men had their IDs ready before knocking. A television could be heard coming from one of the front rooms. Somebody was home. Wil gave a few gentle taps on the door. When there wasn't any response, he knocked a little harder.

'Hello?' A female voice spoke from the other side of the door.

'It's the police ma'am, sorry to disturb you. Could we come in?' Wil spoke back to the door.

'Yes, yes, sure thing,' she replied. The security chain still engaged, she checked their IDs, then let the detectives in.

'Sorry to have disturbed you. We're after Sonja De Bruin, the resident advocate,' Wil spoke in a hushed voice, not wanting to wake any sleeping children.

'It's OK, I'm the only one here, so there's no need to be quiet,' the woman smiled, as she led the two detectives into the living room off the hall to the right. She picked up the TV remote and muted the television.

'And your name, Miss?' Marty asked as they sat down on the couch. He quickly jotted her name in his notebook as she spoke.

'Linda, Linda Madden, and Sonja's not here tonight, she left about two hours ago. I'm here for the night shift,' Linda informed them.

'We need to get in contact with Ms De Bruin, but we haven't been able to get her on her mobile. Would you have a home address and number?' Wil asked.

'No, I've only got her mobile. Oh, and Eddie's,' Linda said, the disapproval obvious in her voice, when she said Eddie's name.

Wil and Marty exchanged knowing nods. 'Not a fan of Eddie's, I take it?' Marty probed, as he flicked back a few pages of his notebook. About the interviews at Tiffany Shelter, Marty had written: *'Housemother' Paige wild poppy red hair—face piercing—suss of Eddie Kovacs 'security guard'.*

84

Wil glanced at the notes over Marty's shoulder.

'He does his job. I don't have to like him, I suppose. I'll get his number for you. He lives close by, only minutes away if he's ever needed.' Linda got up out of her armchair.

'I believe he was needed here recently,' Marty said.

'Yes, we had a husband on the doorstep one night. Not sure how he found us. He was out front calling out the wife's name over and over,' Linda told them.

'Calling out for Jillian?' Wil added.

'Well, yes, it was! How did you know that?' Linda sat back down.

'We're looking for Jillian as part of an inquiry. We need to locate Ms De Bruin, as apparently she took Jillian and her daughters away from the here this morning, but nobody knows where to. If they've been rehoused, relocated, whatever, we need to know, and we need to know now.' Wil's voice rose with each word spoken; he was getting sick of repeating himself.

'I just assumed Jillian was moved because her husband had found her. The fewer people that know of the new shelter's location, well, the better. Eddie had dealt with the husband on the night, and I didn't hear anything more about it. I'm no help, I'm sorry. I'll get that number for you.' Linda left the room.

Wil and Marty left the shelter, and returned to the car. Marty tried the number, but it went directly to voicemail. He tried Sonja's again, same thing. 'Bloody hell! What is with these people!'

'Ring Terry, I want everyone he has available looking for Jillian, De Bruin and Kovacs. This is bullshit!' Wil drove out of the court, and back to the station.

Wil pulled into the police station's car park, parking beside Marty's Jeep. 'I have to go, Marty. I'll see you in the morning.' Marty got out and waved as Wil took off.

*

After parking the unmarked in a loading zone in the CBD, Wil fished about in the glove compartment for the police parking-permit and tossed it onto the dash. For the second time this evening, he took advantage of his position. He left the car and made his way up Little Bourke Street. He turned into Hardware Lane and walked into the first restaurant on the right.

'Detective Saddington, welcome, it's been too long,' the headwaiter approached Wil as he entered the restaurant.

The two men shook hands. 'How are you, Antonio?'

'Very well, thank you. Mr Roach is waiting for you, and a drink awaits you also. Enjoy your night.'

'Ray,' Wil greeted his friend, who stood up as Wil approached the table. They hugged, and then slapped each other on the back.

'Wil, my man, you look in need of a drink.' Ray proffered a glass of red. 'Sit down. Do you want me to order?' Rayden Roach and Wil had been friends since their first day of primary school, forty years ago.

'Yeah, sure, one less thing to have to think about right now would be fantastic,' Wil took a mouthful of his drink and sat back while Ray ordered three courses. Just hearing the food mentioned brought on his appetite—he was famished.

'I heard the news on the way into the city. Fun times, hey?' Ray said wryly.

'Someone in our inner-circle is going to be castrated, and I will personally see to it.' Wil swallowed the rest of his drink and looked around for the waiter. 'Spent the day chasing our tails. Then I learn some cock-head's been blabbing to the press. Then to top it all off, I was almost killed by my parnter on the freeway. It's just one frustration after another. I feel as though I've got my hands tied behind my back most of the time lately.' He sat back and let out a huge sigh.

'Feel better after your little rant then, man?' Ray sat up in his seat, taking a sip of his drink. 'To change the subject completely, Monica was at our house yesterday.'

'Yeah, how's she doing?' Wil asked.

'She's pretty down, what with the divorce...and Lucas being a constant worry. Next week, she and her parents are going to visit relatives in Sydney for a month. I'm guessing you don't know anything about that. She said that she hasn't spoken to you since the mediator.' Ray looked closely at his friend.

The waiter arrived with their entrees. Neither man spoke again until they'd each finished their field mushrooms stuffed with wild rice.

'I can't do much more then worry about Lucas, myself. As for the divorce, she's the one who wants it. She's the one who left. I offered to take her to Sydney last year, when she first said she wanted to leave. I thought what we needed was to get away from things, not away from each other. So I suppose Bob will be looking for a new husband for his daughter.' Wil's voice was thick with sarcasm.

'Come on, Wil, you know that's not the way they are. Mon's parents think more of you than that. You still haven't heard from Lucas either?' Concern coloured Ray's words. 'Monica said it's been weeks since she heard from him.'

'Nothing for over three weeks now. I have to stop myself from thinking the worst. It's ironic, really, isn't it, I wanted to join the army, but my father convinced me not to. Then my son wants to join the army, so I encourage him. Now, well, I've come to think - what the hell was I thinking?' Wil finished off his second drink. He really wanted another, but decided against it.

Their meals arrived, and Wil asked the waiter for water, then turned the conversation around to Ray. 'How are things in the world of demolition? Knocked down any buildings lately, any I may have known?' He attacked his food with gusto.

'Yeah, yeah, going good. Started a big job this week. Remember the old dental clinic in East Melbourne? I recall you had a couple of wisdom teeth removed in there, back in the early nineties,' Ray said.

'Hell yeah, I'll never forget. Sick as a dog I was, had a bad reaction to the anaesthetic. So smash the place up good for me, hey?'

Wil finished his meal and set his cutlery in place on the plate. A waitress hovering nearby pounced when Ray put his knife and fork together on his plate. The two men shared a smile at her exuberance.

'Full yet?' Ray asked.

'Getting there,' Wil sat back in his seat. 'Ray, do you think Mon is missing me, even a little maybe?'

'Mate, that's been the problem all along. She feels you went missing from her years ago. And if you were honest with yourself, you'd accept that was the case,' Ray said.

'You know, I never cheated on her, never. I could have, countless times, I've had opportunities over the years, heaps of them,' Wil muttered.

'Well give the man the medal he so desperately wants! Did you ever listen to her, really listen, 'cause I'm sure she has said all this to you. It's you distancing yourself from her. She didn't have anything to grab onto, to fight with. You can be a right prick at times; you get caught up in yourself and go into a place where it's very hard to reach you. I guess she got tired of trying.'

Dessert arrived and ended the discussion topic. As Wil scooped up the last mouthful of tiramisu, his mobile rang.

'Sorry, Ray, I'd better take it.' He stood and walked outside as he took the call.

Wil walked back in just as Ray was moving away from the counter, having paid for their meal. 'Done deal, you get it next time. Work need you?'

'Yep. Terry's found the source of the leak. I should see Chef, get me a good castration knife.' Wil tried to make a joke of it, but it was an act wasted on Ray.

'Good luck, and remember: breathe, think—then act. That's my motto for demolition, don't want any mistakes there now do we!' Ray laughed as he hugged his friend goodbye.

*

Terry was waiting for him when he walked into the MIR. At this time of night there wasn't the usual crowd or noise.

'Evening, Sads, sorry to drag you back, but I thought you'd best hear this now, and sort out what we're going to do.' Terry looked and sounded tired.

'Who is it then?' Wil asked, but didn't really want to know.

'The new connie, bloody Davis! He's been back to the vic's neighbour's house, again!' Terry said.

'Didn't you specifically tell him not to go back there?' Wil snapped.

'Sure did, but apparently he had given her his mobile number, and she'd been ringing him repeatedly. Anyway, he goes over there, and they did more than chat this time.' Terry looked ready for the expected explosion.

'Oh, for Christ's sake—don't tell me he screwed her?' Wil roared.

'Yep, he gave her one, then he gives her every detail off the board here,' Terry nodded at the Incident

Board. 'Must have made for great pillow talk. Then she goes and sells the story to the networks.'

'Conniving piece of work! What have you done with him?' Wil asked.

'Called him in, got his story, and he's waiting in your office. I told him he'd be suspended to start with. The rest will be up to you, and higher up the food chain. He's been sitting in there for the past hour, so he'll be pretty worked up by now.' Terry shook his head. 'I know what you'll want to do with him, but, Sads, it isn't legal in this country.'

'This case is really giving me the shits, Terry. Anything on the woman and her daughters, or that De Bruin woman, any leads at all?'

'One little ray of sunshine. Melissa managed to contact Jillian Laidlaw's sister, in Canada. She's flying back to Melbourne, possibly arriving tomorrow afternoon. She'll present for interview here once she's organised accommodation,' Terry replied. 'I'm not sure what she can do for the investigation, though.'

'Well, it's something, I guess. You go home, Terry, I'll go deal with Mr Can't Keep It In His Pants.'

CHAPTER SEVEN

Next morning Lexie made her way back to McHale Shelter in Essendon. Her meeting with Paige the previous night had convinced her that her suspicions where not baseless. However, Paige believed that they should leave the investigations to the police. She'd said that she'd told them everything already, even the fact that she didn't particularly like Eddie. Paige had pointed out to Lexie that not being likeable wasn't actually a crime. Lexie had tried already telling herself that one.

Lexie was going to try just once more to speak with Sonja. If she got a reasonable explanation as to Jillian's whereabouts, then she'd let it go. If not, then she would ring the detectives who'd interviewed Frances.

She travelled along Mt Alexander Road, another autumn shower making the road slippery. She didn't want a confrontation with Eddie on arrival, and the thought made her feel uneasy. Slowing the Peugeot to almost a crawl, she turned into Thistle Street. She was only minutes from the shelter, and couldn't decide whether to boldly drive right up and park in the driveway, or park at the Cathedral again, making a quiet approach.

The weather forced her decision, as the shower grew into a downpour. She drove into the shelter's driveway. To her disappointment, she could see that

Eddie's van and Sonja's Audi weren't there. The car parked in front of hers was one she didn't recognise.

Lexie climbed the front steps, thankful not to have slipped as she reached the top. She could hear the sound of a vacuum cleaner coming from inside. She knocked, but the knock went unanswered. She tried the door, and found, to her surprise, that it was unlocked. She called out as she entered, 'Hello? Hello there?'

The vacuuming stopped, and a woman came out from the front living room. 'I'm coming. Yes?'

'Sorry to bother you. I'm Lexie Reed. I was looking for Sonja De Bruin, the resident advocate, would she be about?' Lexie inquired.

'The resident what?' The woman scratched her head. 'No one is here, love. I wouldn't know who was who, anyways. The agency I work for called me this morning and said to get here and give the place a good clean. I don't know who I'm doing the job for. I just get given an address. The place was pretty clean already. They just wanted a dust, polish and good vacuum. So I can't help you, love, sorry.'

'No worries, I'll get going. Sorry to have troubled you.' Lexie returned to her car. How could a women's crisis shelter go from a full-house one day, to empty the next? Lexie was rattled. She had to get help—this just wasn't right.

Before she could think too much about it and change her mind, Lexie grabbed her mobile and punched in the number for Detective Senior Sergeant Wil Saddington.

'Saddington,' the detective said.

'Detective, my name is Lexie Reed, I'm a journalist...' Lexie started slowly, but was quickly cut short.

'No comment!' he snapped and ended the call.

'What on earth...' Lexie looked dumbfounded at her phone. She quickly redialled, but her call went straight through to his voicemail. She hung up without leaving a message. Checking the GPS on her phone, Lexie got the directions to Moreland Police Station. She headed for Coburg, determined to get the detective to hear her out.

Arriving at the station, she charged up to the front counter where a tired looking officer, who looked to Lexie as though he should have retired several years earlier, greeted her without enthusiasm.

Reading his name badge, Lexie spoke with confidence, 'Sergeant Wilks, my name is Lexie Reed, and I wish to speak with Detective Saddington. Could you please inform him that I'm here.' She gave him an expectant smile.

'Hang on a minute, and I'll see if he's here. You go sit over there. And stay out of trouble.' The sergeant returned Lexie's smile, adding a slow wink.

Four floors above in the Major Incident Room, Wil took the call.

'Boss, it's Mick, I've got a gorgeous young blonde down here at the front desk, wants to see you, of all people! What do you want me to do with her?' The sergeant asked.

'Who is it? What's her name?' Wil responded. 'Did she say what she wants?'

'Name is Lexie Reed, full of importance she is,' Mick said.

'Shit, that's the reporter! That's the last thing I want to be bothered with. Let me think. She's probably just after some inside edge. Take her into one of the interview rooms, I'll send Mel down; she can give her the standard public statements. Melissa will be nicer to her than I probably would. Thanks, Mick.'

Mick returned to the counter and signalled for Lexie to head to the door leading into the office.

'Down this way, my dear, take a seat in here, and one of the officers will be with you directly.' Mick left Lexie to sit on one of four chairs placed around a plain wooden table.

Several minutes later, a female officer entered the room. 'Morning ma'am, I'm Constable Trengrove. Detective Saddington is busy at this moment, and asked me speak to you. I have the Statements for Public Address with me, to answer your questions.'

'I don't have any *questions*. I'm not a reporter...Well, I am a reporter, but I'm not reporting...I have information,' Lexie snapped. Who the hell did Saddington think he was, palming her off on a junior officer? Lexie got out her note pad, wrote down her mobile number, then ripped the page from the book. 'Can you give my number to DSS Saddington. If he can be bothered, get him to give *me* a call. I have information as to who may have murdered Mr Laidlaw. Make sure you let him know that, will you?'

Lexie got up and walked out of the room. She caught the desk sergeant's eye and nodded to the door. The door buzzed, she pulled hard on it and stormed out of the station.

She drove with no destination in mind. She drove just to get far enough from the police station, to settle her anger. Realising her location, she made a few turns, then pulled up in the car park of the Royal Melbourne Zoo. She locked the car, leaving her mobile in the glove box, having ignored the last two times it rang. She paid the entrance fee and went straight to the kiosk. Lexie settled herself at one of the outside tables with a ridiculously expensive chicken burger.

Typical of Melbourne's weather, the rain was long gone and it was now quite warm, especially for autumn. The sun on her back had a calming effect. As Lexie ate, she watched people pointing out the animals to each other, and children running around their smiling parents. The animals came out from cover to bask in the sunshine. It was a bizarre world, Lexie thought, the one she was getting caught up in—it couldn't be further removed from right here and now.

At a loss as to what to do next, Lexie returned to her car and headed back to McHale Shelter. Maybe Sonja or Eddie had returned in the meantime. Heading back along Mt Alexander Road, Lexie spotted Sonja's blue Audi coming out of side street and turning right onto Mt Alexander Road. A quick change of lanes had Lexie in the next right-turning lane. A U-turn put her about four cars behind Sonja's by the time she caught up.

Lexie followed Sonja through the traffic, maintaining distance for fear of being recognised. She followed her to Fitzroy, where Sonya turned into a side street. It was a one-way street, as most were in the area. Lexie slowed down and dropped back.

The houses were old and rundown, not an area that Lexie had ever been in before. She didn't know these back streets, but Sonja obviously did. Suddenly Sonja stopped and parked the Audi. Lexie was taken by surprise, and had to wave an apology to the car behind when she slammed on the brakes. The driver tooted her as he drove past. She hoped that Sonja hadn't heard, looked back up the street and spotted her.

Sonja hadn't seemed to take any notice. Lexie could just make her out disappearing into a house about two blocks ahead. Lexie got out of her car and had only walked a few metres towards Sonja's car, when she stopped. Sonja was leaving the house, and she wasn't alone. Lexie jumped between two parked cars and crouched as low as she could.

She could just make out the other person with Sonja—a thin woman, with straight, shoulder-length light blonde hair. The woman stumbled when she stepped onto the footpath. Sonja grabbed the woman as she staggered towards the blue Audi and helped her into the car.

Lexie's heart was pounding. *Christ, is that Jillian? Oh my God!*

Lexie bolted back to her car, prepared to pursue Sonja again. Her mobile was ringing. She wanted to answer it as it was probably Saddington, again, but she didn't want to take her eyes off the blue Audi in case it made a turn and she lost it.

Sonja made a right turn, then another back onto Nicholson Street. Lexie followed. She was starting to panic, she didn't want to lose the Audi, but it was difficult—the traffic was getting thicker, and she was in unfamiliar territory.

She didn't have to worry for long.

Sonja soon turned into another residential street. The Audi parked and the two women got out. Sonja helped the woman, who struggled to walk by herself and was leaning on Sonja. Lexie parked and turned the engine off. She grabbed her mobile and hit the detective's number.

'Hello?' Wil answered on the first ring.

'Detective, it's Lexie Reed. Please, please take me seriously. I think, I think I may have just found Jillian Laidlaw!' Lexie said in a rush.

'Where are you, Ms Reed? Are you at McHale Shelter?' Wil asked.

'I was heading to the shelter but I spotted Sonja De Bruin in her car. I don't really know what came over me, but I followed her,' Lexie replied. 'I tried to speak to you about...'

'Where exactly are you?' Wil cut her off.

She twisted around in her seat and could just make out the street sign.

'Rose Avenue, in Fitzroy. I'm not sure of the number, though, of the house they've gone in. Sonja has a woman with her and I swear it's Jillian Laidlaw. I met her at the shelter, so I know what she looks like, and I know you're looking for her.'

'It would be helpful if you could get the house number. Can you drive up the street, and as you pass the house, tell me the number, and then leave the area. We are on our way there now—stay on the phone until you've got the number.' Wil had grabbed Marty and told him to get a car.

When Wil ran out of the station, Marty was in his Jeep.

'No cars available.'

Wil jumped in. 'Rose Avenue, Fitzroy. That journalist thinks she's spotted Jillian Laidlaw. She's followed De Bruin to a house there.'

Wil hated being the passenger, but had no choice. He put on his seat belt before he spoke again to Lexie, waiting on hold. 'Ms Reed you can start moving now, we're not too far away. Can you see the house number yet?'

'No, I can't move yet. Another car has pulled up near the house, on the other side of the street. There's someone inside the car, they're not getting out, just looking across at the house. It will be too obvious if I drive by now. I'm too frightened to move yet.'

'What's going on, Wil?' Marty asked. 'Put her on speaker.'

Wil gave his mobile to Marty. 'You talk to her, while I use the radio, I think we may need backup.'

'Ms Reed, this is DSS Hanratty. DSS Saddington is radioing for backup. Are you in a safe place?' Marty took over the call.

'Yes, I'm back a fair distance. I don't know what is going on here, but two men have just walked into the house where Jillian and Sonja are. They came from a side street on foot. The person in the car is still there watching the house. What should I do now?'

'Can you safely reverse back out of the street at all?' Marty asked.

'Yes, I think so. I'll just put the phone down for a minute,' Lexie replied. Then a couple of minutes later added, 'I'm at the start of Rose Avenue now. Damn!'

'What? What's happening?' Marty said.

'No, no, nothing on the street. My mobile, it's the battery, I don't think it'll last much longer.'

'Hang up, we'll be at least another ten or fifteen minutes,' Marty said. 'Save whatever power's left in case you need to call back—if something happens.'

'Stay in your car, Ms Reed. Do not, I repeat, do not approach the house, or anyone on the street,' Wil yelled across to the mobile.

'I think she heard you,' Marty said as he handed Wil back his phone.

Marty parked the Jeep on Nicholson Street, looking impressed with himself, and the perfection of the location of the park.

The detectives walked around the corner and Wil got in the front passenger seat, while Marty got in the back of the Peugeot.

'Hello,' they said in unison. Lexie hit her head on the car's window as she jumped in fright.

'Christ! That was uncalled for,' Lexie snapped, 'My nerves were already on edge.'

'This better be good, Ms Reed, we've got the area swamped with the Moreland Major Incident Unit, all on your word,' Wil stated. 'You have a lot of explaining to do, later. For now, which is the car that's watching, and which is the house that's being watched?'

In the rear of the car, Marty finished speaking quietly into his mobile.

'That was Federal Police, and that house in question is a brothel that they have under investigation. And we have been formally told to leave the area. The Unit have already been told to stand down and return to the station.'

'Right, let me think a minute.' Wil stared up the street as his mind raced ahead.

'We can't leave! Jillian is in that house, and from the way she was walking, I think she's been drugged or something. And Sonja is in there too. You need to speak to her, and that's why I wanted to speak to you. I'm sure she and that Eddie have something to do with the murder. You can't leave now!'

'No, we won't, but you have to. Marty, give Ms Reed here the keys to the Jeep, she can drive it back to the station,' Wil said without taking his eyes off the street ahead. 'We'll stay put in your car, Ms Reed, and return it to you as soon as possible. Marty, can you ring Mick and inform him that Ms Reed will be arriving shortly, and to make her comfortable until we get back.'

'But...' Lexie went to object, but as Wil had collected her bag and was gesturing for her to get out, she understood that she didn't have any choice.

Marty leant between the seats with the keys for the Jeep in his hand. 'It's the beautiful black beast, to the right at the corner. Just take it slow.' He gave her a half smile as she exited the car.

Wil thought about climbing across to the driver's seat, but knew it was a ridiculous idea. Marty got out of the back, crouching down, made his way around to the driver's side and got in behind the wheel.

'What's the plan, then, if we're not paying attention to the Federallies?' Marty looked at Wil.

Wil smiled, eyes still ahead. 'Well, the way I see it, both women inside that house are of interest to our investigation—our *murder* investigation. So I don't think we will lie down and roll over. I want to speak to the guy up there, the one watching the house. He isn't Federal Police surveillance, so I want to know what's his interest here.'

'Who's going to talk to him?' Marty asked.

'You are,' Wil looked at Marty, 'Mess yourself up a bit more. So you don't look conspicuous, so you can blend in with the locals.'

'What do you mean by "more"?' said Marty indignantly as he looked at himself in the rear-vision mirror. He rubbed his hair with his palms to dishevel it further and gave Wil a sheepish grin as he got out of the car and crossed to the other side of the street.

Wil watched Marty lumber up the street as if he belonged there. When he reached the car with the watcher, he got down on his haunches and knocked on the driver's window. Wil could see the driver jump—Marty must have startled him as well.

It was around five minutes before Marty made his way back to the white Peugeot.

'Well, what did he have to say? What's he doing?' Wil was getting a bit antsy—it wasn't every day he ignored orders, especially ones from the Australian Federal Police.

'Young Samuel Greenberg is on his own stakeout. When I flashed my badge, he got excited, he thought I was there in answer to his thirty-or-so phone calls.'

'Huh?'

'Apparently, about three months ago, Samuel and his fiancée got into some huge fight. She started hanging out with some new friends she'd met at a café around the corner from here. She cut herself off from all her other friends. He thinks she's got hooked on drugs through these new friends. When she wouldn't talk to him anymore, he started to follow her—yeah, stalk is another word we could possibly use. He reckons they've got her inside that brothel, drugged and working as a prostitute for Madame Lourdes.'

'Jesus!'

'How did this guy not get taken as seriously, Wil?' Marty shook his head. 'He's obviously intelligent; he's studying at RMIT, when he's not here, stalking his fiancée.'

'It wouldn't be an isolated incident. Not enough manpower to follow-up every report such as his, I'd imagine.'

'He begged me to help.'

'What did you tell him?'

'We're on it.'

CHAPTER EIGHT

Lexie parked the Jeep, slamming the door to vent some of her anger. The adrenaline was still pushing up her blood pressure, and her heart rate hadn't begun to return to anywhere near normal yet. She was convinced that it was Jillian Laidlaw being led by Sonja into the brothel in Fitzroy.

'Ms Reed, lovely to see you again so soon,' Sergeant Wilks greeted Lexie as she approached the front desk.

'Yes, yes, I'm sure,' Lexie stood at the door, waiting to be buzzed in.

On the other side, Mick was waiting, as instructed, to lead her upstairs and somewhere comfortable to await Wil and Marty's return.

'Can you get in touch with Detective Saddington, and ask him to please retrieve my mobile,' Lexie asked. 'I must have dropped it on the floor of the car when he and his partner car-jacked me!'

'Yes ma'am, will do. Can I get you a tea or coffee?' Mick asked as he took Lexie into a small room, in which there was a coffee table and several old armchairs. The police station's version of a hospital's quiet room, Lexie guessed.

'As I have no idea how long I'll be here, I suppose I may as well. Black coffee, half a sugar, thank you, Sergeant.' Lexie dropped into one of the armchairs, sighing loudly. She flicked through the magazines on the coffee table, but when she saw they were all at least four years old, she tossed them back onto the table. She wouldn't have been able to concentrate anyway. All she could think about was what was going on back in Fitzroy, and fearing for Jillian's safety.

'Here you go,' Mick placed a steaming cup of coffee in front of Lexie, and a plate with a few biscuits on it. 'Thought you might like a snack.'

'Any word on what's happening?' Lexie enquired.

'Detectives Saddington and Hanratty are still there, but the rest of team have returned to the station. I'm not sure how this will turn out. You just sit tight; I'll let you know when they're headed back. The ladies room is just up the corridor on the right, if needed,' Mick smiled, then returned to the front desk.

Lexie ate biscuit after biscuit, until it was too late—she realised that she'd eaten them all. *Bloody hell! I'd better add a few extra Ks next time I go for a run.*

Time was dragging and nothing was happening. Lexie stuck her head out into the corridor; she could hear voices, but couldn't see anyone about. She ventured out, walking slowly, hoping she wouldn't be noticed. At the end of the corridor was a big, brightly lit room, where the door had been left open. The sign beside the door read Major Incident Room.

Lexie walked in, looking back over her shoulder and making sure that her visitor's badge was in clear sight. The room was massive. There were several uniformed officers seated at desks, concentrating on phone conversations, all of them taking notes. She nodded to one officer as he looked up from his desk, as though she was giving her approval of the work he was undertaking.

She walked to the far end, where the entire back wall was a white board. On it were large photographs, several she recognised as Jillian and her daughters. There were notes written under nearly all of the pictures. She walked along the board and saw what must be the crime scene photos. Lexie was compelled to look out of curiosity, but then felt sickened.

She stood frozen, staring at Sean Laidlaw's corpse. Was that his head: mutilated and grotesque, two ugly halves of a skull? She'd just figured out it was the brain, and what looked like black molasses, which was probably congealed blood, and lots of it, when bile shot up to the back of her throat from her stomach. She turned and ran out of the room, only just making it into a cubicle in the ladies' toilet. There wasn't time to close the door.

Lexie rinsed her mouth out with cold water, and then splashed some onto her face. *I guess now I don't have to worry about the biscuit binge!* She fished out a small makeup bag she kept in her handbag, and repaired her face. With her head down, she walked back to wait where she was supposed to be waiting.

She paced the small room, back and forth. When she couldn't stand it anymore, she stuck her head out into the corridor again. She could hear a lot of activity going on in the MIR. She made her way towards the noise. Recognising the detective's voice, she was about to storm into the room, demanding to know why she'd been kept waiting, but she stopped in her tracks. The anger in his voice stopped her from entering.

'We've been stopped by the Federal Police, no one is to go anywhere near Madame Lourdes. I want a car at that shelter, McHale is it?'

'Yes, Boss! McHale Shelter,' a young officer yelled back.

'Addresses for that De Bruin woman and the security guard, I want cars there as well. I want eyes everywhere—the minute either of them surfaces, haul them in here. I'm getting real pissed at being jerked around.'

Wil stormed out of the room and bellowed at Lexie as she turned, trying to get away. '*You*! Stop there!'

111

Lexie stopped. She could feel the redness creeping up her neck, heading to her face. She turned and started an attempt to get herself out of trouble, feeling about ten years old. 'I'm sorry, I wasn't snooping I was just—'

'Aren't you a professional snoop? Isn't that what you do for a living, under the guise of journalism?'

'Look, don't take your anger out on me. I believe I was the one who led you to Jillian Laidlaw. What other leads have you been following? If you're too impotent to cope with the situation, hopefully the Federal Police will rescue her.' Lexie tried to feel taller, she stretched as much as she could, but the tall detective made her feel diminished.

'Thank you for your assistance. I've left your car keys with the desk sergeant.' Wil stomped off.

Lexie turned on her heel, and took off to the front desk.

*

'I actually think that woman might have something. "Impotent". I liked that. And that she had the balls to say it to your face,' Marty smiled as he sat down. 'I'm not sure whose face was redder—hers or yours. That was so cool.'

'Shut up! What now—how are we going to get round this?' Wil was stumped.

'Our Samuel sounds like he's become a permanent fixture in the street. Madame Lourdes and her gang obviously don't feel he's a threat, otherwise they would've gotten rid of him by now. The feds mustn't care either or they'd have moved him on. What if we get a hold of him, ride shotgun with him on his next stakeout. I've got his address. Can you believe it? He still lives at home with mummy and daddy!' Marty slapped his leg and gave a loud hoot.

Wil sat up straight in his seat. 'That sounds half-baked, but it might actually work for us. You ring him and tell him we'll be around in the morning, about eight o'clock. Don't let on what we want, just say we'd like to ask him a few questions.' Wil got up and got his coat and keys. 'I'm heading out. Mon wants me to come over, she's organised for Lucas' commanding officer to phone us at ho...at her place tonight at seven. Neither of us have had any contact with him for nearly a month now. Its not a good feeling, Marty, I can tell you.'

They were interrupted by a knock at the door.

'Sads, we've got Carmel O'Rourke, the sister from Canada, in Interview Room Two. You two going to talk to her?' Terry said poking his head into the detective's office.

'Shit! She's here now?'

'Yes, she came straight from the airport.'

'All right, be there in a couple of minutes. You want to go or stay, Marty? I don't see us getting much out of this.'

'I might head out, then. I think I'll check on our stalker on the way home, make sure he's OK. He's got me worried, that boy. See you in the morning.'

*

'Call me Carmel, and no thanks, I'm fine, I had enough coffee on the plane,' Jillian Laidlaw's sister replied to Wil's offer.

Wil could see that the woman was stressed, and guessed that she was tired after her marathon flight. 'You and your sister are very alike,' he commented.

'Have you any news on her yet, do you know where she is? The flight from Vancouver is usually long enough as it is, but to be sick with worry for all that distance, well, it was very hard to ...' Carmel O'Rourke wiped away a tear with a handkerchief that was balled up in her hand.

'We have several leads that we're following up.' Wil didn't want to give away too much in case the lead wasn't as solid as first hoped.

'I'm not sure what help I can be to you. I've been living in Canada for the past twelve years. Jillian and I have stayed in touch, but I'd hardly say we were close. Christmas and birthday cards; we send the other photos of the kids in the cards. I'm four years older than Jillian, and as soon as I was able to, I got out of home. I saved as much money as I could, which was hard as my father used to take half my wages for board. But I managed to put some away, and then moved into a flat with a girlfriend. Jillian was thirteen going on fourteen around that time. I hardly ever went back home.'

'You weren't close to your parents?' Wil knew that the mother had died, but as yet had nothing on the father.

'Our mother started getting sick not long before I left home. She was sick for a while before being diagnosed with cardiomyopathy. Our father didn't look after her, wouldn't take her to the doctors, or the hospital when she needed. It killed her in the end. He broke her—and her heart. We used to beg her to leave him. But she believed that we would have been worse off with her a single mother. How she could think that, I don't know.'

'Were you aware that Jillian was abused by her husband? Our last concrete lead on her was a crisis shelter where she went. She'd left Sean as he had allegedly assaulted her, and it hadn't been the first time. Our officers had been to the house before, but Jillian never pressed charges.'

115

'No, no I didn't know. But then it doesn't surprise me. When we were younger, mum was often bruised and sore, but she always said that it was because she fell out of bed. I told her she should sleep in Jillian's old cot—it would have been safer. As we got older, I guess we just got used to it. My father was violent and unpredictable, and when he drank, those two traits were amplified. I felt bad leaving Jillian when I moved out, but I had to—it was self-preservation. Things I assume, got worse. Jillian's visits to me at work got fewer and fewer. Then mum got worse. Jillian rang me at work to let me know that she'd taken mum to hospital. Mum never went home—she died in hospital. I've never forgiven him. I don't know if he ever abused Jillian, we never spoke about him. I pretended he didn't exist.'

'We haven't been able to locate your father. Do you know where he is? Are there any relatives in Australia that might know?' Wil asked.

'The last time I saw my father was at my mother's funeral. I think he would have drunk himself to death by now. Without my mother to look after him, and Jillian eventually leaving, I can't see how he would have survived, in all honesty.' Carmel sat up straight and rolled her shoulders and stretched her neck. 'There aren't any relatives in Australia. He came out here alone, in 1978. He was born in Trondhein, Norway. As far as I know, there'd still be family there. He often talked about them. The drunker he was, the more he hated them. But he always

116

went on about the family tree, and how we'd been added to it, his two little sweeties. Not that I want to know any of them!'

'How long do you think you'll be staying in Melbourne, Carmel?' Wil asked.

'I can play it by ear. My husband is very good. I just want be able to see Jillian and the girls, tell them I love them and that I haven't forgotten them. I feel so guilty. She must feel so alone.' Carmel blew her nose. 'Please let me know the minute you have any news.'

Both stood and left the interview room. 'We have your mobile. I'll phone as soon as there's anything. You look as though you could do with some sleep.' Wil led Carmel out into the reception area.

'Yes, the jetlag is about to hit,' Carmel gave a sad half-smile as she turned and walked out the station door.

CHAPTER NINE

Wil went back to his place to shower, shave and have something to eat before heading over to his soon-to-be ex-wife's house—his house. He let himself into his apartment and went straight to his laptop, logging into Skype. He wanted to be available, should Lucas try to contact him.

The answering machine was flashing, one new message. 'Wil, it's me. Just a reminder for tonight, seven o'clock, please doesn't be late. I...I guess we'll...Nothing, bye.'

The machine beeped, no more messages. Wil could hear the stress in Monica's voice. He looked around the room; it was impersonal, nothing homey about it. It could have been a hotel room. The apartment was one of twenty-five in a secure building, one block back from the beach in South Melbourne, a decent enough suburb. When Monica had asked him to leave, it was the second place he'd looked at. He'd made sure there were two bedrooms, just in case Lucas was ever in town—he could offer him somewhere to stay, other than at his mother's.

While waiting for the microwave to heat his frozen dinner, Wil finished dressing. He picked up his coat from the armchair, checking the pockets for his wallet and keys. Just then, music started playing in one of the pockets. 'Oh shit!' He retrieved the ringing mobile phone, and looked at the screen. *Incoming call from Carla.* Wil hit *Accept.*

'Hi, girlfriend, ready to shake your booty? Remember I'm not taking no for an answer,' Carla's voice was upbeat.

'Hello, this is Detective Saddington. I seem to have acquired your friend's mobile. I retrieved it from the floor of her car, but then forgot to return it to her.' Wil knew what he was saying sounded a bit on the suspicious side.

'I don't understand. If you are the police, what were you doing with Lexie's car? Is she all right? Nothing's happened to her, has it?'

'No, no, nothing is wrong, and I would assume she'd be at home.' Wil didn't really know what to say, he rolled his eyes. 'She was at the Moreland Police Station earlier today, helping us with an inquiry.'

'Well now, I can't ring her to check all this out, can I? We are supposed to be going to City Salsa dance class tonight, in St Kilda,' Carla said. 'Do you have Lexie's address?'

'No, I don't, but it wouldn't take me long to find it—I have connections,' Wil looked at the mobile in his hand, sure that the woman on the other end would now be having some serious doubts about him.

'Can you bring the phone to the Memorial Hall in Acland Street at eight-thirty? I'm picking Lexie up at her place at eight. It'll take me twenty minutes to force her to get changed into something *suitable,* then into my car. Does that suit you?'

Wil put the phone down by his leg so Carla couldn't hear him groan. Then into the phone he said, 'I suppose so. Will I be able to find you if I'm a little late? I have something to do before hand.'

'Walk straight through to the back, past the bar,' Carla was sounding excited now. 'Dress nice, or you won't get past the Russian guy doing security. He takes his job very seriously.'

'All right, I'll see how I go. Bye.' Wil hung up and put the phone in his pocket. This Lexie woman, Wil thought, is getting to be quite an annoyance.

*

Wil knocked, much to his disgust, at the door that had been his home for nearly twenty years. Lucas had been about two years old when they'd bought the California bungalow. Real estate prices in Malvern back then were on the rise. As a young couple with a toddler, they'd dreamed of living in a tree-lined street, close to shops, parks and the city. Fortune came to them when a relative of Monica's, a great-aunt after whom she had been named, died, leaving her estate to Monica.

120

'Wil, come in, I thought you were going to be late. Or caught up at work.' She walked ahead of Wil into the living room.

'Jesus, Mon, it's not even ten to seven. Give me a break. I said I'd be here and I'm early,' Wil responded.

'Well, you've been known to be a no-show before.' Monica sat on the sofa, her legs tucked underneath her as she hugged a cushion close.

Wil removed his jacket and threw himself down in an armchair opposite her. 'Can we move on?'

'Sorry, I'm sorry, Wil. I'm just sick with worry, and it helps me to take it out on you.' She gave him a small smile.

After what felt an eternity to Wil, the phone rang. Monica jumped and sat staring at the phone.

'Are you going to answer it?' Wil said, and got up to snap up the handpiece.

'Hello, Wil Saddington speaking.'

'Lieutenant Colonel Andrew Harris, here. I believe you have been worrying about your son Corporal Saddington.' The man spoke with authority. 'Sir, you and your wife can stop worrying. Your son is fit and healthy.'

'Thank you, that is a massive relief. Are you able to tell us why we've not heard from him, or is that classified?'

121

Wil gave Monica a huge smile, and mouthed, 'He's OK'. He saw tears brimming in her eyes, and knew she could now let go.

'No, nothing quite so interesting as any classified manoeuvres, more a case of on-leave, having a good time apparently. His platoon was on three weeks' break, and they've been in Turkey for most of that time,' the Lieutenant Colonel coughed and cleared his throat. 'Now, Mr Saddington, I've been speaking with your son's Commanding Officer Captain Newell; he is very close with his men, and he has told me that the young corporal has been very angry and depressed over the separation of you and your wife. I hope you don't feel I'm getting too personal here.'

'No, no, not at all. It's better if we're aware of what's going on with Lucas. He obviously can't tell us himself.' Wil slumped back in the armchair. Monica sat forward, trying to hear what was being said.

'He has been drinking, and quite a bit. Lucky for him, he has good friends looking out for him. He's been rescued from trouble on several occasions apparently,' the LTCOL informed Wil. 'Now, Captain Newell feels that, given some time, your son will get his head sorted, and be in contact with you both of his own volition. For now, if you can just sit tight, and be patient. Hard work for parents sometimes.'

'Just so long as he's all right, I guess that's what we have to do,' Wil scratched his head in frustration. 'Thank you for taking the time to check on our son for us, and we appreciate you calling us personally. We will, as you said, sit tight.'

'No problem, I can understand your concern. Goodbye.' The LTCOL cut the connection. Wil put the receiver down.

'What did he say? What's going on?' Monica unfolded her legs and sat up on the sofa, tossing aside the cushion.

Wil got up and sat beside her. He knew what he was going to tell her would hurt. 'Lucas' platoon has been on holidays in Turkey. His captain told the lieutenant colonel that Lucas has been upset, not handling our separation very well. He's been acting up a bit. His lack of communication is most likely a punishment for us. We've been advised to sit back, give him some space. Don't cry, Mon, at least he's all right.' Wil tried to hug her.

She pushed him away, jumping up off the sofa. 'This is all your fault!'

'Yeah, and how do you figure that? Lucas is apparently upset about us splitting up. Like I was. I'm pretty sure that this separation was all your idea.' Wil was astounded.

'If you'd remained the man I'd married, I'd never have wanted it to end. Plus, you're the one who encouraged Lucas to join the army. Was that so he could live out your dream? He should be here, with his family, not in that godforsaken country fighting some insane war.' She'd stopped crying. 'Can you please leave, now, before I say anymore? I can't help but want to blame you, Wil.'

'Yes, I think I'd better go.' Wil had anger in his belly now. 'Do you even know what you want anymore, Mon?'

*

Wil sat in his Honda for ten minutes before he noticed the cold. He turned the engine on to start the heater. He had come out of the house feeling numb; there were too many emotions all at once for him to deal with, so he just shut them all down. He sat in the dark, staring straight ahead. He looked at the clock on the dashboard—it was eight-twenty. His hand went to the breast pocket of his jacket and the mobile phone.

He turned the car lights on, put it in Drive, pulled away from his old home and headed for St Kilda. He found a park easy enough, but struggled to find the correct change for the ticket machine. 'Perfect! I can't seem to get anything right.'

He got back in the car, drove out of the parking lot and parked across the street in a loading zone. From the

124

glove box he retrieved his police-parking card, placing it on the dash.

Wil could hear the Latin American music thumping from the hall before he'd even crossed Acland Street. Lots of people, mostly laughing women, were entering the building, dressed for dancing, ready for a fun night. He pushed all thoughts of Monica from his mind and dashed across the street, careful of a tram rattling along towards him, it's driver ringing the bell.

He started to look for Lexie and her friend Carla. He wouldn't be able to miss the little blonde, she'd be strutting around, ready to have a piece of him—it was just the night for it. It was now eight-fifty, and there wasn't any sign of them waiting for him outside the hall. He stepped inside to the foyer and looked around. The music was loud, the beat thumping through the walls.

There was wood everywhere: panelling up the walls, timber floor and staircase off to the right. He was about to walk straight ahead, through the double doors, as Carla had instructed, when a security guard appeared out of nowhere. He stepped in front of Wil blocking his entrance and mumbled something as he looked Wil up and down.

'I'm sorry, mate, what was that?' Wil said.

'Bar is to left, Salsa classes in hall. Where do you want?' The Russian had a very thick accent.

'The bar will do, thanks,' Wil took a couple of steps back. 'I need a drink before I head on out there.'

He turned to the left and walked into the bar. The music came rumbling through the walls. He climbed onto a bar stool and looked around the room. The bar was central to the room, stools lined up all round it. There were clusters of tables and chairs, many filled with patrons. Poker machines lined the walls, bright lights flashing.

Wil nodded to a couple of serious drinkers sitting opposite him who'd been staring him down as he'd entered. They raised their glasses and returned the nod. The bartender arrived, wiping the bar in front of Wil. It must be habit, Wil noted, as the bar had been perfectly clean.

'What can I get you?' The bartender asked Wil.

'Bourbon should do the trick,' Wil smiled at the young man.

'Make that two, he owes me,' Lexie jumped up on the stool next to Wil and put out her hand.

He took her mobile out of his pocket and passed it over. 'I think it's dead.'

Lexie looked at the phone. 'Yeah, she's a goner.' She opened a small silver clutch bag, and placed the phone inside. She put her hand out again. 'Detective

Saddington, I think we got off on the wrong foot. Do you think we could start over? I'm Lexie Reed, nice to meet you.'

Wil took Lexie's hand. 'Sure, why not. Wil Saddington, and it's nice to meet you too.' Still holding her hand, he turned it over, then back and laughed. 'You've got the tiniest hands.' He let go as the bartender put their drinks on the bar.

Simultaneously, they picked up their drinks and clinked glasses.

Wil turned to Lexie and gave her an approving look, from head to foot. 'So, your friend Carla managed to get you kitted out nicely for tonight.'

'I was actually sitting on the couch, in my pyjamas, sulking, when Carla arrived. I didn't have my phone, as you well know,' Lexie gave Wil a sly look. 'And I didn't think I'd be getting it back until tomorrow. Of course I'd forgotten all about Salsa night. It wasn't a high priority on my list of things to do today!'

'I got the impression Carla was quite excited, especially as I gave her the excuse to get you out of the house.' Wil smiled down at his drink. He was tapping on the bar to the rhythm of music and surprised that he was relaxing and enjoying himself. 'You don't come across as the shrinking violet type.'

'Carla and I have been friends for years. I love her like a sister. But she's more the party girl than I am. She believes dancing can cure most things.' Lexie drained her glass. 'I think you owe me one more drink, Detective.'

Wil got the barman's attention, and held up two fingers. 'So what is it that Carla thinks dancing will cure you of, Ms Reed?'

'There you are, Lex! I thought you'd done a runner on me,' Carla called out as she did a quick-quick-slow step on her way to the bar. 'So, you really are a detective, I hear,' Carla said to Wil as she took the empty stool next to him.

'Wil Saddington.' Wil offered Carla his hand. 'Nice to meet you.'

'Carla Garmendia, a pleasure to meet you.' Carla shook Wil's hand. 'Now, don't take this the wrong way— it's great that Lexie is getting out, meeting new people— but I'm not too sure about this article she's writing, and where it's leading her. I would appreciate it if you could make her see some sense and stay out of this...whatever it is that's going on. It all sounds a bit dangerous to me. What do you think, Detective?'

'Call me Wil. And I couldn't agree more with you, Carla.' Wil liked Lexie's friend. 'You are obviously an intelligent woman—between the two of us, we should be able to make her understand that would be the best thing.'

'I feel the music calling me,' Carla slipped down off the stool. 'My Latina blood is pumping tonight. Come and dance, Wil. Keep our Lexie off the troubled streets for tonight.'

Wil shook his head. But Carla stood, hands on hips, giving him a determined look.

'Oh, all right, why not! Come along now, Ms Reed, finish your drink,' Wil said, and then sculled the rest of his bourbon. 'Let me show you how it's done.' Behind Lexie's back, he gave Carla a wink.

Carla laughed and twirled, then led the way to the ballroom.

The room was packed solid with people. Up on the stage, at the back of the room, was a couple dancing. 'Instructors,' Carla yelled back to Wil. He couldn't hear her, but read her lips. The wooden floor was taking a pounding from the dancers; Wil could feel the vibration from the stamping feet going up to his knees. Carla took off, running into the arms of a welcoming male dancer. Wil turned, grabbing one of Lexie's tiny hands, and smiled. She laughed and nodded acceptance.

He spun her around with expertise, then started the sensuous quick-quick-slow of the Salsa. Lexie glided along with him, the two of them melting together. Each of the couples danced around in their fixed areas on the dance floor, rotating around one another in a tantalising flirtation.

Wil and Lexie each let themselves be swept along with the percussion rhythms. Neither of them had any thoughts for the day and its frustrations; no thoughts really beyond the fun they were having. The drinks had loosened them up enough to be able to relax and be themselves.

The class ended to a cheerful round of applause from the crowd. The instructors encouraged everyone to return the following Tuesday. 'Don't forget, next Tuesday there will be door prizes, and professional dance demonstrations. See you all then. Goodnight all.'

Wil placed a protective hand on Lexie's back as he ushered her out of the hall and onto Acland Street. 'Well, that was quite a work-out,' Wil said as they stepped toward the curb, standing out of the way of their fellow dancers as they turned left and right heading to varying destinations.

'I had so much fun. I must say, though, that cool sea breeze feels delicious—it was getting really hot in there, with all those bodies jumping and gyrating around,' Lexie fanned her face with her clutch. 'Did you see Carla on the way out?'

Both of them scanned the faces of the people coming out, and the backs of those who'd walked away—Carla couldn't be missed in her bright red dress, seven-inch heels, and mass of curly brown hair.

A couple approached them. Carla had her arms entwined around a man who appeared to be happy with the situation. 'Lexie, my love! What a great night!' Carla left her man and ran up to Lexie and gave her a hug, whispering in her ear.

'Sure thing, you be careful,' Lexie kissed her friend on the cheek.

'Now, you two behave.' Carla gave Wil a self-satisfied smile, then skipped off to grab her man as he was walking away.

'Let me guess, she was your ride,' Wil smiled.

'Yup,' Lexie replied.

'Want to grab a coffee, then I'll drop you home?' Wil gestured to the coffee shop opposite.

'Yeah, sure, but it's my treat.'

They crossed the road carefully—even late on a Tuesday night, there was considerable traffic.

Lexie recognised the pretty young waitress as she approached their table.

'Bonsoir.'

'Bonsoir,' the waitress beamed. 'Qu'est-ce que vous voulez?'

'Café latte?' Lexie looked at Wil, who nodded. 'Deux cafés au lait, s'il vous plait.'

'Now you're just plain showing off,' Wil smiled across at Lexie.

She shrugged, and then sat up straight. 'Can we talk now, about Jillian Laidlaw, the shelter, everything?'

'I guess that means the fun is over, finished, that's all folks?' Wil sat back in his seat, resignation written all over him.

'Well, excuse me for feeling guilty,' Lexie blinked at him. 'Here I am dancing the night away, with the man who should be out rescuing that poor woman who has ended up God knows where by now!'

Their coffees arrived and Wil held off his response until the waitress left.

'Look, the Federal Police are onto the brothel. The place is under heavy surveillance. When they make their move, they'll look after her. I was kicked off the street, remember.' Wil sugared his coffee, stirring it vigorously.

'And the shelter, have you been back there? Sonja De Bruin and Eddie Kovacs are up to something. They didn't want me around.' Lexie sugared her coffee as well, and started stirring. 'They made that very clear.'

'I wonder why?' Wil muttered a barely audible response.

'What was that?' Lexie said, pretending she hadn't heard him.

'Nothing. What is it exactly, that you believe that they're up to? Concrete, mind you, something that I could actually use as evidence.'

'To start with, I believe that Eddie is responsible for the murder. Paige, she was working at McHale Shelter on the night that Sean Laidlaw turned up at the shelter. She told me, he was outside on the street calling out for Jillian, screaming her name. Paige ended up phoning Eddie, he arrived and spoke to Sean. Not long after, she heard their two cars drive off.' Lexie scooped up a mouthful of froth from the top of her coffee. 'What time was Sean murdered?'

'Pathologist puts time of death between two and three a.m.,' Wil put down the spoon and finally took a sip of his coffee.

'Well, there you go! Eddie followed Sean away from the shelter at approximately one-thirty. The timing is perfect, the motive is perfect.' Lexie picked up her drink.

'Timing, OK. But why do you believe that Eddie Kovacs would follow Sean Laidlaw home, if it were known that he left the shelter at the same time as Sean? Then enter his house and plant a splitter in his skull? Wouldn't that be just plain stupid? Next, motive: tell me why, if this Kovacs had convinced Sean to leave the shelter, why he would bother to follow him into his house and plant a splitter in his skull?' Wil waited for Lexie to reply.

'Well, it's obvious now, after what I saw this morning. They are taking women from the shelter, and making them work as prostitutes in that brothel in Fitzroy. Sean Laidlaw got in the way by complicating things. Husbands don't usually find their wives at the shelter, so when Sean turned up, they knew they had to get rid of him, otherwise he could jeopardise their plans for Jillian. Either the brothel is theirs, or they are selling women to the brothel owner.' Lexie sounded very convincing.

'So, we're dealing with murdering sex-slave-traders,' Wil raised his eyebrows.

'Aren't you suspicious as to why the Federal Police have a Fitzroy brothel under their watch? It would hardly be small time prostitution, now would it? There has to be more to it, with an international twist?' Lexie scrutinized Wil. 'You aren't exactly throwing yourself into this case, are you? Do you even care about Jillian Laidlaw, or who

killed her husband? What the hell's the matter with you?'
Lexie threw her teaspoon onto the table.

'Feel free to speak your mind, Ms Reed,' Wil bit back.

'Is this your case or not?' Lexie asked.

'Yes, mine and Marty's. You met him earlier today. I bet you have some lovely insights about him too that you are going to share.'

'Whose idea was it that led to the shelter?' Lexie asked.

'Marty's. He's a good detective, but has really bad taste in music,' Wil smirked.

'Yes, I'll vouch for that, I saw the CD covers in his Jeep.' Lexie tried to recover their earlier camaraderie. 'What's been your contribution to the case? You gave me the brush off when I was only trying to help.'

'Yes, you're right, though it hurts to admit it. I've got some personal issues at the moment, and they have been clouding my judgement, stopping me from doing my job to the best of my ability. You know,' Wil looked up from his coffee, 'I am a good detective, usually.'

'Yes, well, I figured you must be, normally. I wouldn't have thought that sloppy work would have got you promotions to Detective Senior Sergeant.' Lexie gave him a smile.

'I have a twenty-three-year-old son: Lucas. He's in the army, in Afghanistan. The thing is, we, his mother and I, hadn't had word from him for some time, and well, we've been worried sick. Only tonight, I went over to my...to my soon to be ex-wife's. We received a phone call from my son's commanding officer, telling us that Lucas was fine, and that there wasn't any need to worry,' Wil swallowed the last of his coffee. 'It was a huge relief, I can tell you. Do you have any kids, Lexie?'

'No, I don't.' Lexie hated answering that question. It was asked far too frequently. 'You have had a lot on your plate. I'm sorry I was so harsh.'

'You're right, though. I've distanced myself from the case, leaving everybody else to run around, getting bits of information here and there, but without being at the helm. Marty and I are partners, but I always take the lead. It's just how we work, and normally it works for us.' Wil paused for a moment before continuing. 'Starting tomorrow, I'll be, as you put it, throwing myself into the case. I'll be one hundred per cent focused. Marty and I have an early start. A plan hatched earlier today in his twisted little brain.'

Lexie gestured for the bill. 'That's good to hear, Wil. Jillian needs all the help she can get.' She placed three five-dollar notes in the bill folder left on the table.

Together they walked out of the coffee shop and to Wil's car, parked around the corner. The five-minute drive was taken in silence, each deep in thought. Wil parked the Honda in Lexie's driveway, but left the engine running. 'I want you to promise me that you will stay away from the shelter, and De Bruin and Kovacs.'

'I'll try my hardest, Detective Senior Sergeant,' Lexie laughed as she got out of the car. 'Thank you for a very interesting day, Wil.'

She shut the car door then ran up the path to her house.

CHAPTER TEN

Wil and Marty made their way along the suburban tree-lined streets of Mount Waverley, heading to the Greenberg house. The plan was to *borrow* Samuel's car. They would be able to park opposite the brothel without drawing attention, as Samuel's car was surely viewed by now as a constant fixture in the street. They could do their own surveillance, undetected by the AFP. Marty had thought his plan ingenious.

'Yes, yes, you're going to bust this case wide open, Marty—you're the man. Now settle down.' Wil slowed the car to a crawl as he entered the street. 'What the hell's going on?'

There were four patrol cars parked in the street. As they neared the cars, they realised that they were out front of the Greenbergs'.

'I haven't heard anything; nothing's come over the radio.' Marty sat forward in his seat.

'Call Terry, see if he knows what's happened.'

Wil parked and got out of the car. He walked up to an officer who was leaning back against the side of the patrol car, and flashed his ID. The constable jumped away from the car, and stood up straight.

138

'Relax. Is all this for the Greenbergs?' Wil asked.

'Yes, sir, well, for Samuel Greenberg. But you'll have to speak to the feds. We're only here for crowd control.' The constable looked around, as did Wil. They smiled at each other, acknowledging the absence of any crowd. Wil turned towards the house. He could hear wailing coming from inside.

Marty was headed towards them, gesturing for Wil to come to him. As Wil got closer, Marty turned and they walked back, getting back in the car.

'We should head back to the station, I'll tell you on the way.' Marty paled as he spoke and Wil sensed something bad. He turned the car around and headed back to Coburg.

'The feds have really fucked up big time, Wil. Our boy Samuel was doing his usual night-shift watch last night. There must have been something going down that Madame Lourdes didn't want Sammy seeing, so one of those Asian fuckers walked right up to his car, and blew his brains out,' Marty put his hands on his head. 'This is my fault! I should have told him to piss off yesterday while he had a chance. Instead, all I was interested in was how to use the poor bastard. Jesus Christ, Wil, what have I done?'

'Hey, come on. Don't go blaming yourself. This has nothing to do with you. If anyone has to answer for it, it'll be the feds. What the hell were they doing? What a cock-up!' Wil sped up.

'I told Terry to have everybody in the MIR, we'll have a meeting a soon as we get back.' Marty went quiet.

'I know what you're thinking— have we lost Jillian Laidlaw, again?' Wil tried to weave through the morning school traffic. 'No point in putting the lights and bells on, I doubt anything would help get through this lot any faster. How many bloody schools are there out this way?'

The MIR was full and buzzing. Terry looked up when he saw Wil and Marty enter the room. He sat at a desk at the far end of the room. the Incident Board behind him. The information on the board was increasing, but wasn't leading anywhere helpful. Terry received the nod from Wil to go ahead.

'OK, people, quiet please. We'll get this meeting started. Anyone with anything to report, be ready, have your notes in order, we've wasted enough time already. Last sighting of Jillian Laidlaw was yesterday—by a reliable witness?' Terry looked directly at Wil for confirmation.

Wil nodded and walked over to the Incident Board. He pointed to his last report written on the board.

'Lexie Reed is a journalist. She had met and interviewed Mrs Laidlaw at McHale Shelter. Yesterday, Ms Reed followed Sonja De Bruin, the shelter's resident advocate to premises at Rose Avenue, Fitzroy, where she believes she saw Mrs Laidlaw being led into a house. Ms Reed is, so far, the only witness to this. The last sighting prior to this was at the shelter on Monday morning, when De Bruin left with Mrs Laidlaw in her car. Where she was the rest of that day and night is unknown.' Wil resumed his seat.

'The Unit arrived on scene at Rose Avenue, but were promptly told to leave, as the house in question is under surveillance by the AFP. Even though our prime suspect in a murder inquiry is possibly inside we were sent packing.' Terry read a page of his notes before speaking again. 'DSS Hanratty spoke to a Samuel Greenberg, who was parked across the street from the house, which we now know is a brothel, run by a Thai woman known to us only as Madame Lourdes. I've not gone any further with ID checks; presumably we're not to.'

Marty took the floor. 'Samuel Greenberg told me that his girlfriend was working as a prostitute inside the brothel. He believed that she been coerced into drugs and was now working to support a drug habit. He said that he'd been trying to get police to help him get her away, but had failed. Now it seems that we've failed him completely.' Marty threw himself back down on his seat.

'The report I have received,' Terry looked back at his notes again, 'is this: At zero six hundred hours, Samuel Greenberg's body was discovered, deceased. He was sitting in his car, in the driver's seat. A local resident, walking to Nicholson Street to catch the tram to work, discovered the body. The triple zero call had Fitzroy Police respond. They were informed by Federal Police to clean up the scene as soon as possible, not to doorknock or canvas the area, as per normal procedure.' Terry shook his head.

'The feds apparently saw the crime committed. In fact, they have video footage of the shooting. Their statement is that a man of Asian appearance entered Rose Avenue on foot, from a side street, walked up to Greenberg's car, tapped on his window to get his attention, them shot him point blank—in the poor bastard's head. The shooter did not come out of, nor go into, Madame Lourdes' at anytime. They believed Greenberg to be dead, and not wanting to jeopardise their investigation, they remained silent. However, they are happy to pass on the picture of the gunman. Their generosity, not to mention their psychic abilities, is very humbling.'

'Who has anything on Eddie Kovacs, the security guard from McHale?' Wil scanned the faces of the officers.

A young uniformed officer stood to say his piece. 'Boss, I have...'

'And you are?' Wil gestured with raised his hands, palms up.

'Sorry, Boss, Senior Constable Ross Ashworth,' he introduced himself, and then confidently continued. 'Mr Kovacs has had several assault charges made against him, with two convictions. We have his home address, with an unmarked on round-the-clock watch. He has not returned to the premises since the car's been there. I don't know whether you want me to attempt to get a warrant to search the place. I don't really like our chances of getting one. What do you think?' Ross shrugged.

Wil thought for a minute before replying. 'Yeah, I agree, and I doubt we'd find anything in there of interest. We just want to talk to him at this stage. But I think we should try and get a warrant for the shelter. Maybe the journalist is onto something—what it is, I'm not sure.'

'I'll get on it straight away.' Ross resumed his seat.

'What about forensics? Who was following up there?' Wil looked across the board to see if any new reports had been written up.

'I went to the Forensic Services Department, and spoke to...' Melissa quickly flicked through her notes, frustrated that she'd forgotten the guy's name so soon. 'Ah huh, Deepak Patel. He's a forensic scientist in the DNA Science Branch, he reckons they are still trying to separate the DNA on three separate prints—the ones

143

found on the picture of the Laidlaw's. Their machine was out of action for a day and a half, which has set them behind for loads of work. But they are still treating ours as a priority.' Melissa clenched her left hand into a tight fist. 'Also, I followed up on what Constable Davis was um...before he was, before he...' she stopped, took a deep breath, then resumed. 'Anyway, I checked and cross-referenced every violent crime committed in Victoria in the past ten years, and nothing stood out. Most of the cases were closed, and the ones that weren't didn't appear to have any relevance to ours.'

Wil, noticing the blush creeping up her neck, gave her an encouraging smile, pleased with her progress. 'Good work, Mel. Stay on top of the forensics, and keep me informed. Anything from Traffic—Kovacs' or De Bruin's cars sighted, glimpsed even?'

Terry answered. 'So far, we don't have either make or model for the van, only that it's white. Nothing registered in either name for a van of any description. There is, however, a bike registered to Kovacs, a Ducati Streetfighter 848. And I'd sure like to know how a security guard at a women's shelter could afford a new bike like that on the scraps he'd earn. No sightings of the blue Audi owned and registered to De Bruin.'

Ross put his hand up. 'We've an unmarked outside her apartment building as well. But again, Boss, no sightings.'

144

'Sarge,' Marty said to Terry, 'what do you think about talking to the Sexual Crimes Squad? They'd have to have something on Lourdes. Do you know anyone in the squad you could have a quiet chat with?'

'Yeah, and if the feds get wind of it, will it be your balls or mine that they bust?' Terry looked at Wil for reassurance. 'I know lots of people, Marty. I want to know now, up front, if you guys are going to be playing cowboys. We all in this room want to catch a killer, but I've seen what can happen to officers if they get in the feds' way. Careers get ruined; hell, I've seen lives get ruined. So think carefully before you go making any grand gestures.'

Wil let out a huge sigh. 'OK, Terry, calm down, no one is doing anything stupid. Yet!' He smiled, attempting to defuse the atmosphere. 'It can't hurt just to enquire, now can it? That would be as far as it would go.'

Shaking his head, Terry replied, 'I'll see what I can find out.'

'OK, get started on that search warrant for McHale shelter,' Wil looked at Ashworth. 'I think in the meantime, Marty and I'll head over there. Let me know the instant you have it. Ross?'

'Yes,' the senior constable started gathering up his notes. 'On it now, Boss.'

Marty followed Wil to their office. 'What are you hoping to find at the shelter?'

'I don't really know, to tell you the truth; I just have a feeling we need to go back there,' Wil shrugged.

*

After many expletives, Lexie was sampling the first cappuccino made from her new coffee machine. *Not bad, not bad at all.* She placed the steaming mug down on her desk. It was time to make a start on the second article for *Contemporary Woman.* She found it hard to concentrate. So many things had happened, and she felt caught in the middle. But she had a commitment to the magazine, and she had to honour it.

After reading the notes from her interview with Frances, emotions bubbled inside her. Lexie went on to open the file containing her first article, the one that Megan had emailed her, the layout copy for the magazine. Reading the article and Jillian's story—told as Hannah—brought back the anguish.

She returned to her notes for the second article and opened a new file. She sat and stared at the screen. Minutes passed, and accumulated. She looked at the clock—she'd been sitting in front of the blank screen for half an hour.

This is ridiculous! She got up and closed the laptop and started to pace her small living room. *Maybe I need a distraction, something so I can distance myself for a few minutes.* She grabbed the TV remote and pressed the power button. She sat down on the sofa and started to flick through the channels. She stopped when she reached one of the morning shows and the news was about to commence.

Lexie sat up straight when she read one of the captions running across the bottom of the screen. *Melbourne man found dead in parked car on a Fitzroy street in early hours.* She turned the volume up with the remote and listened to the newsreader read all the news stories. When the broadcast came to the weather, Lexie turned off the set. *Typical bloody Sydney news! If it didn't happen in New South Wales, it doesn't get a mention.*

She opened the laptop again, and went straight to Google. Typing in *Shooting Fitzroy,* all she found was a small piece on the *Herald Sun* website: *A Fitzroy resident, walking to work in the early hours of this morning, discovered the body of Samuel Greenberg of Mount Waverley. The Coroner has stated that Mr Greenberg died from a single gunshot to the head. The police have a man in custody and expect him to be charged later today. They believe there is a possibility the shooting was drug-related.*

Lexie looked for her mobile to call Wil.

He answered straight away. 'Saddington.'

'It's Lexie, I've just learned about a shooting in Fitzroy this morning.'

Lexie had resumed pacing the living room, fear increasing with each imaged scenario that entered her mind. 'Please tell me, was that the car the one you were concerned about yesterday? The one parked outside the house Jillian went into? Was the man shot this morning...? Was he the one...? Please tell me, what's happened.'

'Hello, Ms Reed, good morning,' Wil said. 'Look, I can't talk about this with you. There is an ongoing investigation, well, two now, in fact, and I am not at liberty to discuss any of the details. And before you ask, no, Jillian Laidlaw has not been found.'

'Have you been into the house yet, at least?' Lexie asked.

'Ms Reed, as you already know, we've been told by the Federal Police not to approach the premises nor any of the occupants. So the answer is no. And you are not, under any circumstances, to go anywhere near Rose Avenue.' Wil's voice was stern. 'For your own safety, please leave this alone.' His voice softened. 'When I have news on Mrs Laidlaw, I promise I will inform you. But that's as much as I can offer at this stage.'

'Fine.' Lexie cut the connection.

She went to the bedroom and changed into her jeans and found a warm jumper, as the weather report had said Melbourne could expect a cold one. Finding her keys and coat, she headed to her car. *The Federal Police haven't barred me from Rose Avenue.* Lexie felt defiant as she drove toward Fitzroy.

*

Lexie didn't want to make her arrival too obvious, so she looked for a park on Nicholson Street, deciding approaching the house on foot was a better option. Trams and cars travelling north and south on the busy street made it hazardous. Putting on a pair of sunglasses and pulling her hair back, Lexie got out and locked the Peugeot.

Looking left and right, she deemed it safe and jogged across to the other side. As she took off, she felt her phone vibrate in the pocket of her jeans. Stepping onto the pavement, Lexie retrieved her mobile, and read a text sent from Wil: *Please don't do anything stupid!!!*

She stopped in her tracks and looked up and down the street. *What the hell...?* She turned back to look across the street, but couldn't see neither Wil's red Honda, nor Marty's black Jeep. Shaking her head, she put the phone back in her pocket and stepped into the first shop she came to. *Nothing to say I can't come to Fitzroy for a coffee.*

149

She walked up to the café counter and ordered her drink. She picked up a newspaper and took a seat at a table by the window. A young woman brought her coffee to the table. As she set the mug down, Lexie could see the track marks on the woman's arms.

'Thanks,' Lexie said, looking up her.

She didn't respond to Lexie, just turned and walked back to the counter in a daze.

Lexie slowly drank her coffee, and finished pretending to read the paper. Satisfied that Wil hadn't been watching her, she got up to leave, giving a final glance around the coffee shop, but no one in there was taking any notice of her. The place looked as though it's last makeover was back in nineteen-eighty—old faded Pepsi and Chiko Roll posters on the walls, the corners curling. The shop hadn't kept up with Melbourne's cosmopolitan look. She stepped out on to Nicholson Street to resume her mission.

Even with her coat buttoned up to her neck, she could feel the bitter cold of the wind and was glad of her warm jumper. Lowering her head, Lexie took off in the direction of Rose Avenue.

She scanned the cars parked around the building where she'd last seen Jillian, specifically looking for Sonja's blue Audi convertible. There were four cars parked along the fence alongside of Madame Lourdes' establishment.

Satisfied the Audi wasn't here, she found the courage to walk up to the door. The building was covered with local graffiti—some good, some bad, and some just plain ugly. The low brick fence at the front of the house had thick faded and peeling purple paint. She looked over her shoulder several times, knowing the Federal Police would be watching her. That knowledge should have made her feel safer, instead she was thinking of the young man shot dead that very same morning.

What could be more important than rescuing a woman in danger? What was going on in this house?

As doubts and fear began to creep into her mind. The face of her friend Ava pushed its way through the darkness in her mind's eye. Lexie's hand went up to the door and knocked.

CHAPTER ELEVEN

'Who are you texting? Not your new girlfriend?' Marty asked Wil, as he parked the unmarked car.

'Not that it's any of your damned business—I was just advising our journalist friend to stay out of trouble today.'

Running out the front door of McHale Shelter, Paige stopped in her tracks, recognition and confusion on her face when she saw the two detectives approaching her.

'How did you get here so...? I just...I don't understand.' Paige looked in disbelief at the mobile phone in her hand, then back at them, then gulped mouthfuls of air as she started sobbing.

'What are you talking about?' Wil grabbed her as she collapsed against him. Marty helped him carry her across the veranda to a cane settee. 'Go see if you can find her a glass of water, Marty.'

'No, no stop!' Paige grabbed Marty's sleeve. 'Don't go in there. *She's* in there.'

'Who's in there?' Wil said looking at Marty, both shrugging their shoulders.

'Son...Son...' Paige took a deep breath. 'Sonja, and she's...she's dead. That's what I was saying—I've just called the police, just this minute. Then...then you walk through the gate!'

Both Wil's and Marty's phones rang in unison.

'Jesus H, Terry! No, no we're at the shelter now. Just this second...Yeah, yeah, we're with Paige now,' Marty replied to Terry. 'No, we've just been informed. Haven't gone inside yet. OK.' Wil put his phone away. 'Who else is inside, Paige?'

Paige sat, her head in her hands, rocking gently back and forth. 'I don't know. I've only just arrived myself, not five minutes ago. Anna rang and asked if I could take over here for a while.'

'Who's Anna?' Wil asked.

'Anna Sellens, she's the RA at Tiffany Shelter; Anna was contacted by the Board. There's been some issues regarding Sonja. Anna wouldn't elaborate, just asked if I could be here as soon as possible, and not sure for how long.' Paige wiped at her eyes. Her mascara had already smudged. 'I knocked, tried the door, it was open. I called out to Sonja from the hall, but the place was quiet. Nothing at all—which is really spooky for a shelter. There's always, always somebody about.' Paige stopped talking, letting out a sigh.

Wil stepped around Marty and Paige. He could hear sirens getting closer. He said, 'I'll go inside and have a look.'

He un-holstered his gun—he still missed his old .38, and knew he still needed more training before he'd feel comfortable with the .40 semi-automatic pistol the Force had chosen. He rarely had occasion to arm himself, so his nerves were on high alert.

'Police, show yourself!' Wil called out as he entered the hall. 'Police! I'm armed, show yourself!' No response from inside.

Outside the sirens had arrived, the flashing blue and red lights reflecting off the shiny surfaces of the posters on the walls inside the shelter.

Wil saw the blood before he saw the body. There was a lot of it. Before he had a chance to step into what he knew to be Sonja's office, uniformed officers where pouring into the entrance behind Wil.

'The place isn't secured yet. There's a body in here, obviously,' Wil said quietly, indicating with his head to the floor. 'That's all I know. Proceed with extreme caution.'

Marty made his way through to Wil's side. Both detectives raised their weapons, looked each other in the eye, and then nodded. Using his foot, Wil pushed the door all the way open. Shoulder to shoulder, Wil covering to the left, Marty the right, they stepped into the room.

Sonja's body lay on the floor just clear of the door. She had suffered what appeared to be a massive head trauma. After a sweep of the room, and certain that Sonja was the only occupant of the room, Marty called, 'Clear.' Both men re-holstered their pistols, and allowed themselves to relax, marginally.

'Man, she must have put up quite a fight to create this mess,' Marty said as they took in the chaos of the room: chairs overturned, papers, brochures and pamphlets strewn all over the floor. The telephone had been ripped from the connection at the wall.

Sonja's body had been brutally beaten. As well as the head wound, her body had suffered many blows. She was certainly dead. No need to check for a pulse. Both Wil and Marty stepped back out of the room as the uniforms returned from upstairs, and the rear of the shelter.

'All clear, nobody else on the property, Boss,' the uniformed officer informed Wil.

'All right, everyone knows what to do. Secure the crime scene—I take it forensics are on their way.'

Wil and Marty walked together out to the front veranda to where Paige was still sitting.

'We'll need a statement from Paige,' Wil said to the officer standing by, then to Paige, 'You up to coming to the station to give a statement?'

She nodded.

The two men walked down the front path.

'So...what did she have to say?' Wil asked Marty.

'Nothing, really, she just entered the room, saw the body and ran back out of the room and called triple zero. She has suspicions about this shelter. There's been talk about Sonja and Eddie Kovacs, but no one knows what's going on, just that something has smelt bad for a while. Some of the women that have come here get moved on, rehoused like they told us, remember? But then, Paige and a couple of the other housemothers, when they've made inquiries as to where certain ones went, they got stonewalled. Frances the volunteer, Paige reckons she went so far as to snoop into the paper work, but came up empty, nothing. No paper trail for some of the women.'

'This is getting to be one giant fucked-up mess,' Wil stood with both hands on his head, looking back up the court. 'Marty, you keep things in order here, at least until Terry can take over. I'm going next door, see if anyone's home.'

Wil walked down the path and out the gate. He was heading up the drive of the neighbouring house when his phone began to ring. Stopping next to the neat rows of stacked firewood, he took out his phone and saw it was Monica.

'Look, Mon, now is not a good time.'

'Well, it never has been before, Wil, so I wasn't expecting it to be now, either. Regardless of that, I still need to talk to you.'

Wil could see the face of an old man with white hair at the front window. He'd pulled the curtain aside to see who was walking down his driveway. Wil just waved and returned to the court. 'Is it urgent? Can it wait until this evening?'

'It's important, but no, it's not urgent. Just make sure you ring tonight.'

'Sure, bye.' Wil wondered, *What now?*

Heading back to the shelter, Wil caught Marty's attention and waved him over.

'That was quick. No one home?'

'Yeah, some old geezer was inside. But I didn't go in, lost interest before I got to the door.'

'Short attention span—early stages of Alzheimer's. How old are you, Wil? I can't seem to recall,' Marty laughed at his own joke, but stopped when he saw Wil wasn't sharing the humour.

157

'So, we hot for Eddie on this too?'

'Pretty violent episode this time around. Sean's killing, though violent, was simple, swift. This Sonja woman had a real fight on her hands. Got chopped at a few times before the head blow.'

*

The door was eventually opened. Lexie's knuckles hurt from the repeated knocking. She'd been on the verge of leaving, convinced no one was going to answer.

'What you want?' A short woman, Thai, Lexie guessed, screeched at her. 'You go way, husband not here!'

Lexie was quick, pushing her foot inside the doorway.

'I'm not looking for a man. I'm looking for a woman.' Lexie had no idea what she was saying, the words just poured out of her mouth. She wasn't sure what she was going to say next.

'Ooh, you want girl-on-girl action?' The woman, Lexie could only guess, was probably in her late fifties. Not pleasant looking by any stretch. 'You want lesbo love. We have plenty, plenty of girls for you. I Madame Lourdes—

you got cash? Must pay cash up front to Madame Lourdes.'

Madame Lourdes looked up and down the street behind Lexie. Satisfied that Lexie was by herself, Madame Lourdes grabbed her arm and pulled her inside and shut the door, locking it. The loud snap of the deadbolt made Lexie jump.

'You first timer!' Lourdes laughed, throwing her head back, displaying a mouthful of gold inlays. 'Show me money, now,' she was back to business.

Lexie brought her hand up to cover her nose. The woman's breath was toxic. She'd obviously spent thousands of Thai Baht on dental work. It's a pity, Lexie thought, that the woman didn't take a few minutes to brush and floss. She took her time fishing her wallet out of her bag while she looked about, getting her bearings. It was dark in what was a lounge room turned into a waiting room.

Couches and armchairs lined the walls. The only light came from a few stray Tiffany lamps: red satin covers, naturally. Lexie raised an eyebrow at the cliché. She thought she could smell the reek that was coming from a torn brown couch. The windows were completely covered. She'd noticed outside that they were also covered with security grilles. There wouldn't want to be a fire in here! WorkSafe must have missed this place.

'No money, no licky-licky,' Madame Lourdes slapped her leg and laughed loudly again, then turned serious and squinted at Lexie. 'What you doing here?'

'Yes, yes, I've got money. But I only want a blonde; she has to be a blonde. I only like blondes. Understand? You have any like that?' Lexie had no plan, no idea.

'One hundred cash, now, you pay now,' Lourdes snapped, putting out her hand.

Lexie took in the Lurex leggings, the chipped toenail polish. As she placed two fifty-dollar notes in Lourdes' hand, she saw the yellow stained fingers— probably a smoker since childhood.

'Only one blondee, she do you nice. Come, come,' Lourdes pulled aside the beaded hallway curtain, waving for Lexie to follow.

As Lexie was about to step into the hall, a man came charging out of a room off the hall to the right. Still tucking in his shirt, his lowered his head when he saw Lexie behind Lourdes. Lexie jumped back out of his way.

'Alak! Alak!' Madame Lourdes screeched at the man. 'You wait. Alak come let you out.'

A young man came running from the other end of the hall. Lourdes yelled in Thai at him as he ran past her. She slapped him across the back of the head, just as he got past. He must have expected it, Lexie thought, because he pulled his head aside so as to avoid copping too hard a blow. He ran to the door and let the customer out onto Rose Avenue.

The light that was let in from the opened door allowed Lexie a better view of the hall and the number of doors. She could see what was possibly a kitchen at the end of the hall. There were six doors off the hallway.

Madame Lourdes slipped the two fifties inside her bra and stood outside the second door on the right, her hand on the doorknob, waiting for Lexie to come to her. Lexie's breath caught in her throat when she heard the front door being dead bolted for the second time. She was further inside the house, there were more people about, and still she didn't have a plan. Panic threatened. She felt her fingers start to tingle, her heart racing so fast she knew that she wouldn't be able to count it. Bile in her stomach bubbled, churning the recent coffee. She took a couple of deep breaths, which took care of the stars that had begun to flash in front of her eyes.

Lourdes took a lanyard from around her neck. On it was several keys. She took one of the keys and unlocked the door.

'You go in, very pretty blondee for you. I give you half hour. Go, go, you don't be shy. She do anything you want, you do anything you want to her, all same to me,'

Madame Lourdes screeched, and shoved Lexie in to the room, pulling the door shut behind her.

Lexie could hear Lourdes' harsh laugh getting further away as she moved to the other end of the house.

'Shit, shit, shit!' Lexie said under her breath, fearful of what she was to be faced within the room.

There was a double bed pushed into the far corner. On a bedside table, a lamp, with what could only be a twenty-five watt bulb, shedding barely any light.

A moan came from under the bedcovers, followed by a slight movement.

'Jillian, is that you? Jillian, it's Lexie, Lexie Reed, from McHale Shelter.'

Cautiously, Lexie stepped closer to the bed. 'Hello?' Another step.

Her eyes now were fully adjusted to the darkness of the room, and Lexie calmed her breathing and took another brave step towards the bed. Hope sprang and settled the bile in her gut when she got the first glimpse of blonde hair as she tentatively lifted the closest corner of the doona.

'Jillian,' Lexie whispered. 'My God, Jillian, what have they done to you?'

162

CHAPTER TWELVE

'Quiet, people, settle down,' Terry roared above the excited voices of the crowd building in the MIR. 'Yes, we're looking at two murders now. Remembering that we haven't gotten far with the first one—this makes things worse.'

'Sonja de Bruin, a person of interest in the case of Sean Laidlaw's murder, is now a victim. Yes, I know their deaths look very much alike, and yes, Eddie Kovacs is still, and again, on our most wanted list of people to speak to,' Wil stood, putting on his gravest face. 'If one word of this gets out in the press before a departmental press release...If I hear one word about a serial killer on the streets of Melbourne, your job will be gone, and charges will be laid. Do you all hear me?'

A collective 'Yes, Boss,' came from the room.

'Good. Down to business. Phone records for the shelter—someone working on that?' Wil acknowledged Melissa's raised hand. 'Did Sonja's mobile phone surface in the search?'

'Techs have it now, Wil. They'll print us a sheet with the text messages.'

Terry wrote the information on the Incident Board, under the first of the latest crime scene photos.

'Paige Townsend is the young lady who found the body. She is here at the station; we'll interview her soon. From what she's said so far to Marty, there's something dirty going on at this shelter. So, whatever Ms de Bruin and the elusive Mr Eddie Kovacs were up to, it's no good. It looks to be tied in with Madame Lourdes' brothel. The AFP are investigating the brothel, but this is tied to two murder cases now,' Wil waved to Marty to come with him. Together they went to their office.

'You think she'd be ready for the interview now?' Wil asked, sitting down behind his desk.

'I'd say yeah,' Marty sat at his desk. 'She's pretty switched on for a do-gooder. I tell you, though, I'm doing all I can not to reach out and touch that girl's hair.'

'What...? What bullshit are you talking about, Marty? Her hair? For Christ's sake!'

'It's just that it's so fake—nobody has hair that red! But I love it—it goes perfectly with her blue eyes.'

'For fuck's sake, Marty, focus! Get your head out of your arse. We have two, *two* dead people, and you're thinking about a woman's hair.' Wil looked closely at Marty, and the vagueness in his eyes; he wondered how he could be so smart, have an IQ of one hundred and

164

thirty-five, and be so switched-on one minute then off to whatever planet it was that he occasionally visited. *No wonder nobody else can stand partnering him!*

'I think I might need to eat. We haven't had lunch yet.'

At that, Marty got up and left the room.

*

Lexie couldn't rouse Jillian. She gently pulled up an eyelid, only to be horrified at the pinned pupil. She knew it wasn't only the poor lighting giving Jillian's face a deathly grey pallor. 'Jillian, wake up!' Lexie said close to her ear. 'It's me: Lexie. Let's get you out of here.'

She tossed back the doona, gagging at the smell that assaulted her nose. Lexie started to cry when she saw the bruising on Jillian's thighs; they were the worst, and most noticeable. The ones to her wrist were not quite as bad. She'd obviously been held down.

'Jillian, I'm so sorry,' her tears fell onto Jillian's legs as she lifted them to the side of the bed.

Trying to sit Jillian up was almost impossible. She kept resisting, trying to lie back on the bed. 'What did they give you, do you know?' Lexie guessed it was heroin when she saw the ugly track marks on both of her arms. The redness and bruising were so severe she must have been injected repeatedly throughout the day and night.

165

Lexie sat on the bed and held Jillian up beside her. 'OK, now I do need a plan!' Jillian moaned, making a weak attempt to push Lexie away and lie back down. 'No way! We are getting out of here. I need you to wake up.'

Lexie knew she wasn't going anywhere without Madame Lourdes' set of keys. That was the first problem, and she had about twenty minutes to think of the solution.

'I've got, what, at least thirty-six centimetres on the old bag, right?' Lexie spoke to the unconscious Jillian who was now lying back across the middle of the bed, her legs hanging over the edge. 'I can put that self-defence training to some good use, finally. That's what we'll apply today: Zero Tolerance. Excuse me for just a sec, Jillian.'

The stench of the bed assailed Lexie again. She raced to the corner of the room where she vomited on the wall and skirting board, just missing her own feet. Reality was hitting her hard; she retched and retched until her stomach was empty.

Wiping her mouth on her sleeve, Lexie returned to try to rouse Jillian. She slapped her face, each slap increasing in harshness, as little by little Jillian began to react. Lexie dug out of her bag a half-finished bottle of water and tossed the contents into Jillian's face. 'Yeah, that one got you going huh?' Bit by bit, Jillian started to rouse from her drugged world and into the disgusting room.

'Ohh...' Jillian moaned, scratching at her arms until they bled.

'Jillian, can you hear me?'

'Ahh...'

'Madame Lourdes, she'll be back any minute. I want you to stay on the bed, like you are asleep. I'll, well...let's just see,' Lexie whispered close to Jillian's ear. 'Just you be ready to run when the time comes.'

The knock came within minutes.

'You there, girlie? You finish now, or pay more money,' Madame Lourdes turned the handle as she spoke. 'Ready or not,' she entered the room and squealed. 'Urf!'

Lexie stepped up to Madame Lourdes, grabbed her shoulders and planted a knee straight up into her diaphragm. Madame Lourdes dropped to the floor, grabbing her stomach. Lexie shut the door, turned and shoved the pillowcase she'd removed earlier into Lourdes' mouth as far in as she could. She removed the lanyard from around her neck and took all the keys off. Dragging the madam towards the bed, Lexie pulled her arms behind her body and tied her wrists together with the lanyard, pulling as tight as she could.

Lexie realised that it wouldn't take long for Lourdes to get free from her bindings, but they only needed enough time to get out of the room, out of the house, and to Lexie's car.

'I wonder if I've got a ticket yet?' Lexie paused for a second. 'Jesus, what does it matter at this stage—stupid, stupid! Jillian, get up—I need you up, now!'

Jillian mumbled, 'I don't feel so good.'

'No kidding. Best don't think about it now. We've only got minutes to get out of here.'

She dragged the bottom sheet off the mattress, gagging over the state of it, and wrapped it around Lourdes' legs. The woman was only just managing to inhale small amounts of air. Lexie looked away when she saw the panicked look in Lourdes' eyes.

Lexie had never deliberately hurt another human before. Even during the self-defence course, she'd struggled when it came to preforming the moves with the instructor. He was padded heavily for protection, and begged her to go all out and try to hurt him. She had grabbed his shoulders with respect, pulled his body into her up-raised knee, and ever so gently kneed his groin. The class had collapsed on the floor in fits of laughter. Even Lexie admitted at the time, it was pretty funny.

But now she was satisfied the Lourdes was tied tightly enough for the time being. She snatched the keys from the floor and hustled Jillian off the bed. Lexie placed Jillian's arm round her neck, and held onto her around her waist. Jillian was groggy and staggering, but at least she was staying upright.

Lexie opened the door a crack and listened for any sounds of movement in the hallway. Satisfied it was relatively safe to move, they left the sordid bedroom and headed for the front door. The third key Lexie tried opened the deadlock.

They were out on Rose Avenue, and the afternoon sun was like a spotlight. They both tripped at the front doorstep, landing on their knees. It was only as they struggled to get up that Lexie realised Jillian was naked from the waist down except for a dirty grey bra. Lexie took off her coat and wrapped it around Jillian's middle, then took off her jumper and dragged it over Jillian's head.

Jillian's knees were bleeding, Lexie's hands were bleeding, but they were both free. Soon they'd be out of time—they had to keep moving.

CHAPTER THIRTEEN

'I need you to put the money back into the joint account—the money you had no right taking, Wil,' Monica's voice came through Wil's phone loud and clear. 'I need that money. I have a credit card bill, and the electricity is due.'

'The money I took was for the rent on the apartment, because you kicked me out of *my* house,' Wil thumped the desk with a fisted hand, but spoke with a calm voice. 'You continue to believe that you can have absolutely everything your way, Monica, but guess what— you can't; it's not going to work that way anymore. Look, I told you I'd ring you later on tonight. We've got a second murder, and as it is, I've been too damned distracted.'

'So what am I supposed to do?'

'As I'm no longer your husband, I don't see that it's my problem. You'll have to work it out.' Wil ended the call.

Marty walked back into the office. He tossed Wil a cling-wrapped roll. 'Dead cow, with a little wilted lettuce to seduce you into thinking you're eating healthy.'

'Don't ever get married, Marty. It'll ruin you both personally and professionally.'

'Jeez, not another happy chat with the missus?'

'Urgh!' Wil ate his roll.

Melissa poked her head in the door. 'You guys going to keep that poor woman waiting much longer?'

'Shit! Sorry, no. We're coming now. Mel, can you do us a favour? Not in a sexist, using-my-rank-to-boss-you-around type favour, but a friend-helping-another-friend-in-need type...'

'What do you want?' she cut Wil off.

'A large pot of coffee and three mugs for the interview. Just thinking of the poor witness.'

'Don't try to do cute, detective. It's just not you.'

'Do you mind if I call you Paige?' Wil started the interview, trying to get the distressed woman as relaxed as possible.

'Sure, no problem.' She fiddled with the hem of her shirt.

'Can you tell us again why you were called to work at McHale?'

'Apparently, yesterday, when a couple of the volunteers arrived, there was an all out brawl going on in the kitchen. Three women were fighting, physically trying to rip each other apart. The volunteers got the women to settle down, sorted out whatever the issue was, then went to find whomever should have been at the shelter that day.' Paige took the coffee that Marty offered her, declining and milk and sugar. Marty nodded with an approving smile.

'That was when it was discovered that there weren't any staff at all in the place. No housemother, and no RA—no Sonja. One of the volunteers rang the head office of DWS. That's Department of Women's Services. They contacted Anna, and she called me. In the meantime, they managed to rehouse the three women to nearby shelters, and locked the place up until I was to reopen today.'

'Do you often get women fighting at the shelter?' Marty asked. 'I would've thought they'd all be pretty scared, and meek and mild types.'

'That's the thing: you get women from all different walks. They're not all middle-class white women whose husbands beat them routinely. Well, there are plenty of those, but we also house Aboriginal, Sudanese, Indian, Asian, you name the race, we've housed the woman. Some come with children, many don't. The youngest are eighteen—any younger and they have to be housed at a juvenile facility. The oldest I've come across was seventy-five. She put up with abuse for fifty years—can you believe

172

it—then simply had enough and walked out one day. I could go on, but that's not going to help you guys much.'

'We saw you first at Tiffany Shelter. Have you had any contact with Sonja since then?' Wil asked.

'No. But you sure did stir things up. A lot of us got talking, and there are a lot of things that people are not satisfied with. Frances did have a look at the paperwork for McHale, and there is a lot missing in the way of content for the paper trail that we're meant to have on all our clients.'

'Have you or any of the other housemothers seen or spoken to Eddie Kovacs?'

'No. Aren't you looking at him for the murder of Sean Laidlaw? Do you think Eddie killed Sonja?' The colour drained from Paige's face, making her hair appear redder, her eyes bluer.

'No, I'm not saying anything like that. It's a case of looking at every person that could have been in contact with the victim. To start with, the ones that we know of,' Wil said.

'What conclusion did these discussions come to, these housemother chats?' Marty asked.

'Well, we wondered why the locations of only certain women have been covered up. What would be in the benefit of that? Some women have virtually disappeared from the shelter—into the unknown—but only from McHale. Sonja couldn't have done it alone. Eddie was always there. We've all seen women leave with one of them. Where have they gone—where would they have taken them?'

The room was quiet as they contemplated what Paige was saying.

'Paige, these women that have disappeared, did Frances say if any of them had children?' Marty asked in a low voice.

'Yes, I'm afraid so.'

Wil felt his mobile vibrating silently in his pocket. He retrieved the phone and checked the name on the caller ID. 'Excuse me, I have to take this,' he said as he removed himself from the Interview Room.

CHAPTER FOURTEEN

Lexie and Jillian stumbled to Lexie's car around the corner on Nicholson Street. Nobody took any notice of the two women, although Lexie felt as though she had a giant neon arrow over her head pointing her out to the world. The suburb of Fitzroy, however, was not unaccustomed to scenes such as the one that Lexie was playing. She couldn't believe that her city had fallen so low as to not care about two women in obvious distress.

The muscles in Lexie's arms were burning from half-carrying, half-dragging Jillian up the street and across the busy road and her back was aching from the awkward position. She was still acutely aware of the stink of Jillian's body, but she was also conscious of her own foul breath, from her earlier heroic act in the corner of the brothel room.

She managed to get Jillian into the backseat of her Peugeot. She was just about to close the door when Jillian started retching. Lexie opened the door wide and helped Jillian as she stretched out far enough to be sick in the gutter. Jillian finished vomiting and drew herself up into a ball on the seat.

As she drove off, Lexie checked the review mirror— incredibly, no one was charging out of Rose Avenue looking for them. She took off towards the city, no real destination in mind. She was on a high of adrenaline. 'I got her out. I actually got her out. *Me!*'

Lexie made a right turn at Johnston Street and headed towards Melbourne University. The streets were teeming with people: students and staff from the university, and medical staff from the nearby Royal Women's Hospital. Lexie pulled up when an opportunity arose. The adrenaline was leaving her body, and now she was suffering from the down side of such a massive experience.

She got out her mobile and punched in Wil's number.

'Wil, I've got her—I've got Jillian! I went in and got her out. Oh, Wil, she's a mess. She's been drugged and raped. But now I don't know, I don't...Hang on a sec...Jillian, are you...?' Lexie undid her seat belt and reached through to the back seat. Jillian was having a full-blown seizure.

'Lexie, what's going on?' Wil's voice was insistent through Lexie's phone.

'Wil, it's bad. She's having a fit. It's really bad. What should I do?' Lexie was getting hysterical. 'Should I call an ambulance? No, wait, I'm right near the Royal Women's. Should I take her there?'

'Lexie, settle down, take a breath. Take her to Royal Melbourne Hospital—they're better equipped for this type of emergency. You concentrate on getting there without killing the both of you. I'll call the emergency room and tell them you're on your way. Look, you're only about five minutes from there. Everything will be all right, I promise. I'll be there as soon as I can. Just take it steady.'

Wil was right—it only took Lexie five minutes to get to the Royal Melbourne Hospital. She drove straight through the ambulance driveway, and to the team that she had hoped would be there to meet her.

They swooped on the white Peugeot. 'How long ago did the seizure commence?' A young man in green scrubs asked Lexie, as he proceeded to put a stethoscope to Jillian's chest.

'Five minutes, six at the most,' Lexie replied.

'What's her name?' a woman with a clipboard asked. Not a nurse, Lexie was thinking.

'Jillian Laidlaw.'

'Are you family or friend?'

'Friend—I guess.'

While the team got Jillian out of the car and onto a gurney, Lexie was told she'd have to move her car, and where she could park. And then she was to come straight back to the ER to answer more questions.

Just as she was starting the car, a nurse ran over to the car. 'Does she have any allergies?'

'I wouldn't know, sorry,' was all Lexie could say before they were all swallowed up by the hospital as the automatic doors closed her out, and them in.

She parked in one of the visitor's temporary emergency parking bays, then walked back to the doors where she'd seen them take Jillian. She was dragging herself now: she'd really hit a wall, and didn't know how she would keep going. She knew there would be a lot of questions.

*

Wil entered the hospital through the ambulance bay. He nodded acknowledgement to couple of ambulance drivers who he recognised. They waved in return.

Lexie looked distraught and lost. She was pacing in the corridor, outside a curtained-off area. She looked up as he approached, and burst into fresh tears, recognition on her face.

'You must be freezing,' Wil said, as he removed his coat and put it around Lexie's shoulders. 'Where's your jumper, or coat?'

'I wasn't cold. I had to cover Jillian—she was almost naked,' she said between sobs. 'Oh, Wil, it's been horrible, horrible!' She proceeded to tell him what she had been through in her rescue of Jillian from Madame Lourdes'.

The curtains opened and Wil could see Jillian on the ER bed, surrounded by eight medical staff: all young, all nationalities, men and women. Jillian lay flat on her back. She had a tube going into her mouth and down into her throat. A medic was kneeling on the bed, holding over her mouth a mask with a large ball attached, which she squeezed every so often—she counted and squeezed, counted and squeezed. Tubes ran from both Jillian's arms to bags of fluids: on the right side was a bag of clear fluid, on the left, a bag of blood.

A young man approached Wil and Lexie. 'I'm Dr Marcos, I'm the Emergency Department Registrar,' he held out his hand to Lexie first.

She shook his hand, but Wil could see that her eyes weren't leaving Jillian.

'Hey, Cookie,' Wil returned the young doctor's handshake. 'Here we are again.'

'Yes, Detective, one of the joys of the ER at Royal Melbourne, all those victims of crime—from both sides.' He looked back to Jillian. 'She's in a very bad way. The grand mal seizure she had was very dangerous. We've

179

given her drugs to induce coma, which stopped the seizure, but because of the narcotics already in her system, we're concerned about her recovery. There could be brain damage. Wil, could I speak to you?'

Wil and the doctor both looked to Lexie for her reaction, but she was still staring at Jillian, not really grasping what was being said.

'Lexie, come and take a seat for a minute,' said Wil. Turning to Cookie, he asked, 'Do you think someone could get Ms Reed a tea or coffee? She's had a big day herself.'

Cookie waved to the ward clerk to get her attention. 'Margaret, could you get Ms Reed whatever she'd like to drink.' He spoke to Lexie, 'Ms Reed, we're going to move your friend to intensive care now. You wait here. Margaret will get you something to drink while I have a chat with Detective Saddington.' Dr Marcos led Lexie to a nearby chair and gently squeezed her shoulder as she sat.

Wil had always been impressed with the young man's bedside manner. Once the team had wheeled Jillian's bed, and all the paraphernalia attached to it, into a lift at the end of the department, he followed Cookie into a small office next to the lifts.

'Your patient didn't look too good.'

'Don't know if she could be any worse—dead, maybe. That poor woman has suffered brutal treatment. By the bruising on her arms, she's been force-fed narcotics—we won't know until the toxicology report comes back, but my guess would be heroin. It makes for docility and compliance, plus it is, as you'd be aware, fast to addict. We did a rape kit—horrendous what has been done...' Cookie stopped for a moment. 'If she survives, she might well wish that she hadn't. She is going to require surgery as soon as she is stable enough to handle it. Her rectum has been torn; the drugs would have masked the pain that she would have felt otherwise. We've done every imaginable STD screening. She was dehydrated, malnourished. Her haemoglobin was dangerously low; she's already on her third unit of blood. For now, we've intubated her, and she'll be kept in the induced coma. IV fluids, total body scans for any possible fractures, then surgery as soon as the surgeon deems she is stable.'

'So she's critical?'

'Yes. Now I have to get back my other patients,' Cookie shook hands with Wil as they both left the office.

Wil walked slowly toward Lexie. He saw that someone had attended to her bloodied hands.

He sat alongside her, taking the empty cup from her. 'You know I have to take you into the station so that you can make a statement.' He turned so that he was facing her.

She leant forward and put her head onto his shoulder and mumbled, 'Yes, OK.'

'Give me your keys. I'll go and move your car into long-term parking so it doesn't get towed. Then I'll drive us back to Coburg. Sit tight, no more heroics, please!' Wil patted her knee, and then left her sitting.

CHAPTER FIFTEEN

'You've done really well to talk for so long,' Wil said to Lexie, wrapping up her interview at the station. 'I'd drive you home myself, but as you can imagine I have my hands pretty full at the moment. I'll get Mel, see if she's got a minute.'

'It doesn't matter who drives me. I just want a shower, then to curl up in bed.'

Wil saw she was looking paler as the minutes passed.

'You know, you're going to have a decent parking bill when you eventually get your car from the hospital.'

'Last thing on my mind, at the minute,' Lexie said with her eyelids at half-mast. 'I'll get Carla to drive me back there. Tomorrow will have to do.'

Wil opened the door and waved to the first officer he spotted. 'Ross?'

'Yes, Boss?'

'Any chance you, or whoever, could run Ms Reed home?'

'I was about to finish my shift anyway. I'll be happy to drop her home,' the young man replied. 'Where does she live?'

'Elwood. Not out of your way?'

'No, not at all, I'm in Elsternwick. I'll just go and sign out and grab my stuff, Give me five.'

Wil stepped back into the room.

'Thank you, Wil. Thank you for not yelling at me and telling me how stupidly I've behaved. Because, you know, I'd do it again if I had to.'

'Yeah, I'm starting to realise that about you,' Wil shook his head, but smiled at down at her.

*

Lexie pulled the woollen standard police jacket tightly around her. An officer—she wasn't even aware of when—had placed it on her when she'd first arrived at the station. She put on her seat belt and watched as Ross put his on and started the car.

He looked across at her. 'Cold? It takes a few minutes before the heat kicks in with the old girl. Sorry.'

'Not to worry. Thanks for doing this. I don't think I could have driven myself.' Lexie let out a huge sigh she felt she'd been holding in for hours.

'You just sit back and relax. We'll be hitting peak hour, so it'll be slow going,' Ross said as he pulled the car out of the station's car park. Headlights flashed at them off the rainwater pooling on the road.

They had an easy run along Moreland Road, but hit a wall of traffic at the entrance to the Citylink freeway. Another light shower started.

'Getting dark earlier every day now,' Ross spoke after ten minutes of silence.

'Yes.' Lexie looked toward her driver. 'You don't have to talk. In fact, I don't think I can manage a conversation. Is that OK with you?'

'Sure, I understand. I just didn't want you to think I was being rude.'

Lexie settled back, staring out at strangers they passed. She started to mull over everything she had seen and done in this incomparable day.

Ross pressed the stereo power button, and soft classical music sounded throughout the car. Lexie smiled to herself—he was still trying to make her feel comfortable.

She was exhausted but a long way from being able to feel comforted. She thought about Jillian and the way she'd been treated—a piece of human flesh for the desires of others to do whatever their perverted minds could imagine. She cringed inwardly that this was going on in her home city.

How naïve had she been? Lexie rested her head against the cold glass of the window. The city looked sinister now, and vile as darkness descended over it.

New York had been fun at first—the excitement of the Big Apple had been infectious. She and Doug had done all the tourist things straight away: cruised the East River, toured the Statue of Liberty, viewed the entire city, by day and into night from the top of Rockefeller Centre. They'd eaten real New York cheesecake at Junior's off Times Square. Things were good then: just married, great careers, no pressures. But disappointment and loss had marred those memories too.

'Ms Reed, wake up, you're home,' Ross was gentle as he shook Lexie's shoulder.

'Huh...?' Lexie sat up straight. 'Sorry, I must have nodded off. Yes, yes, this is me.'

They both exited the car, but when Lexie got to the gate she stopped dead in her tracks. The house was in total darkness, as were both her neighbours', either side. A dog barked in the distance. Her hand froze on the gate's latch.

'What's the matter?' Ross was by her side.

'I...I can't move. I don't think I can go in there,' she said staring at her home, her beloved grandmother's gift.

'Give me your keys. I'll go in and turn all the lights on.' Ross took the keys from Lexie's hand. He looked her in the eye and smiled. 'You'll be all right. Just a little bit of shock I would imagine. Will you be right standing there? I'll only be a couple of minutes.'

The porch light came on first, bathing the path in yellow. Lexie watched as lights blinked on in each room in the house. It gave her the confidence to walk up the path. By the time she reached the door, Ross had returned to the front of the house.

'All safe and secure, madam,' he saluted her. 'I'll be off then.'

'No!' Lexie heard the desperation in her voice, and was quick to cover it up. 'No, please, stay and have a drink. You're off duty now. Please. Let me thank you for driving me home.'

Without waiting for Ross's response she took off to the kitchen, where she grabbed two wine glasses and a bottle of Sauvignon Blanc from the refrigerator. 'Do you want red or white?' she yelled back over her shoulder.

'Whatever you're having is fine.'

Lexie poured two large glasses of wine. She took a huge mouthful from one, then topped it up and carried

187

the glasses to the coffee table, placing one down in front of the young man.

'I'm really quite embarrassed. For the life of me, I cannot remember your name. I'm so sorry,' she said taking a drink from her glass.

'Senior Constable Ross Ashworth, at your service,' he said, 'but you can call me Ross. I am, as you pointed out, off duty. Cheers.'

Lexie sat down on the couch beside Ross, curling her legs underneath her. She'd taken off the police jacket, replacing it with a throw from the back of the couch.

'Like your car, the heater should kick in in a few minutes or so. Can I offer you cheese and crackers, or something more substantial?' Lexie had another long drink from her glass. It was close to empty.

'No, I'm fine thanks. I'll be off home soon.'

Lexie drained her glass and got up to get another. 'Drink up, I'll grab the bottle.'

Returning from the kitchen, she saw Ross texting on his phone.

'Sorry, I'm probably keeping you from something. Or is it someone? Girlfriend, or wife maybe?' Lexie started on her second glass of wine.

'No, no, that's fine. Just letting a mate know I've been waylaid. No drama.' Ross picked up his glass. 'You've had a big day. We'll have to make sure that you get some form of counselling. What you saw, and the trauma of the event that you've been through, well, it is going to hit you, and probably hard. You should probably slow down on the wine.'

'Oh, it was bad all right. That was undoubtedly the worse thing I've ever been through.' She'd half finished her second glass. 'It'll be a long time before I'll be able to get the image of that poor woman, lying on that bed, in that condition, out of my mind. Actually, you know, I bet I never do.' She drained the glass.

'I might just take a look in your fridge, if you don't mind me being so forward,' Ross said. 'I'll see if I can rustle us up something to eat. I am getting a little peckish, and you really need to eat something before you have anymore of that wine.'

'Help yourself. Anything for our boys in blue,' Lexie laughed. 'Do you like my house? It used to be my grandmother's. I inherited it when she died.' Lexie suddenly started weeping.

Poking his head back into the living room, Ross said, 'Yes, I like it very much. You're very lucky.'

'I miss my gran...I wish my mum was like...' Lexie was sobbing now. 'I wish I...'

'Sorry, what was that?'

'Nothing, don't mind me.' Lexie blew her nose and recovered her composure. 'Find everything you need in there?'

'One Spanish omelette coming up—it's my specialty.'

'You're very kind. You'll make someone a wonderful husband one day.'

Lexie sat up straight as Ross returned to the room. He placed a tea towel across her lap, handed her a plate in one hand and cutlery in the other.

'Not for a long while,' he responded with a grin. 'I'm far too young. I'm thinking maybe in my forties, that should be soon enough to settle down.'

'This looks and smells divine. Suddenly I'm starving—I had no idea...' she stopped talking and started eating.

Now seated himself, Ross said, 'Sounds like it tastes good then?'

'Oh yeah,' she said with her mouth full.

They ate in silence.

Together they washed and dried the dishes. When Ross started to make a move to get going, Lexie put on the coffee machine.

'This machine is virtually brand new. I've seriously only made two coffees with it. You have to stay and have a latte. Or would you prefer a cappuccino?'

'Cappuccino will be fine,' Ross resumed his place on the couch.

'Cappuccino it will be,' Lexie got busy in the kitchen making noise.

Shortly, she placed the steaming mugs on the coffee table.

'I don't think I can be alone tonight. For the first time in my adult life, I'm scared stiff. The thought of you walking out that door, well, my breath just catches, I have to gasp for air.' A fresh river of tears streamed down Lexie's cheeks.

'Would you like me stay with you?' Ross put his arm around her shoulder.

She nodded her head as she buried it in his opened arms that then wrapped round her.

CHAPTER SIXTEEN

Wil was already awake when his alarm went off at five-thirty a.m. Today was going to be a big day: the case had been going from bad to worse, and so far they hadn't made any headway. It was time to get everyone's arses into high gear. He had so far been reactive, but from now on, he planned on being proactive. Today he was taking charge.

But first he had to get rid of all the crap in his head from last night's confrontation with Monica. And nothing worked better for Wil than a long, hard run along the bay. It was still dark, but he wouldn't be the only runner. Beaconsfield Parade was a popular running track.

The temperature was in single figures, but Wil still chose to run in shorts. If it got really cold, he'd put on a windcheater, and maybe a beanie. He never ran listening to music. Running was his time to sort out his mind, as well as his body.

Earlier the previous day, Wil had told Monica that he didn't have to care about her anymore, but he'd still phoned her that evening. He wanted to keep things amicable with her—if not for his sake, then at least for Lucas'.

192

He ate a banana while he got dressed, then put on his runners. As he was about to walk out the door, he stopped and looked back into the apartment. On his way home from work several days ago, he'd stopped on a whim at a florist's. He'd purchased a plant and several prints that they'd had hanging on the wall. What he was looking at now was starting to resemble a home. He locked the door and left.

He checked his watch. He would allow himself forty minutes. That would give him time for breakfast and a shower, and he also wanted to make quick stop and check on Lexie; he'd get to the station by seven-thirty. He was happy with that.

It had taken Wil a long time to get to sleep the previous night. He'd kept going over the trivialities of the things Monica said she felt burdened with, and comparing the way Jillian Laidlaw's life had turned out. What Lexie had said to him at the hospital was affecting him the most, striking out at his emotions: *If her husband hadn't been murdered, would anyone have even noticed that she was missing?*

Wil pounded the pavement as he headed north. The rain had eased overnight, the city felt clean and fresh, very fresh—he was glad he'd grabbed his beanie. He thought about what Monica had wanted from him as a husband, but he had disappointed her. He didn't want, the divorce, but probably more out of laziness than any sense of love and affection. He didn't want to have to make it on his own. He'd been comfortable with things the way they were. It had been a relationship he didn't even have to think about. Now he realised how unfair that was.

Monica had been at university when they'd first met, just finishing a degree in accounting. They'd married almost right away, then not long after came Lucas. She'd never really worked. She did the books for her father's dry-cleaning business, and as that progressed and got bigger, her involvement took up more time. The business had twenty shops across the city now.

Since Lucas had joined the army and left home, she'd just had too much time on her hands. That was when, Wil assumed, she noticed what their marriage had become. He was now starting to see how, to her, his distancing himself was a form of abuse. Not abuse to be compared to that of the women at the crisis shelter—but still.

Wil overtook three young women jogging side by side by side, ponytails swinging in unison. 'Morning,' he called out before passing, so as not to startle them.

To the east, the sun was starting to hint at rising. Wil kept up a good rhythm, overtaking another, larger group. Wil assumed it to be a boot camp fitness group, as the leader was yelling orders.

Checking his watch, he saw it was time to turn around and head home. He noticed that it was the first time he'd actually thought of the apartment as home. He had his home now, and Monica had hers. Lucas was an adult now; if, or when, he was to get out of the army, he'd make his own home. There was no going back with Monica. They had a history, and that was that. He was making a new life for himself from this point onwards.

Wil slowed down as he came to the group he'd earlier overtaken. They were down on the beach now, getting yelled at. Push-ups in the sand—not the easiest thing to achieve, Wil thought as he jogged on the spot, not wanting to cool down. He hoped that their leader was first aid trained, as some of his class looked as though they might soon be in need of assistance.

He resumed his steady pace south. He thought back to Jillian Laidlaw now, and how she was fighting for her life; how he and the unit were to start to fight for her. Thinking of her condition, and what Cookie Marcos had said, of the brutality she'd been dealt, Wil was now running fast. He knew he couldn't outrun his emotions; he had to feel them, and then deal with them. In the past he'd become expert at pushing them deep down, never to be seen again. His friend Ray had tried to tell him, and not just on one occasion. He didn't want to live that way anymore. He let the sadness wash over him, and then felt the resolve to do something about replacing the sadness.

By the time he had the key in his front door, he was feeling full of a new determination and drive to get on with the job. He went straight to the kitchen and put the coffee maker on, then went to shower.

Half an hour later, Wil was fed, suited up, and heading towards Elwood. He felt like a new man: new attitude, and a new resolve, someone who was going to get the job done. He remembered exactly where Lexie's house was, even though he'd only been there the one time. He smiled as he remembered back to their salsa dancing. He hadn't let on to her at the time, but man, he had been so turned on during that dance that he'd been worried it would start to show.

He turned into Browning Street and slowed the Honda to a crawl as he approached Lexie's house as something, or someone caught his eye. He stopped the car, killing the headlights. Standing on Lexie's front porch was a man, stretching. Wil slid down in his seat.

The man stretched his arms above his head, then behind his head. He twisted his body left, then right. He leant over forwards, stretching down to touch his toes.

'What the...' Wil muttered.

The man walked down Lexie's front path, let himself out of the gate, and went to a car parked directly in front of the house. The car was parked under a streetlight that was still on. Wil noted that the car was covered in dew, an indication it had been parked overnight.

The man stopped and looked up and down the street before getting into the car. Wil slid further down into the seat —but only after he'd gotten a good look at the man's face.

*

'Where the fuck is everyone, Terry?' Wil barked as he looked around the room, taking a head count. 'Two homicides and this unit has achieved fuck all so far. I want a meeting in half an hour, and there will be a shit-fit if the entire unit isn't present.'

'Jesus, Sads, what bug crawled up your arse overnight?' Terry returned his attention to his computer screen. 'Most of them are already here; they're in the canteen getting breakfast. So take some deep breaths now, and compose yourself. Don't want you to make a fool of yourself in front of the others when they come back in a couple of minutes.'

'Humph!' Wil walked over to the board and glared at the information. So far, the biggest lead was the location of Jillian Laidlaw at the brothel in Fitzroy. Both Jillian and Sonja de Bruin had been sighted at the

197

location in Rose Avenue, and the house at Kay Street, but as yet, the Federal Police had barred them from going near either property.

'What, now you're not staying?' Terry looked up from the computer terminal. 'You need to lighten up, Sads. I was just...'

'You run the meeting, or get Marty to. I'm going to follow up on something.'

'You want back-up?'

'No, thanks, I'll be right.'

'Here, take one of these at least,' Terry grabbed a radio off a nearby desk, and tossed it to Wil. 'You never know, hey?'

Wil didn't have far to travel, but the morning traffic was the usual beast. When he mused about how he'd felt when he'd recognised Ross as the man leaving Lexie's house earlier, he turned up the volume on the radio to stomp on his thoughts.

He turned right, illegally, into Kay Street, where the first house that Lexie had spotted Jillian and Sonja was located. He drove slowly along the street, trying to spot the undercover surveillance of the Feds. He didn't know if this place was on their radar or not. Nothing seemed out of the ordinary. He got to the end of the street and parked the unmarked police car. He'd locked the car, but then had second thoughts about leaving the police radio. Unlocking the car, he retrieved the radio and turned the volume to low—just in case, as Terry had said.

At the last block before number thirteen he sat on a low brick fence, pretending to be making a call on his mobile, as he casually looked up and down the street.

Number thirteen was a single fronted, double storey terrace house, painted a sickly pale green with a dark grey trim. The top storey balcony had peeling cream paint on its old timber-framed windows. The internal window coverings were dirty looking venetian blinds. Half of the upper balcony was enclosed. Wil presumed it to be an added bedroom—he wondered if it had ever been council approved. He also wondered if this was an active brothel, or just a place to hold the women before placing them elsewhere.

Wil heard the motorbike before he saw it. It came from a laneway running behind the row of terrace houses. The licence plate was the one registered to Eddie Kovacs, and the colour and make fitted the description—Wil had the first sighting of the elusive bouncer.

Still pretending to talk on his phone, Wil got off the fence and took long strides toward the bike that was now headed directly at him. In what must have looked like a game of chicken, Wil pocketed the mobile and threw himself at the rider. They both went flying over the bike, hitting the tarmac of the road. The bike fell onto its side, spinning three hundred and sixty degrees, and then stalling.

Luckily for Wil, Eddie took the main force as they plummeted to the ground, breaking his fall. Unluckily, though, Kovacs's helmet bounced off the road, forcing it up and into Wil's forehead. He lay on top of Eddie, stunned, for a matter of only seconds but it was enough time for Eddie to gather his wits and push Wil off.

Will lay on the road, unable to get up, concussed. He could just make out Eddie on the road beside him, struggling to get to his feet. Eddie swore and cursed as each attempt to get to his knees resulted in a scream of pain.

Wil remembered his police radio and got it out of his jacket. Trying to sit up again made his head spin, so he lay back down.

Eddie had rolled onto his side, and was dragging himself towards his motorbike.

Wil made the call to PCC—the Police Communications Centre—using MMR Call Priority Function. 'Code 9—Repeat, Code...' Then his world went black.

CHAPTER SEVENTEEN

Lexie woke to an empty house, relieved to discover that Ross had already left. She hadn't wanted to be alone the previous night but this morning company was the last thing she wanted.

She went about making her breakfast. She planned to phone the hospital to check on Jillian's progress, but wasn't really expecting that they'd give her any information, not being in any way related to her. Wil had told her about Jillian's sister arriving from Canada.

How devastating was it going to be for the poor woman to learn what had happened to her younger sister? Lexie thought about how she would feel if anything remotely similar were to happen to her sister Dana.

Lexie decided that the best thing that she could do for Jillian at the moment was to get on with the article. She wanted now, more than ever, to get the world to hear and understand.

She started 'Breaking the Cycle', her second article for *Contemporary Woman,* this time with statistics. She knew that in reality, the numbers didn't reflect the truth of the number of women touched by domestic violence: the emotional, verbal, social, and economic abuse, as well as the spiritual, physical and sexual. During her research, Lexie had found that the government had committed $14.9 million to repeat the Personal Safety Survey of 2005. There were surveys and studies, and conference workshops on bridging gaps and filling cracks. The police had repeatedly stated that there weren't enough shelters for women to turn to for refuge.

Lexie believed that the work being done in the community, with men, and the changing of attitudes to women was the real light, the real hope. The invaluable work being done through White Ribbon—Australia's campaign to stop violence against women: that was the answer. Working on the source of the trouble.

And then it was all starting to sound like mumbo-jumbo to Lexie. What she wrote she felt was inadequate, inept. How could she possibly make a difference to anyone's life?

She was alone. She was a failure as woman. Millions of women the world over were having babies, many unwanted. And she couldn't even get pregnant. She had failed to be a wife that her husband wanted to keep. Even her career, she thought now, was a flop. She'd just got by in New York; nobody had been chasing her down to work for them. It had been all Doug's money that had allowed them to live a decent Manhattan life.

Melancholy took hold of her. She couldn't write anymore. She should have gone and had a shower, she knew, but instead she threw herself onto the couch in a funk. She stared up at the ceiling, examining the intricate work of the rosette moulding surrounding the light fitting. *Some people have talent*, she thought of the person whose work she was looking at. *But not me, I'm just a hack.*

The knocking at the front started out softly but grew louder and more insistent the longer Lexie ignored it.

'I know you're in there, young lady. I can see you through the lace,' Erica Reed had her face up to the lounge room window. 'Plus, your car is sitting in the driveway.'

'Coming, Mother.' Lexie got up and tightened the belt around her robe. 'Shit, shit, shit!' she mumbled to herself.

'Alexis, it's twelve-thirty in the afternoon, for goodness' sake!' Erica walked past Lexie, eyeing her messy hair, down to her bare feet, disapproval written across her face. 'Aren't your feet freezing without slippers at least?'

'No, I can't say that they are. But if it will make you feel more comfortable, I will go and find a pair.'

She returned from the bedroom, feet appropriately covered. 'Mother, why are you here?'

'And it's lovely to see you too, darling.'

'Sorry. Hello, Mother.' Lexie gave her mother's cheek a faint peck. 'And what brings you to Elwood this...' she pulled the lace curtain aside, 'grey dull autumn day?'

'Don't you read any of your text messages? Your father comes home today.'

She snatched her mobile from the coffee table and scrolled through the messages that she'd ignored yesterday. 'Oh, yes, here it is. Dad arrives at Tullamarine today at four-forty.' She thought back to yesterday, and what she'd been through, what she had seen; Jillian and the condition she'd been in.

'Whatever is the matter? You've gone as white as a sheet.' Erica went to her daughter, and helped her to sit back down on the couch. 'Are you sick? You look terrible. Maybe I should take you to a doctor.'

'No, no, I don't need a doctor.' Lexie took the glass of water her mother offered, and drank. 'I've had, well, I've been through...'

'What, has something happened? You're starting to worry me now, Alexis.'

Lexie slowly drank her water. She desperately wanted to confide in her mother. She wanted to tell her everything. Everything that she had seen at the shelter, what had happened at the brothel and the horrendous things those bastards had done to Jillian. She wanted to bare her soul now to her mother; to tell her she was feeling as low as she had ever felt, that her despairing thoughts had been leading her to a very dark place—that the knocking on the door had saved her.

Lexie drained the glass. 'I feel much better now.' She looked at Erica. 'So where did you decide to take me to lunch?'

'It'll be a surprise. No surprise, of course, that I'm paying,' Erica said, looking relieved. 'Quick, jump in the shower. I won't be seen in public with you looking unwashed.'

In the shower, Lexie let the hot water wash away her tears.

*

Lexie waved goodbye to her mother, and watched her BMW disappear as it headed off to the airport. Lunch had been uneventful; she'd sat back and listened to her mother prattle on about the things that Lexie found irritating. She found it exhausting.

She still had to collect her car from the long-term parking at the Royal Melbourne Hospital. And she knew that she wouldn't be able to sleep, not until she'd seen Jillian and checked on her progress. She'd been right—they wouldn't give out information to her earlier when she'd enquired over the phone. Lexie was hoping, though, that when she got to the hospital, someone would remember her from the previous day, and let her see Jillian.

She entered the hospital, then found her way to the Intensive Care Unit. She walked confidently up to the nurse's station. 'I'm here to visit Jillian Laidlaw.'

'Are you a family member?' the nurse said as she stabbed a syringe into the top of a small glass vial.

'Well, no. I'm a friend. A very close friend.' Lexie watched the nurse turn the vial on its side and with one hand draw up the solution in one deft movement. 'I brought her into hospital yesterday.'

'No visitors, I'm afraid. She is still critical. Only one family member at a time.' The nurse looked at Lexie. 'I'm sorry, it's hospital policy.'

Lexie thanked the nurse, and walked out of the unit. She made her way to the Emergency Department— and her backup plan.

'Yes, he's here!' Lexie waved to catch the young doctor's attention.

Dr Marcos smiled as he walked towards her, recognition on his face. 'Ms Reed, how are you?'

'I'm fine, thank you, Doctor. And thank you again for yesterday.'

'Call me Cookie. All in a day's work. Have you come to visit Mrs Laidlaw?'

'Yes, I tried, but they won't let me see her. Because of hospital policy, and my not being family.' Lexie gave the young doctor her saddest, most desperate expression. She didn't have to work too hard: sad and desperate were very close to the surface of her emotions.

'Not a problem.' Cookie turned and said something to a passing nurse. 'I was just going up to check on our patient myself. I can bend hospital policy just a little bit this evening. Well, that is until someone higher up catches me out.'

The got into the lift and headed up to the ICU.

'Cookie isn't your real name, is it?' Lexie asked when the lift door closed.

'No, my Philippine mother had me christened with the auspicious name of Fortuna. But naturally, growing up in Australia—and having very clever friends—Fortuna became fortune cookie: Cookie. Since my early teens everyone, even my family, have all called me Cookie. Only my mother calls me Fortuna.' He smiled at Lexie, and placed a hand on her back as they exited the lift and entered the Intensive Care Unit.

Tears pricked at Lexie's eyes. All of the tubes were still keeping Jillian alive and breathing. She looked so fragile.

Lexie looked up, and saw a woman at the nurse's station. She did a double take—the woman looked exactly like Jillian, only slightly older, with short hair. This woman had a confidence about her, the way she held herself, her mannerisms. Both she and the nurse were looking towards Lexie and Cookie as they stood beside Jillian's bed.

'That's our cue to leave,' Cookie said to Lexie.

'Oh, OK. Thanks for getting me in to see her, Cookie.'

'No problemo. Look after yourself, Lexie Reed,' Cookie said as they both left Jillian's room.

Cookie nodded to Carmel, Jillian's sister, and winked at the nurse behind the desk as he waved and left the unit.

'Hello, you must be Jillian's sister.' Lexie put out her hand to Carmel as she approached her. 'I'm Lexie Reed; I brought your sister to the hospital. I hope you don't think me intrusive, getting in to visit Jillian with the doctor's help.'

'Is there somewhere were can go and talk?' Carmel leant over the desk and asked the nurse.

The nurse this time was injecting a solution into a large bag of clear fluid. She did so again with skill and speed. She pointed to a room, the other of the nurse's station.

Carmel headed to the family room, and Lexie followed.

Carmel shut the door behind them. Before Lexie knew what was happening, Carmel swept her up in an enormous hug, her arms wrapped tight around Lexie.

'Thank you, thank you so much,' she said as her tears flowed, wetting Lexie's coat. Then she held Lexie back at arm's length, having a close look at her. 'Detective Saddington has told me everything that you have done for my sister.'

CHAPTER EIGHTEEN

'Nurse! Quick, I think he's going to chuck!' Marty yelled, to anyone and everyone in the Emergency Department. He emptied a green kidney dish that sat on Wil's bedside locker, tipping out the scissors and tapes.

'What's going on? How did I get here?' Wil said as he handed the full kidney dish back to Marty.

'Jesus, Sads, that's disgusting.' Marty dry-retched as he passed the dish to the nurse who approached in answer to his distressed call.

'How's the head, Detective?' the nurse enquired of her patient. 'That's a pretty good concussion you've got yourself there. I'll just get rid of this and then do another set of obs on you, OK? And you,' pointing at Marty, 'no more yelling.'

'You don't remember what happened?' Marty picked up the little white torch off the locker, flashing the light into Wil's eye.

'What the hell are you doing? You idiot!' Wil said, snatching the torch from Marty's hand. 'I remember driving to Fitzroy, parking, walking up to observe the house where Jillian was first spotted with de Bruin. But, no, nothing after that.'

'You will remember our disgraced Constable Davis. He was working PCC—banished to Police Communication Centre, that's pretty awful punishment for giving one to a witness...'

'Marty!'

'Sorry, anyway, he'd received a couple *dirty 30s...*'

'What the hell are you talking about?'

'Code 30—Officer-arresting-a-drunken-citizen. Then comes over a Code 9—you know that one? Police-in-trouble. Then no response when he tried to communicate back. He tried all the Crime Department channels but there wasn't a response to the priority call function, the dispatcher, Davis, had to start a role call of all units logged on the channel. Terry had that radio logged, and it was the one he gave you.'

'So, I called for help?'

'Yeah, but you must have blacked out right after making the call. We found you through the GPS in your phone. You were lying on the middle of Kay Street, unconscious, about a block away from your car. Looked as though you'd had a run-in with something, or someone.'

The nurse returned and started taking Wil's blood pressure and pulse. She waved the lighted torch in front of his eyes. 'Both equal and reacting. BP's up a bit, but that's understandable,' she said looking, unsmiling, directly at Marty.

'Detective! Two days in a row. Should I be worried about you?' Dr Marcos stepped into the room.

'Hey, Cookie,' said Wil, rubbing his sore head. 'Just wanted to see the place from a different perspective.'

'I've just been upstairs with your friend Ms Reed. Do you want me to let her know that you're here?'

'No!' Wil replied a little too loudly and quickly. 'She's not a friend, she's a witness.'

'Relax, just asking.'

'Can you check and see if I'm right to be discharged.' Wil summoned a pleasant smile. 'Please.'

'Well, your obs are all stable.' Cookie looked at Wil's chart. 'You wouldn't stay anyway, would you?'

'Look, I feel fine.' Wil started to move slowly. 'I know the bed will be needed for someone else.'

'OK, I would advise though, against being alone for while,' Cookie said, looking at Marty, who was fiddling with the oxygen and suction units attached to the wall near the head of Wil's bed. He turned back to Wil, and shook his head. 'That way, if you start to go downhill, someone can do something about it.'

'Marty will look out for me. Marty! Did you hear the doctor?'

'Sure. Can we get out of here now?'

Wil closed the curtain around the bed, and put his clothes back on. There was a piece ripped from the elbow of his jacket, where he must have hit the road. He started to feel dizzy, and sat back down on the bed. He waited a minute, and then resumed dressing. He didn't want any of the nursing staff to see him feeling light-headed; they'd want to keep him longer. So he told himself to toughen up and get on with the job. The nausea was starting to come back, but he'd be able to get something at the pharmacy to deal with that.

Dressed now, he went to the nurse's station and signed the necessary discharge paperwork, Marty standing close by.

The cold hit Wil as they stepped outside. The even temperature inside the hospital had lulled him into a false sense of comfort. He pulled his torn jacket close over his chest.

Both detectives looked up as they noticed a woman waving to them. Lexie Reed.

'Shit!' said Wil.

'What's the matter with you?' Marty asked.

'Wil, hi. Detective Hanratty, hello,' Lexie said as she approached. 'Perfect timing. I was just about to start the search for my car. You didn't tell me yesterday where you parked it. I thought I'd be wandering around here for hours.'

'It wouldn't have taken long if you started in the basement. You're pretty resourceful; I've no doubt that you would have found it. I bet you get what you want most of the time, Ms Reed.' Wil kept walking. 'Where's the car, Marty?'

'Um, in the ER short-term. I hadn't planned on staying all day.' Marty hurried along beside Wil. He pointed the key and unlocked the unmarked car.

'What are you talking about?' Lexie asked as she stopped several metres from the two men.

'Basement, about third row on the left.' Wil got into the passenger seat and shut the door, ending the conversation.

Marty shrugged, waved to Lexie and got behind the wheel.

Wil looked in the side mirror as they drove away; Lexie was still standing in the same spot, staring at the back of their car. He turned his attention forward, away from the hospital, and her.

'You want me to take you home?' Marty asked.

'No, straight to the station; I must have been on to something. We have to figure out what happened, who I had a run-in with.' Wil stopped to think for a minute. 'The Shift Manager has a recorded PSM shift report from D24, right?'

'Yeah, well, the priority call function activations, anyway, like your Code 9, are definitely recorded.' Marty sat up straighter.

'If I listen to myself making the call, it might trigger my brain to wake up.'

*

Wil and Marty entered the station on a mission. Wil was aware that he knew something—he hoped they were about to find out just what that was. .

'Terry, you've got the tape?' Wil asked as he crossed the threshold of the MIR.

'Yes, Sads, as requested.' Terry had the tape ready to play. 'How's the head? You're looking a lovely shade of grey, matches your hair beautifully.'

'A few scotches later will fix that. Can we have some quiet in here, guys?' Wil took off his jacket and hung it over the back of the chair at his desk in the Incident Room.

Marty did the same, sitting opposite. 'You ready?'

Wil nodded for him to press play, and the recording started.

'Code 9—Repeat, Code...' static. Wil's voice sounded panicked then cut out.

'This is D24. Please identify yourself, over.'

'D24, go ahead—we have received your Code 9, over.'

'Play it again.' Wil closed his eyes, and held his head in hands.

On the fourth playing of the tape, an image popped into his head. He jumped up from his seat.

'A motorbike! A bright yellow fucking motorbike! It came out slow, from the laneway, from behind the house. Then, as I started towards the bike, he made a charge at me. When he was right at me, I leapt at him. Knocked him off the bike. I landed on top of him, that's when I got this.' He raised his hand to the egg on his forehead. 'I smacked into the guy's helmet.'

'It had to be Eddie Kovacs!' Marty was up off his seat this time. 'Finally—I was beginning to think he was a ghost.'

'He was in a world of pain. I remember now, he was screaming each time he tried to get up.'

'Maybe he broke something in the fall,' Terry said. 'I'll get a step up in the KALOF. See if I can't get more eyes out there on the road.'

'He was taking a chance, don't you think, coming back to that house?' Marty said. 'He must know by now that we'd be looking at the place, as well as Rose Avenue.'

'Yeah, you're right. So, that must mean there's something of importance to him there.' Wil went to the Incident Board. All the warrants that were still valid, were listed on the board. 'We have to get into the Kay Street house, and then Rose Avenue. I don't care what the Federal fucking Police say—we're going in there today, now! Marty, got your balls intact today?'

'Sir, yes, Sir. Balls-of-steel today,' Marty said, grabbing himself. 'Just checking—right to go.'

'And how, might I ask, am I to handle backup for two cowboys?' Terry said, shaking his head.

'Get onto the Chief. This bullshit has gone on for too long. And Terry, I want to reinterview Frances Spencer, and that Paige whatever her name is. Get them to come in tomorrow morning, early as possible.' Wil walked to the door, calling to Marty, 'You ready, pardner?'

Lexie parked the Peugeot in her driveway. She dragged her feet as she walked into her house. As hard as she tried, she could not come up with one logical reason to explain Wil's behaviour in the hospital car park. She put her bag down on the sideboard, and then dropped onto the couch. He didn't look too good; must have taken a knock to the head, judging by the huge bruise forming on his forehead.

'Brain damage, that's all it could be,' she said to the empty room. 'There's just no other explanation.'

After getting herself something to eat, Lexie attempted her article again. She sat at her desk, a large glass of wine in front of her. She sat staring at the condensation covering the glass. She couldn't shake the feelings of inadequacy; it seemed to her that she'd never quite been good enough through her entire life. She hadn't been the good enough daughter. Certainly she hadn't been the good enough wife. She wasn't even good enough as a woman.

She'd been self-denying in an attempt to overcome whatever it was that she'd been lacking in all her relationships. She was emotionally restrained with her family, for fear of embarrassing either them, or herself. Now, whenever she was with her family, even her father whom she loved dearly, she behaved in an unnatural way.

She now believed that her own family—mother, father and sister—had no idea who she really was.

Her marriage had been much the same in the end. She'd made personal sacrifices for Doug to move forward. She wanted to move to New York, that was no sacrifice. But she'd moved away from family and friends, all the same.

The moisture began to drip from the glass, making a puddle around its base. She took a sip, admitting to herself that tonight she wasn't going to be getting any work done. The house was empty, and she felt empty.

'God, I need help.' Lexie roused herself, picked up her mobile, and hit speed dial. 'Carla, want to go get a drink? I need a spark from somewhere and, hopefully, you're it.'

'Cool, I could do with a drink, and I have goss for you.'

'Your choice for location.'

'Nice new place, aptly called *Spirit Bar*, give me fifteen minutes. I'll pick you up.'

*

The following morning, a slightly brighter Lexie waited in the cafeteria of the Royal Melbourne Hospital. Carmel was meeting her there at ten a.m. as they'd arranged the previous day. Carmel knowing Lexie wouldn't be allowed access to visit Jillian, not without herself present.

'Good morning.' Lexie rose as Carmel entered the café. The two women leaned in and kissed each other's cheek. 'Any change overnight?'

'Nothing overnight, but the doctors are going to attempt to bring her out of her coma this morning.'

'Coffee?' Lexie asked.

'Yes, please,' Carmel replied as she took a seat. 'Black, no sugar, thanks. I can't stand the milk in Canada, so I had to get used to drinking my coffee without. Now it's the only way I like it. Funny isn't it, what we get used to?'

'I know. My time in the States was the same. I couldn't get a decent coffee anywhere, so I just gave up in the end. But since I've come back home, I've turned back into a latte junkie.' Lexie felt sick at her choice of words. Jillian was upstairs with untold number of tubes stuck in her body, an unwilling addict, her body was in crisis.

Lexie turned away from Carmel, hoping that she didn't take to heart the crushing words she had just uttered. She returned and placed their drinks on the table.

'Can you stay in Melbourne for a while?' Lexie moved the conversation on.

'I can take as long as I need. I have a very understanding husband and, luckily, a great support-group of friends, who will help with my boys.' Carmel looked into her coffee. 'I try not to imagine the worst, but it's hard, you know. I've got to try to stay positive; Jillian is going to need a lot of help. I can't even...'

Lexie put her hand over Carmel's—it was all the comfort she could give. She didn't have any words. They had no idea of what the future held for Jillian.

'It just rips my heart in two when I think about the life that Jillian has led. She must have been so very sad and lonely when I left home. I couldn't wait to get out of there. I didn't think too much about her and what she would have been dealing with. Then when Mum died, I just didn't want to know. I was only just out of my teens; I didn't want to feel responsible for a little sister, so I blocked her out of my mind. The old man had gone all religious when Mum for got sick.'

'I don't really know anything about your father; Jillian didn't say much about him when I interviewed her,' Lexie said. 'She mentioned the abuse that your mother endured. I only guessed that he would have been abusing her, too.'

'When our parents first went to get married, the church wouldn't marry them. Mum was Catholic, the old man, he wasn't any religion. He actually became a Catholic so that they could marry in the church. Mum used to love telling that story—like he did this great, wonderful thing just for her. After they got married, that was the end to the churchgoing for him. That was, until Mum got cancer. In his twisted, alcohol-addled brain, God was punishing him for not going to church, by making mum sick. He kept on drinking—the Catholic Church doesn't seem to worry about the evils of drink. And he became very, very devoted. Almost, I suppose you could say, zealous. After Mum's funeral, I never saw him again. He will have rotted away, somewhere, all alone. I'm sorry about that, I don't usually talk about him. We'd better get going.'

Half an hour later Jillian's ventilator had been removed and an oxygen mask placed over her mouth and nose.

'The drugs used to keep her in a coma, have been reduced at a slow rate over the morning,' the doctor said. 'Now, we wait.'

'Do you have any idea how long it could take before she wakes up?' Carmel said, then blew her nose—she'd been quietly crying since they'd entered the ICU.

'No unfortunately, we don't.' The doctor shook his head. 'Every case is different. Because of the drugs your sister had been taking -'

'She wasn't taking drugs! They were forced on her,' Lexie interrupted, raising her voice. Carmel patted Lexie's arm, nodding in agreement.

'I'm sorry. I didn't mean anything. A poor choice of words on my part.'

'No, I'm sorry, I shouldn't have snapped at you,' Lexie said, guilty over her own earlier comment.

'We're all anxious; it's a very stressful situation. We wait, we observe.' The doctor checked the monitors at the bedside, then left the room.

They didn't have to wait long. Lexie noticed it first: Jillian's hand clenching into a fist, then releasing. She did this several times before Lexie said anything; she wanted to make sure that she hadn't imagined it.

'Her hand, she's moving her hand, look!'

'Yes! I can see.' Carmel was up on her feet and at her sister's side, scanning her body, looking for whatever she could find to give them more hope.

She placed her face near Jillian's, just as two nurses entered the room.

'Talk to her,' one nurse said, looking at the monitor. 'She can hear you.'

Lexie could see the monitor was showing an increase in Jillian's heart rate.

'Yes, Carmel, keep talking, her heart started to beat faster just then when you said her name.'

'Bean, I'm here, wake up, sweetheart,' Carmel said. 'I've been waiting for you to wake up and talk to me. I've missed you so much. I love you, sweet girl. Please wake up.'

Jillian's eyes snapped open. She stared straight into her sister's eyes.

'Hello.' Carmel bent over the side rail of the bed, and kissed her sister's forehead.

Jillian's eyes followed Carmel as she moved back a little.

'What a scare you've given us,' Carmel said as she brought Jillian's hand to her mouth and kissed the back of it.

'Hello, Jillian.' Lexie spoke now, her voice cracking.

Jillian's gaze never left her sister's face, but the sound of Lexie's voice obviously triggered some kind of stress in her. Her heart rate and breathing increased rapidly. The automatic blood pressure monitor switched on, the nurses alarmed at the extremely high BP reading.

'She could be having what's called an ICU psychosis, or delirium. It happens on occasion, when a patient comes out of a coma,' the nurse said, pressing the nurse assist call bell. 'We need to give her something to calm her, before she gets hysterical.'

'We can give her some Ativan,' the second nurse said, looking at Jillian's drug chart. 'That'll help settle her down.'

'Lexie and I have been waiting here, waiting for you to wake up,' Carmel spoke in a soft voice. She indicated to Lexie to come around to where she was standing.

Lexie walked to the other side of the bed, trying to stay out of the way of the nurses, who were darting in and out of the room, checking monitors and charts.

'Hi there, Jillian.' Lexie bent down so that Jillian could see her, but eyes were still fixated on Carmel.

It started as a low growl coming from deep inside Jillian. Her eyes were still locked onto Carmel's, but she appeared to be acknowledging Lexie's presence. Another growl, then came a loud animal howl.

Jillian clasped Lexie's hand and Lexie jumped.

'Where—are—my—babieees?' Jillian's shrill scream cut straight through Lexie's heart.

CHAPTER TWENTY

'You sure you're up to this? You could have brain damage.'

'I'll give you brain damage, Marty, if you don't shut up. Knock on the door, I've got you covered.' Wil stepped to the side, out of the line of sight. 'Balls-of-steel ready?'

'Locked and loaded.'

'Jesus, don't say anymore. I don't want that picture to be my last—just in case this goes bad.'

Marty knocked hard on the front door of the Kay Street residence. A minute passed, he knocked again. This time the door opened, and there was a slight movement behind the door, but not enough to determine who or what was standing there.

Marty showed his badge to the darkness behind the door. This got the door opened further. Marty pushed the door wide. Wil was at his back, looking over Marty's shoulder. Simultaneously they said, 'It's a kid!'

The boy was Asian in appearance, and Wil guessed he was about eight or nine years old.

'You speak English, kid?' Marty spoke down to the boy.

The boy just smiled, and put out his hand for Marty's badge.

'That's a detective's badge, not a toy. You can't play with it.' Marty shook his head at the boy.

'Give the kid a look, I don't think he speaks English.' Wil looked up the corridor. 'Give it to him. Distract him while I have a look about.'

The first room to the left off the corridor was empty of any people. There were two old faded green couches, and several dirty beanbags strewn about the room. In the corner was an old television, with a DVD player in the cabinet beneath. There were some DVD covers on the floor. Wil picked two up; both were children's movies.

He went back into the corridor. The walls were devoid of any pictures or family photos. Marty pocketed his badge and fell into step behind Wil as he headed further down the corridor. The boy trailed behind.

At the end of the corridor, they walked into the kitchen. The sink was covered with food-crusted plastic bowls and cups. Wil shuddered when he saw a large roach run across a plate investigating what scraps remained.

'Jesus, kid, your mother needs to lift her game,' Marty said to his shadow.

The boy grinned innocently up to his new hero with the shiny badge.

'Let's have a look upstairs; there's an enclosed part of the veranda I saw from the street.'

All three made their way upstairs. Wil counted four double mattresses and ten singles.

'That's a lot of bodies sleeping in one house.' Wil looked at their tag-along. 'What do you say to that, little buddy?'

The upstairs rooms also lacked any personal items. The mattresses weren't made up but had sleeping bags and old blankets tossed on them. Their stale, musty smell made Wil's stomach queasy.

'This feels more like a halfway house,' Wil remarked, 'than somebody's home. I'll check out the bathroom, you see if there's a laundry; maybe we can get an idea from any dirty washing who or how many live here.'

'Great—choice job, thank God I always, *always* carry gloves.' Marty turned to the kid, who was still smiling and said, 'Come, Kemosabe,' as the three of them headed back down the stairs.

'Wrong nationality, Marty, but it works for him.' Wil turned into the bathroom shaking his head. 'I like it.'

Black rings encircled the bathtub it at varying levels. A bucket sat in the empty tub, filled with broken bits of toys. Wil upended the bucket, tipping out the contents along with the stagnant water that had been sitting in the bottom. He shuddered at the thought of small children being put into such a filthy environment.

Again, no personal items; everything was in bulk: large pump bottles of generic-brand shampoo, conditioner and soap. The bench surrounding the hand-basin was littered with bits of rubbish: dirty cotton wool balls, used tissues, a broken-toothed comb and a brush full of hairs in a variety of colours, Wil noticed.

A sparkle caught Wil's eye. On closer inspection beneath a used tissue he found a hair clip—pink, purple and sparkling. There was something vaguely familiar about the clip.

He was about to put it back on the bench, when he heard shrill women's voices coming from the back of the house. Wil dropped the hair clip into a small evidence bag, slipped it into the pocket of his jacket, and went to see who was making all the noise.

Wil found Marty cornered in the laundry by two short, ferocious women. They had him bailed up against an old twin-tub washing machine. He had his badge out, waving it in their faces, but they kept pushing his hand back and away.

'Hey, Tonto, you ready to go?'

'Hell yeah,' Marty pushed his way between the two women. 'I think I need to learn to speak Thai, or Vietnamese, Chinese—whatever it is, those are two scary mammas.'

The women continued screaming at them, until they were out the door and on the street.

'As filthy as the place was,' Marty said, once they were safely in the car, 'I think it was clean. I didn't find anything. My guess is that was son, mother and grandma. And I've seen the dirty underwear to confirm.'

'No longer feeling quite so steely, huh?' Wil turned the car around and headed back towards the station. 'I might have figured some things out. But just let me think for now.'

'No music?'

'No music.'

*

The MIR was full, hushed murmurs buzzed back and forth. The entire unit had been called in; off duty, days off—didn't matter. Wil knew if these cases were ever to be closed, all hands needed to be on board. If what he was thinking was correct, they had a massive job to do.

'Right, everybody, settle down.' Wil walked up to the board and stood facing the Major Incident Unit, all eager faces paying attention. 'Marty and I have just been through the house at Kay Street, Fitzroy—the first location where Jillian Laidlaw was seen. The place was set up like a child-minding centre, but there weren't any children there except for a young Asian boy and two women, who I think we can assume are his mother and grandmother.

'We know that Rose Avenue is a brothel. We can assume for now that Sonja de Bruin sold Jillian Laidlaw to the brothel. We know from Frances Spencer, a volunteer at McHale Shelter, that Jillian left the shelter with de Bruin. And we know from Lexie Reed, the journalist, that she saw Jillian's daughters being driven away from the shelter in a white van by Eddie Kovacs.

'I think Eddie took the children to the house in Kay Street. I would put money on it being a transfer station for stolen children. Where to from there I have no idea.' Wil stood in front of the photographs of the two little blue-eyed blondes. He felt sick to his stomach.

'Wil, we have to get the Feds on board with this now,' Terry spoke up. 'For all we know, this is what they're working on.'

'I actually have some information on that, which might be helpful.' Ross stood up. 'My housemate is presently working for the Federal Police, specifically the case involving Rose Avenue.'

'And you're only just now sharing this information,' Wil raised his voice. 'You didn't think that speaking up sooner might have helped us with our two fucking murder inquiries. Not to forget that poor bastard who had his head blown off outside the place. How the fuck did you end up on this team?'

'I'm sorry, Boss,' Ross held his ground, 'but you must be aware that neither of us would be discussing cases and details. I do have one piece of information that has been shared quietly: the brothel isn't so much under their surveillance, as is a certain customer that uses the brothel.'

'That's something, I suppose.' Wil stared at Ross until the young man looked away and sat down. 'When Sean Laidlaw turned up on the doorstep of McHale Shelter, Eddie would have been worried about losing Jillian and the girls. They might have already sold them at that stage, I don't know. But he was a threat to their business, so Eddie had to get rid of him.

'What happened with Eddie and de Bruin, who knows? Fighting over money is usually a good motive. But his killing her upset more than just the apple cart—she was the centre of the business and without her running the shelter there was no business.

'When I ran into Eddie at Kay Street—and I would bet Marty's Judas Priest collection—he'd just finished cleaning out all trace of his ever having been there.'

'Now, now...' Marty started up.

'Your collection's safe, Marty,' Terry said, then put one hand beside his mouth and looked about the room. 'No one's interested in that shit.'

Some of the older officers laughed; the younger ones shook their heads, not having a clue what a Judas Priest collection was.

'Paige what's-her-name, and Frances Spencer are to be re-interviewed.' Wil turned to Terry. 'Terry, they're both coming in tomorrow morning—there has to be something we've missed.'

'We should be looking at all the records of the women that have gone through the shelter since de Bruin was running the place.' Marty walked up to the board. 'We still have warrants that cover all the paperwork for the shelter. Christ, Wil, I can't believe this. I wonder how many have disappeared?'

CHAPTER TWENTY-ONE

By the time she got back to the sanctuary of her little house, Lexie was drained from beating herself up. She regretted her earlier decision that morning to catch public transport.

She was certain that the other passengers on the tram could see right through her, and what a horrible person she really was. She was sure that they would all agree with the universe, it was the correct move not allowing her to be a mother.

People looked at her, but were quick to turn away, embarrassed, she was sure of it. They could see her disgrace. She had dragged herself off the tram allowing herself to be swept along with the busy foot-traffic.

Lucky for Lexie, she was swept along in the right direction, towards her next tram stop. She had forced herself to focus; she had to make sure that she caught the right tram so she could get home and fall apart in private.

Aboard the 67 tram, she turned her body towards the window, away from prying eyes; she didn't think that she could take any more reproachful looks. She tried to distract herself with the familiar sights of the Botanical Gardens' floral clock, the War Memorial, sights that belonged to the Melbourne she loved. But she couldn't take comfort so she'd closed her eyes.

Home finally, again on her couch, lost and alone. She didn't even have enough strength to remove her coat and scarf.

'How could I have forgotten her children? What sort of person am I?' Lexie said to her empty living room. 'I was so caught up in my own little crusade, I couldn't see...'

She pulled her mobile from the pocket of her jeans. It was still turned off from her hospital visit; she hadn't thought to turn it back on. She wasn't sure now what the point of turning it on was. Who would want to have anything to do with her now?

Carmel had told her not to blame herself, that she wasn't responsible for Jillian's daughters. She knew that: the part of her brain that didn't want to accept responsibility was saying exactly that. It was the fact she hadn't thought of them at all that was killing her.

She had thought she was going to change things with her articles; she was to going to make some sort of improvement in the lives of battered women. She would somehow make amends for not being there for her friend Ava, back in New York, who had been battered and murdered by her husband. If Lexie had been any sort of friend she would have known what had been going on.

But she'd been oblivious then, as she felt she had been now. No wonder she couldn't have children—she didn't deserve to.

She turned her phone on, and was alerted to two voicemail messages.

'Hi, Lex, gives us a call, would you.' Message left by Megan Kestler at 10:00.

'This is your editor calling, again. I will need to see the first draft of your second article pretty soon. Call me today, Lexie.' Message left by Megan Kestler at 15:00.

'What's the point?' Lexie looked at her phone as it rang, then clicked it on.

'Lexie, did you get my messages?' Megan's tone was not exactly friendly. 'I want to see the draft tomorrow; we have to start on the magazine layout for next month. I need to know how much space your article will need.'

'It's coming on a bit slow,' Lexie said. 'I'm struggling with this one. Things have been going on that...'

'Look, Lexie, I don't want to be a hard-arse, but you are on a contract, and been paid an advance. I will expect to see you around four p.m. tomorrow. That should give you plenty of time. See you then.' The call was over.

'I'm useless *and* I'm screwed.' Lexie sat back on the couch when her mobile rang again.

'Ms Reed, Wil Saddington.' Wil's voice sounded cold to Lexie. 'We are re-interviewing a few of the people involved with the cases connected with McHale Shelter. I was hoping you'd be able to come down to the station, tomorrow morning, say around nine-thirty?'

'I don't think I...' Lexie started to cry. 'I don't think, well, I'm no good...'

'Ms Reed, Lexie—are you alright?'

Wil's voice lacked any real concern, which made Lexie cry even harder. She pressed *end*. She couldn't speak. She was sobbing uncontrollably.

'I've ruined everything,' she said, and threw the phone to the other end of the couch.

Getting up, Lexie took of her coat and scarf and tossed them onto the armchair. In her bathroom mirror she saw a mess. Two large black panda eyes, pale face. She shook her head and turned on the hot tap and grabbed a flannel and the face-wash. She scrubbed her face and removed all the makeup. She brushed her hair and tied it back.

She thought about running a bath, but didn't feel that she deserved that luxury. She had to eat and then get to work. She had nobody else to support her. If she lost her contract with *Contemporary Woman,* she would most definitely be screwed.

Forcing down two poached eggs, toast and a cup of tea, Lexie started to feel slightly better. She was still numb from crying, washed out and tired, but she at least felt that she was ready to sit at her computer, and get something down.

Writing about statistics, and the relationship between the crisis shelters and the police, kept Lexie busy for some time. Her research had been thorough and she had plenty of material. It was the emotion that was missing. But she would be able to attempt to put that in when she did the second draft.

She was lost in writing, when her attention was pulled back to her lounge room by a banging at her front door. She checked the mantel clock—it was eight-thirty at night, pitch black outside. Who would be visiting at this hour?

'I'm coming,' she called out as she headed to the front door. The outside light was on, the security sensor doing its job. 'Who is it?'

'Detective...It's Wil, Lexie. Open up.'

'Oh!' she said, opening the door. 'Come in. This is a surprise.'

'You're kidding!' Wil said, staring at her. 'I got the impression over the phone that you were in a really bad way. I came as soon as I could, not knowing what I was going to find!'

'I'm sorry, I was in a pretty bad state.'

Wil shut the door behind him. 'You hung up on me.' He bit his tongue on the real fears that were scurrying around his head...suicide or self-harm.

'I'm sorry...' she turned and went to the living room.

'Stop saying that.' He followed her for two steps and then grabbed hold of her arm. Turning her round to face him, he looked into her eyes. 'Tell me, what the hell is going on?'

Lexie leant into Wil, her arms encircling his waist. She laid her face on his chest and started to cry again.

His arms went around her shoulders, and he drew her close to his body. She felt his lips gently touch the top of her head. She was amazed at how much comfort that simple action gave her. She felt the temperature rise in her veins. Her tears began to subside.

She let go of him, and wiped the tears away from her cheeks.

'Do you want to let me know what's wrong?' Wil's voice was softer now.

'Take a seat,' Lexie said, indicating the couch, 'this could take a while.'

CHAPTER TWENTY-TWO

'Thanks for coming back in, Ms Townsend.' Wil ushered Paige into Interview Room One.

'Please, call me Paige,' she said as she took the offered seat. 'Ms Townsend makes me feel as though I'm in some sort of trouble. I'm not, am I?'

'No, not at all,' Marty said, and sat opposite Paige, before Wil could take the seat. 'We're hoping that by going over your original statement we might be able to find something we missed.'

Wil opened the file containing Paige's earlier interview.

'We want to go back to the first time you came in contact with Jillian Laidlaw.' Wil concentrated on her written statement while Paige talked about the Laidlaws' arrival at McHale Shelter. She talked for nearly ten minutes—nothing differed from her original statement.

'What about the night her husband turned up at the shelter?' Marty looked at the woman keenly.

Christ, I hope he can keep his hands to himself! Wil thought. He moved on, and caught up to where she was talking about in her statement: the night Sean went to the shelter, calling out for his wife.

'Eddie convinced him to leave, and Mr Laidlaw walked to his car. I went back inside. I heard him drive off, and then the second car,' Paige looked at Marty as she spoke. 'I assumed Eddie was going to follow him, just to make sure that he was well and truly gone. That was it for the night, no more drama.'

'Can I have that for a sec, Wil?' Marty reached over and took the file. 'Now, you said that you heard two cars. What car did Eddie drive off in, because here, in your original statement, you said: "Eddie arrived on his motorbike." But just now, you didn't actually say how he arrived, just that he arrived, and then left by car. Which car?'

'Oh?' Paige looked confused.

'Think very carefully, Paige,' Wil said. 'Don't rush this, it could be important. Have a drink of water, take your time.'

She took a few mouthfuls of the water that had been poured for her. She looked nervously from one detective to the other.

'Now I'm totally confused,' Paige took another drink. 'I remember now—he definitely arrived on his bike. I remember clearly him wheeling it around the side of the shelter where he always kept it, out of sight from the street. But, now this is where I'm stumped—I definitely heard a second car drive off, *after* Sean Laidlaw drove away.'

'Were there any other vehicles at the shelter that Eddie could have taken that night?' Wil asked. His detective-feelers were sensing something.

'No, none! I'd be been dropped off earlier, and my mother was picking me up the next morning when my shift finished. The other two housemothers live nearby, and walked together.' Paige grimaced. 'I feel so stupid, what a God-awful mistake to make. I've probably upset your entire investigation now.'

'No, this is our mistake,' Wil said. 'We should have picked this up sooner. This does put a different light on things.'

'Do you recall hearing the bike later that night?' Marty asked.

'No, but that's not unusual. Eddie would push the bike down the court before starting it, so not to wake any sleeping children.'

'Very considerate of him,' Marty said, sarcasm lacing his voice.

'You've been great, Paige,' Wil said. 'Thanks for taking the time to come in to see us.'

'It's nothing,' she said. 'Any word on Jillian and the girls yet?'

'Nothing that I can speak of at this stage,' Wil said, standing, letting her know that the interview was over— and that he couldn't share any information.

Next they interviewed Frances Spencer. They used the same room, both men bringing in their morning coffee.

'Hope you don't mind,' Wil said to Frances as they entered the room. 'No time for a break this morning I'm afraid.'

'That's OK, I've brought mine along as well,' she said, smiling as they took their seats.

'Thank you for coming in this morning,' Wil started the interview.

'Look, I don't know if this is of any help or not,' Frances opened her own file. 'I've been doing a little snooping of my own for a while. Whenever I got the chance when I was at McHale, I went though Sonja's paperwork. I never really knew what it was exactly that I was looking for, but I always figured I'd know when I saw it. You know what I mean.'

'Yes, we often work that way ourselves,' Wil said.

'Normally there is a paper trail for any resident at any shelter,' Frances looked from one detective to the other, making sure that she had their attention, 'but it wasn't always the case, not here anyway. So, I started to keep my own records, what I could manage in the times that I worked at McHale.'

'So you're telling us you have names of women that may not have a paper trail, ones that should have?' Marty was sitting up and on the edge of his seat now, at full attention.

'Well, yes, but...'

'Going back how long?' Wil interrupted, his feelers standing to full-attention.

'Twelve months or so,' Frances said shaking her head. 'But that's not all. I've found that, repeatedly, there were bills and documents for a different address: a place that doesn't have anything to do with McHale Shelter, nor any of the other shelters. The addressee wasn't anybody I knew, nor could I find out who it was.'

'Where is the place?' Marty was almost standing now.

'Port Melbourne.' Frances pushed photocopies of all the bills and statements for the property in Port Melbourne across the table to the detectives. 'It's probably illegal, what I've done, but whatever. Let them take me to jail—I felt I had to do something.'

'Frances Spencer,' Wil leant over the table and offered her his hand, 'you have my word—you will not be going to jail. I think you have just given us a massive break. Can we keep this?'

'Yes.' Frances's voice shook with emotion. 'You get that bastard Eddie. And find those poor missing women and children. Will you do that for me?'

*

The MIR was in full motion. The Incident Board was filling with information. A team was assigned the task of going through the names in Frances's file. Missing Persons needed to be brought in, names needed to be run through their databases.

A second team was put to the task of going through all that pertained to the property in Port Melbourne. Search warrants would have to written up for the place. Everyone was busy—finally, they were making progress.

Wil went to his office; he needed quiet to think over Paige's revelation about the second car not being Eddie's, and what that meant. It wasn't long belong Marty joined him.

'Good pick up back there, Marty,' Wil said, 'the second car. What do you make of it?'

'It's funny, isn't it, something can bug the shit out of you, but you have no idea what it is, even though it's there, staring you down the throat.'

'I'm proud of you,' Wil said. 'You kept your hands to yourself today. I was shitting it in there at the start—I didn't know what I was going to do if you put your hand out to touch her hair.'

'Don't be a dick,' Marty said. 'Balls-of-steel, remember? I can handle any situation.'

'Sorry, I forgot,' Wil said, relief allowing him to laugh. 'I take back every bad thing I've ever said about you.'

'What, what bad things have you said about me?' Marty was staring Wil down.

'I was joking; don't you be a dick,' Wil said. 'So, now what, back to the neighbourhood, door knocking?'

'I think we're getting close,' Marty said. 'I'm just not sure to what exactly.'

CHAPTER TWENTY-THREE

'Hey, Frances, wait up,' Lexie jogged across the street.

'Lexie, hello,' Frances stopped, her car keys in hand.

The two women hugged, a mutual bond already formed. Lexie took a close look at Frances; she could see emotion close to the surface on the older woman's face.

'Have you just been interviewed?' Lexie asked.

'Yes, you too?'

'Yes, I'm done, though. Would you like to have a coffee?' Lexie smiled. 'And a debrief? We could leave our cars here. There's a coffee shop not far from here, on Sydney Road.'

'I'd love to.'

They walked into the cold wind, pulling their coats close.

'I'm wishing we'd driven—this breeze is a little on the brisk side,' Frances said.

'We'll be right when get a warm drink inside us.'

As soon as the waitress took their order for hot chocolate and jam doughnuts, Lexie started.

'There seemed to be some excitement in the air after you left the interview room. I'd finished my interview, but hung around because Wil, DSS Saddington, told me earlier that you and Paige were to be re-interviewed as well. Did you give them something helpful?' Lexie looked at her hands as she spoke. She felt bad that she'd been listening, but she'd felt compelled to.

'Yes, I think I've given them something that they can actually use.' Frances gave a half-smile, and raised an eyebrow. 'I've been doing my own snooping, and an address has come to light that has given the police a lead, at last. I feel awful that I didn't say anything before this, but until Sonja's death, it was really only speculation on my part.'

'What did you find?' Lexie looked up now.

'An address the detectives think could be where the children have been taken.'

'Where, Frances, what is the address?' Lexie's stomach tightened.

'Um, well, I'm not sure I should tell you, Lexie. The police will handle it and I'd hate for you to get mixed up in any trouble.'

'Oh, no, you don't have to worry about that,' Lexie looked into her steaming drink as she stirred the marshmallows around. 'I'm just curious, you know, from a journalist's point of view. I wouldn't get in the way of a police enquiry.'

*

Lexie parked the Peugeot in the busy car park of the Port Melbourne Yacht Club. The *Spirit of Tasmania* ferry was docked at Station Pier and cars were lining up to board the huge ship for the overnight journey across Bass Strait to Davenport.

Maybe I'll do that one day soon, Lexie thought as she grabbed her scarf from the back seat. *Here I go again!* The wind coming off Port Phillip Bay was icy.

Again with no plan in mind, just sheer determination to make something right, she charged ahead. She crossed the road then started to walk the two blocks north-east along Bay Street. At Little Bay Street, she turned left.

Lexie knew what she was doing was probably reckless but she had convinced herself, after her grand saving of Jillian, and how righteous she'd felt, that her failure to consider the woman's children was inexcusable. She had to prove to herself, first of all, that she was better than that. She could fix this—she could get that family back together.

Trying to walk at a casual pace was hard, but she didn't want to draw attention to herself. Her phone vibrated in the pocket of her jeans. She pulled it out, her heart jumping slightly when she saw Wil's number. She hesitated before answering—could she lie to him? Now?

'Hello?' Lexie stopped and turned her body to shield her face from the wind.

'Stop right where you are!' Wil's voice barked through the phone.

Lexie spun around, again thinking he was there watching her.

'Frances Spencer has just left here. She had a feeling that you were going to get into some trouble,' Wil continued, his voice loud and clear in Lexie's ear. 'And going on your past behaviour, I know you *are* going to get into trouble.'

'I'm not...'

'Turn around, walk back to your car, and get the hell out of there,' Wil was yelling.

Lexie could hear a siren drowning out Wil's orders. She had stopped, but she wasn't about to turn back. Up ahead, she could see the signage for Little Bay Street, and she picked up her pace.

'Wil, Wil, listen to me, turn off the siren,' Lexie raised her voice, begging. 'You'll spook him!'

'Cut the bells, Marty. Say again,' Wil's voice could be heard now. 'We're on our way. Get the hell out of there, Lexie, now!'

Lexie closed her phone without saying anything. Wil and his unit would arrive and arrest Eddie, save the children—Jillian's two girls, and God knows who else's, from what Frances had been telling her.

What could Lexie Reed do to make her peace with the world? She heard her mother's voice in her head: *Step out of the way, Alexis, let the professionals do the job. Let the men do what they have to. You're only in the way.*

She heard her ex's voice: *You're just not enough for me, Lexie. I mean, you're a wonderful person, don't get me wrong, I loved you, once. But you're not enough. You can't give me what I want, what I need.*

She heard her own voice from just the night before: *You're no good for anybody. You think that you're going to make a difference in peoples lives with your stupid little articles, huh! You can't even cut it as a journalist. You forgot about the poor woman's children, for Christ's sake!*

'You are all wrong about me!' she said to the street and the passing traffic as she made the left into Little Bay Street.

Lexie didn't know the area, but her smartphone map was showing her a lane running behind the houses in the first block—behind number twenty-four. She started to jog, casually looking for a gap between houses that would lead to the lane. Eddie's white van wasn't parked on the street, and all of the houses were close to the pavement: no off-street parking. There must be parking at the rear of the property.

She spotted the small walkway as she ran past it, then jogged across the street and made a run for it straight through, up to the laneway. She counted the houses, and when she was behind the one that should be number twenty-four, she stopped, her breath clouding in the cold air.

As she slowed her breathing down and tried to calm herself, she listened. She could hear chattering, little voices talking, coming from behind the high fence. This must be where the van entered, access protected by a roller door.

Through a slight gap in the fence palings, Lexie could see into the garden. Next to a tarpaulin-shrouded van was a sandpit where three small children sat—two little blonde girls about four and six, and a little brown-headed boy of about four.

Lexie almost squealed when she spotted the girls. She couldn't believe it was this simple. She frantically looked about to see how she was going to get to them. She looked up and down the lane, hoping something would jump out at her that she could use to break into the back yard.

She spotted a wheelie-bin two doors up the lane, lying on its side. She ran and pulled it to the fence. Gingerly she climbed atop the bin, careful to put her weight on the edges of the plastic frame. She stayed bent, only getting up high enough to spy over the fence.

Lexie could see the children, but no one else in the garden. The back door to the house was open. The girls chattered to each other.

She took the chance and waved to them.

'Psst,' Lexie hissed. 'Charlotte, remember me?'

All three children stopped, turned and stared at Lexie.

'I'm a friend of your mummy's.' Lexie grabbed the fence. 'Hello, Bonnie, do you remember me?' *Time to prove your worth, girl.* Lexie said as she put her left foot up onto the fence, grabbed hold with both hands and jumped over and into the back yard. 'Now, you guys, there's nothing to be afraid of. I've come to take you home.'

Her first priority was to try and open the roller door, so they could all escape into the laneway and get away from the house. Lexie picked up a shovel from a pile

255

of rusty garden tools, discarded in a heap by the rear fence. She bashed repeatedly at the lock to the roller door. It eventually gave in, and the door released. She forced it up several inches. Bending down, she gripped the bottom of the door, and pushed up as hard as she could. The door stopped about a metre from the ground and Lexie couldn't budge it any further. It didn't matter—it was enough for all of them to get through.

She turned back to the children. They were still staring at her, fear on all three tiny faces. 'I know, I look like a crazy lady, but really, I'm not.'

There was lots of yelling and banging and crashing coming from inside the house. Lexie reached her hand inside her pocket and brought out a hair clip.

'I found this in another sandpit,' she held her hand out, the hair clip lying in her palm. 'I was wondering if know who it belongs to? It's very pretty, isn't it?'

'That's mine,' said the older of the two little girls. 'I never thought I'd see them again, they're my favourite.'

'Would you like me to put it in your hair for you?' Lexie approached the children.

'Do you know where my mummy is?'

'Yes, I do. I saw her yesterday, and she was asking about her girls,' Lexie said. 'Who is your friend?'

256

'Oh, that's Charlie. He's a sook.'

'Hello, Charlie,' Lexie held her hand out to the little boy. 'You're probably very scared. Would you like to go home now?'

All three children nodded their heads. Lexie herded them through and under the roller door and lowered herself, ready to crawl under the gap.

She was half through when someone grabbed both her ankles. She quickly flipped herself onto her back, surprising her attacker, who then lost their grip. She was now in a position to kick, and kick hard. The struggle only lasted a matter of seconds.

Wil stuck his head under the gap. 'Do you ever, ever, listen? I thought I was very specific.'

CHAPTER TWENTY-FOUR

Eddie Kovacs sat at the table, his head drooping. Both hands were in his lap.

'How long before my lawyer gets here?' Eddie mumbled.

'What, you anxious to get back to Lockup, Eddie?' Wil sat back in his seat, it was going to be a long night.

'Yeah, looking forward to starting your new life?' Marty smiled. 'Life is what you're going to get, by two. How do they work that, Wil? When you die, they resuss you, so that you can do it all over again?'

'What do you mean, by two?' Eddie looked from one detective to the other. 'I thought I'd was being done for Sonja. What the fuck are you talking about?'

'So, is that a confession to the murder of Sonja de Bruin?' Wil picked up his pen, making out he was ready to write.

'No—fuck you!' Eddie looked back down. 'I not saying nothing til my lawyer gets here. You're just twisting my words.'

'We know you were at McHale Shelter the night Sean Laidlaw turned up there. He was out front calling

258

out for his wife. We know that Paige Townsend phoned you, and that you arrived shortly after. We know that Sean left the shelter, and then you left the shelter. Sean went home, and then someone dropped a splitter into the back of his head.' Wil sat with his hands behind his head, watching Eddie's response.

'You've got to be...' Eddie stopped talking. Lowered his eyes again.

'Go on, say it,' Marty put on a sad face. 'It wasn't me—I didn't do nothin'.'

There was a knock at the door to the interview room and Marty responded.

'Lawyer's here,' Marty said to Wil, 'the honourable Bart Clegg.'

'Yeah, yeah,' Wil said, getting up out of his chair. 'You want some quality time alone with your client. Don't take too long—Eddie's pillow's already been plumped, the doona is fluffed, and his cell-mate is awaiting his arrival.'

The lawyer rolled his eyes at Wil—they all had their parts to play in the game.

*

The canteen was deserted, apart from the cleaner who was polishing the vinyl floor. Wil and Marty helped themselves to coffee and sat at an area that had armchairs.

259

'It did look like Eddie was surprised when Sean was brought into the conversation,' Marty said.

'I know, I agree. But I still think we'll push him in that direction. First, get him all riled up about being accused of something he didn't do, so when we go for what we're pretty sure that he did do, he'll crumple.'

'That sounds pretty damn good,' Marty smiled. 'I like how you think, Sads.'

*

Back in the interview room, Wil and Marty sat opposite Eddie and his lawyer. Eddie was sitting up straight now. Wil figured Eddie believed that his lawyer was going to save his arse.

'Eddie, I want to talk to you,' Wil began, 'about the first murder. The night you killed Sean Laidlaw.'

Eddie's head snapped around so he could face his lawyer.

'Aren't you going to say something?' Eddie said in a loud whisper. 'They can't fucking say that!'

'I, you, we, don't have to say anything at this stage,' Bart went to pat his client's arm, but must have had second thoughts, Wil noticed, as his hand stopped before it made contact. 'Let's just wait and hear what they think they know.'

'Was it your idea, Eddie,' Marty asked, 'to kill Sean, or was it Sonja's? We can see the why—now that we know the full story about the human-trafficking.'

'Sean's turning up like that, looking for his wife,' Wil jumped in, 'that would have made a shit-awful mess of things, right? Had you already made a deal with the brothel for Mrs Laidlaw? You must have made a small fortune on her—good-looking woman and a natural blonde, don't see many like her these days.'

Eddie went to open his mouth, but Bart Clegg quietly raised his hand to silence any outburst.

'Did you ring Sonja that night, from the shelter? Did you have to ask permission to get rid of the problem?' Wil asked. 'Or did you have equal partnership? 'Cause, from what I've gathered so far, Sonja was in charge, and you were just there to do the dirty work.'

'She was the brains behind the operation,' Marty pointed at Eddie, 'and you were just the dumb muscle man. I must say though, Eddie, your muscles are impressive. I could never get muscles like that—my attention span is far to short. Couldn't focus on one thing for that long.' Marty made out he was feeling his biceps.

Wil looked at the manila folder in front of him. He decided it was time to wake Eddie up—his eyes were starting to look a bit glazed. He slid the crime scene photos from the first murder out of the folder one by one, and placed them on the table in front of Eddie and his lawyer.

'This is what happened to Sean Laidlaw,' Wil looked at Marty.

'Probably within an hour,' Marty replied, 'an hour from when he left you at the shelter—when you followed him home. We assume, as there wasn't a break-in, when Sean went into his house, you followed him straight through the front door. The weapon, the splitting maul— that one has us tossed, though. What were you doing with one? Was it Sean's? But then his house doesn't have a fireplace, so why have a wood splitting tool? We were hoping that you'd be able to enlighten us.'

'No fucking way, man! No way,' Eddie made a move toward the photos, pushing his chair slightly. Wil's expression told him not to bother.

'Please refrain from speaking, Mr Kovacs.' Bart Clegg moved his chair, as Eddie's had moved closer when he'd sat back down.

'They're trying to pin this shit on me,' Eddie yelled at the man, spittle dribbling down his chin. 'And you— you're just sitting there on your fat fucking arse. You fucking say something.'

'My client has no comment,' Bart looked Eddie in the eye, then turned back to face Wil and Marty. 'You have nothing. You cannot tie this murder to Mr Kovacs solely because he saw the victim some time that night. This won't even make it to court.'

'All right.' Wil put the photos back in the folder. 'We'll move on.'

Wil was satisfied that Eddie was starting to get nervous; he was starting to sweat now, his shaved head glistened. Eddie kept stretching his neck—he was certainly looked uncomfortable.

'Which charge do you want to ask about next, Wil?' Marty had all the files in front of him. 'The kidnapping, child abduction, human trafficking, or the other murder? Your choice.'

Eddie wasn't looking quite so tough now.

'The child-abduction case please, Marty. We know we have plenty of evidence on that,' Wil said.

Marty selected the file and pushed it across to his partner. Wil opened the manila folder, and took out the photographs of Charlotte and Bonnie Laidlaw. There were two individual shots of the girls and one of the two little girls together—professional portraits most probably taken in some shopping centre. Marty also had a photograph of Charlie, taken only hours before. His surname was yet unknown. Charlie wasn't speaking to anyone, yet.

Wil turned the photos around and placed them in front of Eddie.

'We have an eye witness state they saw you putting these two girls into a white van. You were seen leaving McHale Shelter with them in the van. They'd been staying at the shelter with their mother.'

'No comment,' Eddie sat back in his seat, his hands behind his head.

'You'd killed their father the previous night, and then you removed the girls from the shelter to a house in Kay Street. We have DNA evidence that puts at least one of these girls in that house.' Wil put the evidence bag containing the hair clip found in the bathroom at Kay Street on the table for Eddie to see.

'You will be interested in this, Eddie,' Marty said, 'we managed to find a translator for the three generations living at Kay Street. I know what you're going to say—how did you work out which nationality? Chinese, Malaysian, Vietnamese: the list could go on. We're pretty multi-cultural around here, so yeah...'

'Marty,' Wil gave his partner a look that said *shut the hell up*. 'I don't think all those details are really necessary.'

'Anyway, we got onto the fact that the family are Thai. The mother and grandmother had plenty to say,' Marty said. 'I liked that kid, he made me laugh.'

'So we have a witness who saw you taking the girls. We have forensic evidence puttin one of them at Kay Street. We have witness statements from the two Thai women who live at Kay Street. They have managed to cut a deal to save their arses - by giving us yours. We haven't determined yet, just how many women and children have been through the place. I gather that it's been used as a transfer location. Do you have anything to say at this stage?'

'No comment.'

'We believe that you then moved these two girls,' Marty tapped the photographs, pushing them closer towards Eddie. 'Moved them to the property in Little Bay Street, Port Melbourne, where we located them, plus young Charlie here.'

'This would be a good time,' Wil yelled, slapping his hands down hard on the table, making Eddie jump, 'to inform us, as to what was the next stage for these innocents? We know of the Thai connection—the two women at Kay Street—we'll get onto the brothel, Madame Lourdes, soon. Do we assume that the next stage would have been putting two little girls on a boat or a plane bound for Thailand? Is that where this sick, fucked-up situation was heading?'

'My client has no comment,' Clegg jumped in before Eddie could say anything.

'How can you represent something as disgusting...?' Wil felt sick, he didn't want to think about the destination Eddie had in mind for the girls.

'Innocent until proven guilty, blah, blah, blah!' Clegg said. 'This is all pretty sketchy and, I must say, farfetched at best. My client admits to removing the children from the shelter, as instructed by his boss, Sonja de Bruin. He admits to taking them to the house in Port Melbourne. He was minding the children until their mother was to come and collect them. He doesn't know what happened to the children's mother, or her whereabouts. He has no knowledge of any brothel in Fitzroy. And you have no proof otherwise.'

'Yeah, well your client is lying to you, Mr Clegg,' Marty said.

'Marty, I'm quite sure that Mr Clegg is used to having his clients lie to him.' Wil looked directly at Clegg. 'It's all par for the course, as they say.'

'This is all starting to get a bit old,' Clegg said, making out he was ready to pack up and go home. 'Either charge my client, or we are leaving.'

'Fine, fine,' Wil looked at Marty, who nodded in silent agreement. 'I'm formally charging you, Eddie Kovacs, with Child Abduction. I was going to wait until we'd moved a little further along, but as your lawyer here looks in a hurry to get on with...'

'Hey, what the fuck!' Eddie yelled, saliva spraying onto Clegg's suit sleeve. 'You told me they didn't have enough to do that.'

Taking a handkerchief from his trouser pocket, Clegg wiped his sleeve, a look of distaste on his face. 'Looks like I was wrong. We'll talk tomorrow.'

The two detectives and the lawyer rose from their chairs.

'While you're resting up in Lockup tonight, Eddie,' Wil said, packing up the folders from the table, 'work on your story about what happened to Sonja. Tomorrow's going to be a big day.'

'That's right,' Marty added before leaving the interview room. 'Forensics on that lot should be back. Sleep tight, don't let your cellmate bite.'

'Fuck you!' Eddie screamed as he stood and kicked his chair away.

CHAPTER TWENTY-FIVE

Lexie was nervous but excited to be seeing Jillian's girls. They had been in a state of shock following the events of their rescue. When she last saw them, they were being placed in a police cruiser by a female constable. Wil said they would most probably be checked out by medical staff, and then temporary custody would be given to Jillian's sister Carmel,as the grandparent might not be the appropriate choice. They weren't coping with the death of their son, or with the fact that he had been an abuser. Wil had his suspicions that Sean had learned his abusive behaviour from his father—a common enough scenario. Lexie wondered if Sean's mother's coping mechanism was to stick her head in the sand and hope all the bad stuff would simply go away.

She knew that's what her own mother did, which was why, Lexie figured, she herself had such lousy coping skills. But she was feeling like she had made some major breakthroughs in the last few days. She felt stronger than she'd ever felt in her life. She could handle anything that life threw her way now.

Flowing with the traffic along Kings Bridge, she saw the Melbourne Aquarium with its posters advertising the famous penguins. She thought might be a place they could visit. That is if Jillian wanted to pursue a friendship with her. While she felt a connection to Jillian and her daughters, only time would tell whether that was something that would be reciprocated.

Lexie parked and locked the Peugeot in front of Carmel's hotel, going straight to the doorman to inform him that she was there to collect hotel guests. He just shrugged. *He's obviously not as excited about that as I am,* Lexie thought.

'I've just got off the phone with Cookie,' Carmel said to Lexie as she closed the door to her room. 'How nice is that guy? All doctors should be like him. He said that Jillian is improving. Her condition has been downgraded from critical to serious-but-stable. And I bet it has everything to do with these two gorgeous creatures—my nieces.'

Carmel hugged both girls, squashing them together. Charlotte looked at Lexie and rolled her eyes. Lexie winked at her.

'So, girls, how do you like your aunt's hotel?' Lexie said as casually as possible. The children had been to many different places since their mother first took them from their family home. When she took that first brave step to leave her abuser, only to be abused again.

The younger of the two girls cuddled up closer to her sister as they climbed up onto the sofa together.

269

'I'm wearing my hair clip,' Charlotte spoke in a tiny voice.

'I can see that,' Lexie smiled. 'You look very pretty. You both look very pretty. Are you ready to go and visit your mummy?'

With that, both girls jumped off the sofa and headed to the door.

'They're ready,' Carmel said with a laugh, grabbing the hotel key and her bag.

*

As the doors to the hospital elevator opened, Lexie felt a small hand take hold of hers. Fighting back tears, she looked down into Bonnie's eyes which were wide with fear.

'Everything will be OK,' Lexie said. 'You don't have to be scared anymore.'

Gingerly, they all entered Jillian's room. The head of her bed had been raised and she was still taking oxygen, but via small nasal prongs now, not the mask she'd previously had to wear. The monitors tracked her heartbeat and the automatic blood pressure cuff was still attached.

Jillian looked at her girls. Tears spilled down her face and into the corners of her smiling mouth. Putting her hands on her heart, she then looked to her sister.

270

'Hey, Bear,' Jillian said, 'you brought me my babies.'

'Hey, Bean,' Carmel said, as she placed an arm around Lexie. 'I can't take any credit for that. This girl here is Wonder Woman.'

Lexie stepped towards Jillian's bed, and patted her foot. The two women shared a watery smile.

'Can they get up?' Lexie asked Jillian, indicating the girls.

'They sure can,' Jillian opened her arms to embrace her children. 'I love you both so much. I've missed my girls.'

'Mummy?' Bonnie said.

'Yes, baby girl?'

'Why did you just call Aunty Carmel a bear?'

'Those are the first words I've heard that child speak!' Carmel exclaimed.

'Well, Bonnie,' Jillian said, gently rubbing her hand up and down her younger daughter's cheek, 'when Aunty Carmel and I were little girls—just like you and Charlotte are now—our father used to call us his two little sweeties. Aunty Carmel he called Caramello Bear, and me he called Jilly-Bean. You know, like jelly beans? We shortened the names to Bear and Bean. Only us, though, nobody else ever called us that. It was a secret.'

'How are you feeling, Jillian?' Lexie looked concerned. 'You let us know when you want us to leave.'

'I tire very easily, but I don't want any of you to leave me,' then Jillian hugged Bonnie, and patted the bed beside her. 'Charlotte you can come closer, you don't have to be scared of the tubes and things—it's alright.'

'The white-haired giant called Charlotte Bean!' Bonnie giggled.

Charlotte sat on the bed, not moving, deep in thought.

'What was that? What white-haired giant?' Jillian sat up straighter in the bed.

'When we were playing tea sets,' Bonnie said. 'He would have a cup of tea. He said we were his little sweeties, too!'

Charlotte placed her hand to her head, touching the hair clip Lexie had returned to her. Lexie looked at Carmel, who was looking at Jillian—both women looked troubled.

'Charlotte, honey,' Jillian said. 'Can you tell me what Bonnie is talking about?'

'When we were at the place, you know... The other place?' Charlotte looked to Lexie for help.

'The place where I first met you and your mum?' Lexie asked.

'Yes there, in the sandpit, when Bonnie and me was playing and the white-haired man from next door would talk to us through the hole in the fence. We gave him his very own cup for tea. He called me Bean.'

'He goes to church and prays to God for us, Mummy,' Bonnie said. 'Can we go to church?'

'That can't be!' Carmel said in a quiet voice. 'It can't be him...'

'Do you know what they're talking about, Jillian?' Lexie asked. 'Who is he?'

'Think really hard and tell me again, Charlotte,' Jillian said. 'What happened?

'At that place...'

'Where we went to stay after we lefthome,' Jillian interrupted.

'Yes. Me and Bonnie played in the garden and the sandpit, and the man with the white hair, would come to the holes in the fence and talk to us.'

'Were you scared of him?' Lexie asked.

'A bit the first time, but he already knew who we were. So I knew that it was OK.'

'Oh, Carmel,' Jillian said to her sister. 'It couldn't...you don't think...'

'Bean, I know what you're thinking and I think I don't want to go there. But...Lexie, can you call Detective Saddington,' Carmel said. 'I'll take the girls back to the hotel. Come on, girls, give your mother a kiss and a hug, we'll come back tomorrow. Mummy needs her rest now. Have you ever had a ride in a taxi?'

Charlotte started to protest but Jillian soothed the child. 'Charlotte, look at me. Everything is fine, you didn't do anything wrong. I'm just tired, and Lexie and I need to talk to the policeman about something before I have a nap. You go with Aunty Carmel, and I'll see you tomorrow. I love you both.'

While the girls solemnly kissed their mother and climbed off the bed, Lexie sent a text message to Wil, asking him to come to the hospital, and that it was urgent. She didn't understand exactly what was unfolding, but something had Jillian and Carmel spooked.

As the door to Jillian's room closed behind Carmel and the girls, Lexie stepped closer to Jillian's bed.

'The white-haired man isn't a stranger?' Lexie asked.

274

'My father!'

'I didn't think that you had any family, besides Carmel. Well, your in-laws, of course.'

'I haven't given my father a thought, not since I left home. When I walked out of that house, I didn't take anything with me. I never went back, and I...' Jillian stared out the window. 'Well, I was hoping, I guess, that he'd just disappear.'

'So, if this man is your father, what exactly does it mean?' Lexie didn't understand the implication—the dire concern that Carmel and Jillian were showing.

Fifteen minutes later, Wil arrived, and Jillian gave him the new information.

'I thought your father had passed away some time ago,' Wil said, shaking his head. 'I'm sure that was the information your sister gave us when she was interviewed.'

'That would be wishful thinking on her part,' Jillian sighed and lay back on the pillows.

Lexie could see the little colour she'd had earlier slowly seeping away. She didn't think Jillian would be able to handle much more conversation, let alone an interrogation.

'Carmel hasn't had any contact with him since our mother's funeral, and me, not since I left home.'

'Where was that?' Wil asked. 'What would have been his last known address?'

'Scott Street, Moonee Ponds; not all that far from where the shelter is actually,' Jillian said. 'My mother was Catholic, and she would go to mass at St Agnes's, which you would have seen when you drove to McHale Court.'

'Jillian, how would Sean have known that you were there, staying at that particular shelter?'

'We'd been at the shelter for at least three weeks, and I was starting to feel claustrophobic. I remembered the park around the corner, Lincoln Park. Carmel and I used to play there when we were kids. I took the girls one afternoon, even though Sonja had advised against going out anywhere public. I didn't think anyone would be around. As we were leaving the park and crossing the road, one of our neighbours drove past. She must have seen us, maybe even followed us to the shelter, then told Sean. It's was the only time we'd left the shelter.'

'The neighbour—it wouldn't have been Julie Asling?' asked Wil, but before she could respond, two nurses entered the room. 'Enough now, visiting hours are over. Our patient here has had a big day, with far too many visitors. Say your goodbyes.' The older nurse confidently ushered Lexie and Wil out of the room.

276

Together they walked to the lift.

'How did the father come into any of this?' Wil asked.

'One of her daughters mentioned a white-haired man who talked to them through the fence when they were at McHale Shelter. He must live next door.'

'Yeah, I think I saw him looking out the window at me. But I didn't go in. I don't...' Wil scratched his head. 'Oh shit! I remember the driveway—all the neatly piled firewood. The second car leaving so soon after Sean, the night he was outside the shelter. Jesus H Christ!' Wil fished his mobile out of his pocket.

'What...?'

Lexie suddenly clicked as Wil barked, 'Jillian's father—he killed Sean, not Eddie Kovacs!'

CHAPTER TWENTY-SIX

'So, Mrs O'Rourke, you understand what this means?' Wil spoke to Carmel on his mobile, as he and Lexie exited the hospital. 'Good then, we'll be in touch with you as things develop.'

'She knew straight away!' Lexie was jogging in order to keep up with Wil.

'Marty,' Wil was on his mobile again, 'I'm on my way back. Get started on a warrant for one Lars Claussen. That's C-L-A-U-S-S-E-N. The address is McHale Court, Essendon—next door to the shelter. Yes! I'll explain when I get back to the station.'

Pocketing his phone, Wil retrieved his car keys. He stopped, his hand on the car's door handle, realising Lexie had followed him to the car.

'You look good, well I mean...' he stumbled over the words. 'Things are going to be crazy for a bit, but we'll talk soon, I promise.'

Lexie took a step closer to him, into arms that automatically wrapped around her.

'I am good, thanks,' she said.

Wil placed his lips onto hers, felt their warmth and welcome. He looked over her face, as if making an inventory of her features.

'Can I trust you to stay out of trouble?' he laughed.

'Always,' she smiled.

He got into the unmarked car, waving as he left the hospital car park.

＊

Wil hurried into the MIR. Another board had been set up.

'What's all this, then?' Wil put a hand on Marty's shoulder.

'Sads!' Marty stopped writing, his excitement bubbling. 'The house belongs to St Agnes's Cathedral.'

'We've been told to tread very carefully here,' Terry joined the two detectives. 'The house is the presbytery for the cathedral.'

'It's a what?' Wil asked. 'And what does any of this have to do with my warrant?'

'The house belongs to the Catholic Church,' Marty said. 'It's the accommodation for the clergy, you know, the priests and some of the staff.'

'Since when have you been our religious expert?' Wil looked at Marty.

'I was raised a good Catholic boy—Christian Brothers education.' Marty looked back to the board.

'Explains a lot!' Terry added to the conversation. 'Anyway, any dealings with the church have to be approved from higher up, so as soon as the address was flagged, I had to go to the chief.'

'I doubt Lars Claussen is a priest,' Wil said. 'From what I've gathered, he was a wife beater, and child...' He went on and told them of the information he'd gained from Jillian and Carmel.

'I'm thinking he works for them, possibly lives in the presbytery,' Marty said, serious now.

'So, do we get our warrant or not? We need to move fast,' Wil urged.

'I'm working on the search warrant for the presbytery. The unit is just about ready. Just waiting on Ashworth and Mel to return from the courthouse.' Terry lowered his voice to a whisper, and looked back to the room. 'Apparently, Ashworth and the Fed— Steve—well, they're more than just housemates. Davis had the intel— trying to get back on my good side.'

'Looks good for the arrest, though,' Marty said, ignoring Terry's comment. 'How do you want to play it, Sads?'

'I want unmarked cars used—we don't want to spook him. Though I'd say he's probably thinking, at this stage, that we're clueless to his existence. Jesus, how many times have we been to that bloody court?' Wil shook his head in frustration. 'I walked up the driveway, ready to talk to the prick myself. It didn't take much to distract me. Meanwhile, a killer just gets on with his daily shit.'

'Focus, man.' Marty looked at Wil. 'And?'

'Officers watch the church, while you and I'll go to the house, suppository, whatever you called the place! We'll make like we're doing routine canvassing of the neighbourhood in regards to the shelter death. Make our enquiries as to who's home, who lives there.'

'We're still coming up short on any information on Lars Claussen,' Terry said. 'Last known address was Moonee Ponds. Not far from Essendon. Do you want someone to go there, make inquiries?'

'Yeah sure, any information will be helpful,' Wil said. 'What about a driver's licence, car registration, electoral roll?'

'Nothing,' Terry said. 'There's no death registration—it's kind of like he vanished, years ago. The undead. Nothing with the ATO, so he can't have been paying his taxes.'

The three men turned as two officers entered the MIR, making a lot of noise. Waving a large white envelope, Constable Melissa Trengrove hurried across the room to join them at the incident board.

'The forensics is here, from the Laidlaw crime scene,' Mel enthused . 'They finally fixed the machine, the one working on the DNA that was lifted from the photo frame. Remember the guy said they had trouble separating the DNA of the prints? Well, they've done it. They found Sean Laidlaw's, Jillian Laidlaw's and that of a third person. The report states that the mitochondrial DNA of the third...'

'Mel,' Wil interrupted, 'get to the point, we don't have a whole lot of time.'

'The third print lifted is 95.5 per cent likely to be the paternal parent of Jillian Laidlaw!'

'We've got him!' Terry said.

The unit packed what it needed, assigned and fitted radios and the teams headed out. Leaving Terry to man the MIR, the phones, and to await the warrants for the presbytery.

Wil didn't stop Marty this time as he slipped a CD into the player. Some charge-music would be appropriate.

'I have just the thing,' Marty said with a sly smile. 'It's Lenny time!'

They took off out of the station car park, Lenny Kravitz blasting from the car.

*

In McHale Court, the two detectives walked to the front door of the presbytery. Marty gave three loud knocks, then stepped back to stand beside his partner.

Wil was been just about to knock again, when he heard a shuffling approaching the door. The door was opened by a little old balding man. Wearing baggy black trousers and a greying, once-white shirt, which was Wil thought, possibly two sizes too big. He noted the collar.

'Hello, Father,' Marty stepped forward, showing his ID. 'We are detectives with the Moreland Major Incident Unit. Could we come in and speak to you, please?'

This was a polite and reverent side to Marty that Wil hadn't seen before. He decided to follow Marty's lead— he appeared comfortable with the old man.

'Yes, come in, lads. Sad unfortunate case next door, that you have on your hands. Come and sit down. I'm Edward Ward—everyone's always called me Father Teddy.'

They followed the priest into the dark living room, off the hall to the right. Wil remembered being watched from the window of the room off to the left. The room smelt musty and dank. Wil didn't really want to sit on any of the furniture.

'Father Teddy, does Lars Claussen live here?'

'Yes he does. Lars, we all call him Snow—because of his white hair. He's lived here...I don't know, I have to think about this. It would have to be well over ten years. His poor wife died. She was one of my parishioners for many years.'

'Did Mr Claussen come to church with his wife?' Wil asked.

'No, I think he only started coming to church when poor Barbara was first diagnosed. He felt a sense of guilt, that he'd somehow brought on her illness, because of his lack of faith at the time. I believe he came seeking forgiveness. He became quite devout. After Barbara's passing, he helped around St Agnes's and then around here,' he waved his arm, indicating the house. 'When his daughter moved out of home, he was completely at a loss. Both daughters appeared to have abandoned him. He immersed himself in the church, studied and went on to become a lector.'

'A lector?' Wil asked.

'He does the readings and commentaries during the service,' Marty said.

'Oh,' Wil replied with raised eyebrows, shaking his head as he looked again at Marty. *How did I not know this about him?*

'Yes, he is part of the fixtures at the cathedral, and here at the presbytery. When Snow lost his house to bankruptcy, we offered him a home here. He works around here: cleaning and maintenance. We have our meals cooked by two ladies, parishioners, who take turns. Oh, and he cuts all our firewood. You would have noticed the driveway—all the neat stacks of firewood. He is quite obsessive with the job.'

Wil and Marty exchanged looks of anticipation.

'Father Teddy, is Mr Claussen here?' Marty asked.

'He'll be at St Agnes's. Today he was to do the lawns, and the trimming. I don't think he'd have any knowledge of the events that occurred next door, and what happened to that poor woman.'

'Father,' Wil said, 'would you give us permission to look in the garden shed?'

'Of course, son,' Father Teddy said. 'You can look about the place as much as you want. We don't have anything to hide here. Do you know what it is that you're looking for?'

'Just a quick look in the shed will do for now,' Wil said. 'I won't be a minute.'

Wil followed the directions the old priest gave him, and found the garden shed in the back corner of the yard. He also saw the gaps in the fence palings; he could see the sandpit of the shelter, where the two little girls had played.

Pulling a pair of latex gloves from his pocket, Wil walked to the shed. It took a few seconds for his eyes to adjust to the darkness. There were heaps of tools, and the one he wanted was right in front of his eyes, as if on display. It was clean—the Go-devil. And there wasn't any doubt in Wil's mind that it was the weapon that killed Sean Laidlaw. He didn't doubt, either, that forensics would find evidence on it.

Wil left the shed without touching anything. He didn't want to jeopardise any future legalities by doing anything inappropriate. They'd wait for the Search and Siege Warrant. He was satisfied that they had their man— they had the weapon.

Returning inside, Wil waved for Marty to get up. It was time to leave.

'Thank you for your time, Father,' Wil said as they left the house.

'God bless you both,' Father Teddy waved them off. 'Catch the sinner.'

'Weapon's in the shed!' Wil told Marty, as they headed to the car. 'We may as well leave the car here, we can walk it from here.'

'Was it clean?'

'No, it was mounted on the wall, blood still dripping from it! Course it was clean. There'll be trace on it, though, don't worry.'

They started to jog, hurrying to join the rest of their unit.

CHAPTER TWENTY-SEVEN

'Hello?'

'Hey, Dana, it's me,' Lexie said to her older sister when she answered.

'Lexie?' Dana replied. 'Is that you?'

'Yes, it's...'

'What's wrong? Are you crying?' Dana said. 'Are you hurt, Lexie?'

'No, no, I'm all right. It's just that...Well, a lot's been going on,' Lexie tried to rein in her emotions. 'I was hoping that you'd be home—I need my big sister.'

'Then you'd better get your arse over here then,' Dana said. 'I'll make us some lunch. How long will it take you to get here?'

'Forty, forty-five minutes,' Lexie replied. 'Thanks, Dana—I'll see you soon.'

Lexie took her bag, jumped in her car and headed for the Mornington Peninsula. She didn't want to think anymore—for the moment anyway—so she put in a disc, and turned up the volume, using the music to drown out all her thoughts.

She arrived at Dana's, admiring the house and its vantage point overlooking Red Bluff and the bay, with its million-dollar view back towards the city. Dana and her husband Karl had put a lot of work into the house making it a home.

'Hello,' Lexie knocked and called, then entered the front door off the veranda. 'I'm here.'

She heard them before she saw them—two sets of little feet running towards her from inside the house. Her nephews attached themselves to a leg each when they reached her.

'Hello, boys,' Lexie patted their heads, 'where's your mum? Making our lunch, is she?'

'Nate, Joey, let go of Aunty Lex,' Dana called out from inside. 'Come to the table boys, you can start eating now that she's here.'

Dana walked up to Lexie, looking her over from head to toe.

'All intact, still,' Lexie laughed. The sisters hugged. 'I'm so glad you were home. I really need this.'

'I'm nearly always here, Lexie,' Dana said looking at Lexie. 'It's been you not wanting to be around me. Well, that's the impression that I've had. Go on, boys, start on your lunch, Aunty Lex and I will just have a bit of a chat first.'

Lexie followed Dana into the kitchen.

'I know, I'm sorry,' Lexie apologised. 'I suppose I have been avoiding you. Well, not so much you, but your family is more what I've tried to keep away from. I was struggling with what I don't have, I guess.'

'It's sad, Lexie, God knows I feel for you—to not be able to have children—I can't begin to know how you feel. But I am still your sister, and a woman, so I can feel empathy for you. I didn't plan on treating you any differently once I knew you couldn't have kids. I assumed that we'd still be sisters; that you'd continue to be an aunt to my children. That we'd still get together periodically to debrief over encounters with our mother.'

'I know—I want that too. It's been hard adjusting to being, well, just me. I thought of myself as Doug's wife for a long time. Back then, I was always going to be the mother of his children. I wanted what you and Karl have; I assumed that was the course my life was on. Now I hear comments like *you wouldn't understand, you're not a mother,* and *I wish I was free like you, to just up and travel half way round the world*—this from people I thought were my friends.'

'You should know me better than that, Lex,' Dana shook her head. 'Do you honestly believe that I would say anything like that to you, let alone anybody else?'

'I know, I know that now,' Lexie cried. 'I've been stupid and self-absorbed. In the past couple of weeks I've had to face life, and myself. I can see more clearly now. I see that you and Karl and the boys are my family. Motherhood, or the lack of it, doesn't make a person who they are. I am a whole person, and I can say now. Say also that I'm a brave person.'

'Well, little sister, I never doubted that for a second,' Dana had finished making their tea. 'Let's see if those two have left us anything to eat.'

CHAPTER TWENTY-EIGHT

The unit had closed off the street and warned all local residents to stay indoors until further notice. They had St Agnes's Cathedral surrounded. Wil stopped and spoke to the first officer he came to. The officer was Ross Ashworth—normally Wil didn't listen to gossip, but what he'd heard earlier in the MIR regarding Ross, well he was happy to take it on board. His suspicions about Ashworth and Lexie were obviously groundless.

'He's supposed to be here doing the lawns,' Wil informed Ross. 'Any sign of him yet?'

'No, Boss, but the grass has just been cut. He must have finished.'

Wil gave the order for the uniforms to wait outside while he and Marty looked inside. He could hear a few grumbles from the officers nearby. The sky was threatening to erupt into the predicted thunderstorm. In their anticipation to catch the killer, not one officer had given wet-weather gear a thought—now there were regrets.

Wil and Marty entered through the main entrance to the cathedral. Wil could see two see men near the altar, and assumed they were priests. Wil indicated for Marty to take the left side aisle, while he would take the right, each detective approaching the altar from the side.

Tension built inside Wil as he slowly made his way forward. He had his hand ready, his holster's safety clip already released. As he got closer to the altar, Wil noticed a third man ahead in a darkened area of the church. He was kneeling in front of a table, on which were several lighted candles that illuminated the man's head.

Wil clicked his fingers twice, a signal to attract Marty's attention. He waved him over, pointing directly ahead at the praying man with white hair.

Together they approached then stood behind the man, weapons drawn and pointed down. The other two men were now staring at Wil and Marty. One of them made a move towards them, but Wil held up his left hand and shook his head.

'Lars Claussen, you are under arrest for the murder of Sean Laidlaw,' Wil said. 'I want you very slowly, to place your hands on your head. Don't turn around until both your hands are on top of your head. Do you understand?'

'Eternal Father, I offer Thee the sacred heart of Jesus, with all its love...'

'Hands on your head, NOW!' Marty cut in on the man's prayer.

'All its sufferings and all its merits; to expiate all the sins I have committed this day, and all during my life,' Lars continued, unmoving. 'Glory be to the...'

Marty grabbed the man's left wrist while Wil grabbed his right. Together they pulled his arms behind his back, clapping on handcuffs. Marty radioed the unit. Instantly the cathedral erupted, loud and thunderous, as the officers poured in from all directions. The two priests stood stunned at the altar, looks of horror on their faces. Wil handed over their prisoner to the officers, told Marty to handle things, and went to talk to the priests.

'Detective Senior Sergeant Saddington, Moreland Major Incident Unit,' Wil flashed his ID and badge. 'I am sorry for the intrusion. Can we sit, I'll explain what's going on?'

'I'm Father Bill Walkley, and this is Father Dominic Hall,' the older of the two priests said, pointing to the nearest pew.

The men sat, but their attention was on the arrest—it wasn't going very well. Lars Claussen was refusing to stand and kept up with his repetitive prayer. Wil could see Marty calling for more officers to assist. Eventually, four officers lifted Claussen by his arms and legs, carrying him from the church. Wil turned back to the priests.

'We've arrested Mr Claussen for the murder of his son-in-law, Sean Laidlaw.'

'Murder, Lars? Murder? I don't believe it!' Fr Walkley said, a bewildered look on his face.

'No, this is wrong!' Fr Hall said. 'It was a woman that was killed—you're talking about the shelter. It's just been all over the news; they've arrested the man. He's in jail now. And besides, when she was killed, Lars was here with me working on a special mass program. We saw the police arrive, we watched them together.'

'There is no confusion, I'm sorry. You are right—we have a man in custody for the murder that took place at the shelter. The murder Mr Claussen has been arrested for occurred at an earlier time. We've been to the presbytery and spoken to Father Teddy, and he told us that Mr Claussen was here. The murder we are investigating happened Sunday, 20 April. Late to the early hours of the Monday morning. Do you know where Lars was that night?'

'He was at home, at the presbytery. He never goes out, especially at night,' Father Hall said. 'He spends his time between here and the presbytery. This is his whole world. No friends, besides us. No family—well he had two daughters, but I don't know where they are now. They seemed to have abandoned their father.'

'You weren't aware of the abuse?' Wil asked, shaking his head at their lack of knowledge. 'Apparently, Mr Claussen abused his wife during their marriage, and then after her death, he took to abusing their youngest daughter. It is that daughter's husband who was murdered.'

Both priests sat speechless, disbelief and shock covering their faces.

'Does Lars have a car?' Wil asked.

'No, he lost everything when he lost his job,' Father Hall said, his head bowed. 'His house was foreclosed on, the car repossessed. He had declared bankruptcy. He was here often at the time, praying for guidance. We had a meeting with the bishop, and Lars was offered a roof over his head, food and clothing. In return he worked for the parish. He's never been paid a wage, but he has never gone without.'

'Is there a car kept at the presbytery,' Wil asked, 'one that Lars would have access to?'

Wil saw that the reality of what he'd been saying was dawning in the minds the two priests. Their heads hung lower. Each man had his hands clasped together, as if in prayer.

'Yes,' said Father Hall in a hushed voice. 'I have a silver Lanos registered in my name.'

'The prayer that Lars was saying, just before,' Father Walkley said, 'it's called a Prayer of Reparation.'

'What does that mean?' Wil asked.

'I think that you are going to find that it is significant,' Father Walkley continued gravely. 'Reparation is the making of amends. To make up for an injustice that one has done to another. There are several reparation prayers—the ones that Lars was using, *Prayer of Reparation, Act of Reparation to the Most Blessed Sacrament, Acts of Reparation to The Holy Trinity...*'

'Have you heard him use any of these prayers before?' Wil interrupted.

'Yes,' Father Hall said, his eyes moist and red. 'He has been lighting candles, and repeating all of them, and also the *Pardon Prayer,* for, well...Now, that I'm thinking about it, since some time after Easter. I never thought anything of it, really. Possibly he was still enthused by the Easter celebrations. He has always been an odd man, but I never would have believed that he was a violent man.'

'That is the sad fact about domestic violence— abusers can portray themselves outside the home as gentle, caring, loving people. But behind closed doors, they turn into monsters. Monsters that sometimes kill.' Wil rose from the pew, handing his card to Father Walkley. 'You'll have to be formally interviewed at the station. I'll ring and organise a time that's suitable. I'm sorry for the way things have turned out.'

'It's we that should be apologising, for our...' Father Hall said. 'I don't know what we are guilty of—ignorance most certainly, to start with. This is all just so, so devastating.'

'I'd better be heading back.' Wil shook hands with the priests, then walked out of the cathedral.

As Will left the grounds of St Agnes's, the heavens opened. He pulled his jacket up over his head, and started to run back up McHale Court. Once inside the car, he sat quietly and listened to the sound of the rain on the roof. Two murder cases—two killers caught. He knew there was lots of work to do still on both cases, to ensure that both Eddie Kovacs and Lars Claussen remained behind bars, but for just this moment, Wil wanted to enjoy the pleasure of success. Also, he wanted to share the feeling.

It had been many years since he'd shared any of his work details with Monica—either good or bad. However, today was different, he had a desire to tell someone; someone who would appreciate what it meant, and what it had taken to get here. He took out his mobile, scanned the contacts, and pressed *call*.

CHAPTER TWENTY-NINE

By late morning Lexie was getting hungry, and needed to rest her feet. She'd been walking around for hours, reacquainting herself with the city's streets, killing time before an early afternoon appointment with Megan Kestler at *Contemporary Woman's* head office. She entered a café opposite the State Library on Swanston Street and ordered lunch.

Just as her meal arrived, her mobile rang. The waiter rolled his eyes as he placed her food in front of her, and walked off with his nose in the air. She answered the call.

'Hello, Wil?'

'Lexie, I just wanted to...' Wil paused for a second. 'Look, this is all off the record, right?'

'Yes, I understand,' Lexie said, though she wasn't too sure that she did.

'It's just that you can't write about anything I'm about to tell you,' Wil said.

'I'm not a tabloid reporter, Wil. Besides, you should know by now that you can trust me.'

'Yes, yes, I do.' He went on to tell Lexie of the events that had just occurred at St Agnes's Cathedral.

After the phone call, Lexie was left with her thoughts. It was all very bizarre. All that time she'd been so convinced of Eddie's guilt, that theory being compounded when Sonja's body was discovered—another violent slaying.

Wil's urgency in telling her had surprised her and she realised what a huge risk he was taking by giving her details of a case that was ongoing. It was as if he had to tell her, had to share with her. She found that she was excited by the development. She felt a closeness growing. She only hoped she wouldn't blow it, disappoint him in some way.

But then she pulled herself up—*Stop thinking that way! New attitude, girl!* She had made a pact with herself: to move forward with her life, to stop thinking that she was never quite good enough, to quash the urge that she constantly had to reform and improve—not only herself, but everybody else as well. Her friend Carla didn't call her The Reformer for nothing!

Lexie could see now how her relentless pursuit of the *ideal* had led to her having a hard time relaxing and enjoying life. She'd become emotionally repressed and was uncomfortable expressing any tender feelings.

But now she was beginning to think that she wanted something to develop with Wil. This was a nice feeling, and she would take things slowly, just sit back and see where it went.

Looking at her watch, Lexie jumped with panic: she would now be cutting it fine to get to her appointment on time. She swallowed the last half of her now cold coffee, wiped her mouth on the napkin, and then quickly reapplied her lipstick. As she approached the counter to pay, she caught the waiter again rolling his eyes. She decided to keep the tip that she'd planned to give him— teach him to be an arse.

She didn't have far to walk: the *Contemporary Woman* HQ was in the office tower of Melbourne Central, on the tenth floor.

'Can I help you?' a receptionist greeted her.

'Yes, Demi,' Lexie read the young woman's nametag. 'Lexie Reed, I have an appointment with Megan Kestler.'

'Yes, Ms Reed, 12:30, take a seat. I'll let Ms Kestler know you're here.'

Lexie was kept waiting the obligatory fifteen minutes, making her aware that Megan was her boss, not her friend—another of the small and precise details to remind her of her position.

'Lexie, love, come in,' Megan said waving Lexie into her office. 'Sorry to have kept you.'

Lexie felt inelegant in the sophisticated presence of her editor, even more so when she sat down and noticed the drop of mayonnaise on her skirt. In one swift move, Lexie placed her bag on her lap.

'I apologise, Megan, for any concerns that you may have had regarding my being finished on time.'

Megan ignored Lexie, her attention focused on her computer screen.

'Your deadline was yesterday,' Megan said, still not looking at Lexie, 'however, I expected I'd receive it before 11:30 that night!'

Lexie had emailed the article off to Megan without phoning ahead, due to the late hour, and her embarrassment at her own tardiness. Within minutes, Megan had replied, asking Lexie to be in her office the following day at 12:30. Lexie had been sick with worry about her professional future ever since.

'Is this true?' Megan asked. 'Some women take out AVOs just to get back at their partners or exes?'

'Yes, but that is a rare occurrence. The police officer I interviewed believed that Apprehended Violence Orders are only really worth anything if they are adhered to.'

302

'These statistics, from between 2009 and 2011—well, they seem to say that they're not really worth anything!' Megan looked at Lexie. 'This is quite shocking—less than fourteen per cent of the 1550-odd men breaching these AVOs were jailed!'

'From the police point of view, they can only do so much. Government change is what is needed, in the policies and practices of institutions. Political action for social change could be greatly assisted...'

'Yes, yes,' Megan cut Lexie off. 'This is all very informative. I thought that we'd include a piece from the White Ribbon people as well.'

'Is that the story about women and children living in their cars, because they didn't feel safe in the family home?' Lexie asked.

'Yes, how did you know about that?'

Lexie smiled, 'I have a source on the inside!'

'Oh, do you now?' Megan said.

Lexie wasn't too sure how to take Megan's comment.

'That's why I haven't said too much about that particular subject,' Lexie decided to carry on. 'I had spoken to the Housing and Homelessness Minister, but then, when my source informed me of the details given to the magazine, I decided to leave that interview out of the article.'

'Well, Lexie, I have to say I'm impressed.' Megan finished reading the article. 'You haven't let me down; maybe made me just slightly anxious until I received your email last night. But, no, quite the contrary, it's quality work. These articles monthly, leading up to...when is White Ribbon Day?'

'November 25,' Lexie replied.

'These articles should be concluded by then.' Megan got up from her desk, and picked up pages from a counter nearby.

'The seeds of the next series are germinating as we speak,' Lexie said, cautious not to push too soon for more work.

Megan waved a controlling hand, a signal Lexie took to mean *we'll get to that another day.*

'Here, the first print of your first article.' Megan handed Lexie the glossy pages, her story in print.

The photos of Jillian and Frances were taken from behind to conceal their identities. Still, Lexie recognised them and their stories flooded her mind and heart in an instant.

CHAPTER THIRTY

In the MIR, Wil and Marty sat in front of the screen, observing Lars Claussen in his cell. He appeared to be oblivious to the surveillance camera mounted on the ceiling, and had been kneeling beside the cot for the past hour.

'He looks all innocent, like a kid saying his bedtime prayers,' Marty said, shaking his head.

'So, you can relate to him?' Wil smirked. 'Is this stirring up childhood memories for you? Say, were you ever an altar boy, Marty? I can picture you in the long dress and the frilly collar. Or is that a choir boy?'

'Shut up, Sads, you don't even know what you're talking about.'

'Are we ready to interview?' Wil looked around the room for Terry. 'He lawyered up yet, or what, Terry?'

'Waiving his rights.' Terry came over to join them. 'And I quote: *Holy Jesus will illumine me, so I shall be protected by His light.* We had to go looking for a bloody dictionary—nobody knew what *illumine* actually meant!'

'What about getting a psych evaluation?' Wil asked.

'Yeah, I've got that organised. Won't be happening until tomorrow, though. All of the assessors are tied up today. Says quite a lot about our city, hey? Oh, and I've organised Legal Aid—I figure, once reality sets in, our boy there,' Terry pointed to the screen, 'might want some back-up besides light!'

Wil phoned downstairs to Lockup, requesting that Lars Claussen be brought to Interview Room One. He and Marty waited for an hour before joining him there, the theory being that he'd be getting impatient and fidgety by then and his frustration and discomfort would make him react and say things before thinking. It usually worked a a treat.

The two detectives entered the room to find Lars seated, hands clasped together in front of him on the table. His hands were still, and he looked to be entirely comfortable. Wil thought he looked to be in a trance.

Wil turned on the recording equipment, both sound and visual.

'Detective Senior Sergeants Saddington and Hanratty present to interview Lars Claussen. Twenty-fifth of May 2012, the time is 1700 hours. Mr Claussen has waived his rights to legal counsel. Mr Claussen, Lars, do you understand that you've been arrested for the murder of Sean Laidlaw?'

Lars didn't respond but sat staring at his hands. Marty and Wil exchanged questioning looks. Wil nodded to Marty ask a question.

'When did you first realise that your daughter and granddaughters where staying at the shelter next door to the presbytery?'

'Charlotte and Bonnie—your granddaughters,' When it became obvious that Lars wasn't going to answer, Wil said, 'You didn't even know that you had grandchildren, did you, Lars? There are three grandsons too—Carmel's boys. They live in Canada. But, you wouldn't know that either. Father Teddy was under the misguided opinion that your family abandoned you. He was shocked when we enlightened him with the knowledge that you had abused them, and their mother before her death.'

Lars remained unmoving.

'It's quite ironic isn't it, that the women's shelter that you have been living next door to is there because of men just like yourself. It's sad, that women need all these community service systems and domestic violence resource centres, all because men like you assume an entitlement to abuse and exert power over the women in your lives.'

Wil was getting angry, so Marty kicked him under the table.

'Lars,' Marty said, 'we know that you spoke to your granddaughters. Charlotte told us that you would play tea parties with them. She also told us that you called her Bean. We know that this is the nickname that you had for her mother, Jillian, when she was a little girl. This confirms for us that you knew who they were. We are assuming, living at the presbytery for the previous ten years, you would be fully aware of what goes on at McHale Shelter. Earlier, on the night that Jillian's husband, Sean, was murdered, he'd been outside the shelter, calling out for her. We believe you heard the commotion, realising what was going on.'

Lars remained silent, fixated on his hands. Wil slammed his hand down onto the table, wanting a reaction, any reaction, from the man.

'You were watching, weren't you, Lars? Standing in the dark, in the driveway?'

The two detectives sat in silence, waiting. They let several minutes pass.

'I too was a miserable sinner, unworthy. I didn't know him but I recognised him—his blasphemous tongue spitting words of filth, denigrating the fairest of God's creatures,' Lars spoke his voice barely audible. 'I had prayed for redemption. I have been serving the Lord to compensate for my deficiencies. I thought they were my daughters, there—Jillian and Carmel—playing in that

308

sandpit. That night, I was offered the opportunity to restore myself in the eyes of God.'

'You are admitting that you knew exactly who Sean Laidlaw was?' Wil sat back, astounded.

'Do you have knowledge of what was going on at McHale Shelter?' Marty thought it was worth going for all they could. 'The investigation into the death of Resident Advocate Sonja de Bruin, and the disappearance of some of the women and children that had resided at the shelter?'

'He took them?' Lars sat up stiff and straight. For the first time, his pale grey eyes met Wil's.

'They are all safe,' Wil said. 'Jillian is recovering in hospital, and the girls are with their aunt. We have Eddie Kovacs in custody.'

'And don't worry,' Marty added, 'we'll dish out the justice this time!'

'Legal Aid has been organised for you, Lars,' Wil said as he began packing up. They had enough for the moment. 'Take my advice, use them. You're going to need all the help you can get. Interview ended, time is 1800 hours.'

Wil and Marty left the interview room and told the officer waiting outside the room to escort Mr Claussen back to his cell.

309

'They have a shift change while we were in there?' Wil asked Marty. 'Davis wasn't on before, was he?'

'Nah, they must have changed over,' Marty said. 'He's hanging by his teeth, that one. Terry's waiting to pounce on his next stuff-up.'

They went to get coffee from the canteen, before returning to the MIR to discuss the interview. On arrival, refreshed and ready to continue for a few more hours, they went straight to the screen to view Lars Claussen back in Lockup. Expecting to see a man unburdened by confession. What they saw was an empty cell.

'Terry!' Wil bellowed. 'Where the fuck is Claussen?'

'In his cell. You finished with him didn't you?'

'I'm looking at his cell. *It's empty!*'

'Let me look. What the...' Terry snatched the phone and called down to the cells. 'Davis, where the fuck is Lars Claussen? No, I'm looking at the screen now, he is most definitely *not* in cell four!'

'Give me that,' Wil grabbed the phone out of Terry's hand. 'What cell did you put the prisoner Lars Claussen in?'

Wil hung up the phone, and charged out of the MIR, the others on his heels.

'Wil,' Marty called out to his partner as he ran to catch up, 'what's wrong? What's happened?'

Wil didn't waste time waiting for the lift, he ran down the stairs, two at a time, to the Lockup.

'Our white-haired giant,' Wil yelled back over his shoulder to Marty. 'Dip-shit Davis has gone and put him cell six. He's in there now, rooming with Eddie!'

'Jesus, he's fucked!'

'Who?' Wil threw open the door to the basement. 'Eddie, or Davis?'

Marty caught up to Wil as they approached the holding cells. Wil could hear the others pounding down the stairs behind him. There was yelling coming from the back cells. Marty hit the alarm on the wall near him—more cops would flood the area within seconds.

Wil ran towards the cells, yelling. He came up behind Davis, who was screaming into a cell.

'Let him go, back off, do you hear me!'

'Give me the keys!' Wil snatched the keys out of Davis's hand. 'Don't do it, Lars. Snow, listen to me, he's not worth it.'

Inside, Lars and Eddie were together on the cot. Lars was sitting up behind Eddie, his arm wrapped around Eddie's neck. Lars had Eddie's jaw in the crook of

311

his arm, his other hand resting near Eddie's chin, his thumb on one side and three fingers on the other.

'He needs to be punished,' Lars was nodding in agreement with his own statement, 'and I, I will again be redeemed.'

'Lars! Lars!' Wil yelled. 'Don't do it!'

His voice was drowned out by the sound of booted officers charging in. Wil and Marty were shoved further into the cell by a wall of men arriving to help. As they neared the two men on the bench, in the pushing and shoving, they heard the horrible crack.

Wil lunged at Lars just as he let go of Eddie. Eddie fell forward onto the bench, his head lolling at an unnatural angle.

Lars began to pray.

'Have mercy on me, God, in your goodness; in your abundant compassion blot out my offense. Wash away all my guilt; from my sin cleanse me.'

CHAPTER THIRTY-ONE

Lexie arrived at the ICU with flowers for Jillian and treats for the girls. Her stomach dropped as she approached Jillian's room, seeing it empty. She pivoted on the spot, her eyes darting around the ward, looking for any familiar staff. A hand came to rest on her shoulder. A kind voice spoke to her.

'Everything is fine. She was moved to one of the surgical wards yesterday to recuperate.'

'Cookie!' Lexie almost burst into tears at the sight of the caring young doctor. 'You must have been reading my mind. I felt sick there for a moment. Always ready to assume the worst. Terrible habit, I know!'

'Your friend is stronger than she looks. She is recovering and remarkably well.'

They entered the lift together. Cookie pressed the button six for Lexie and ground for himself.

As Lexie left the lift, she turned and waved.

'Say hello to our favourite girl for me,' he called out as the doors closed.

Lexie felt a heart-warming boost as she approached the ward where Jillian had been moved. She could hear the giggles coming from the little girls. How quickly children bounced back Lexie marvelled.

'Hi, guys, you all look happy,' Lexie gave Jillian the flowers, and a peck on the cheek. 'What's going on?'

'Making plans for our future,' Jillian said. 'These are gorgeous, thank you. You remember Frances Spencer, from the shelter? When I get discharged in a week or two, she is going to move in with me and the girls for a while. Just until we get on our feet.'

'Jillian, that's fantastic news!' Lexie hugged her. 'If anyone knows how to get back up and onto their feet, it's that woman. I have a lot of respect for Frances, she's one of a kind.'

'Carmel has to head back to her family,' Jillian's eyes moistened as she spoke about her sister. 'She'll be leaving the day after my discharge. We've promised to keep in touch, now that we've found each other again.'

'Nothing will stop you two now. I can see trips back and forth across the globe in your future,' Lexie laughed.

'Lexie! Lexie, look!' Charlotte was tugging at her sleeve. 'Look what the policeman gave me. He founded it for me, just like you did!'

Lexie looked at the little girl's hair, as she shoved her head near Lexie's face.

'The other hair clip! Now I have all my diamonds back!'

'How lucky are you?' Lexie said as she tickled her under the chin.

'Detective Saddington was here, earlier this morning. He found the clip in his travels,' Jillian said, the lowering her voice. 'He also told me about my father, and what all that...'

'It's OK, Jillian,' Lexie patted her arm, 'you can tell me another day. When you are feeling stronger.'

'Oh, Lexie, if I'd known you were coming,' Carmel entered the room carrying two coffees in take-away cups, 'I'd have got one for you too.'

Carmel gave the drink to her sister, giving her a questioning look.

'We're going to talk about all that later,' Jillian said, 'when we get home!'

'Yeah! Home!' Both little girls squealed in unison.

'I have something that both you ladies will be interested in.' Lexie handed Jillian a copy of *Contemporary Woman.*

'Is that what I think it is?' Jillian reached out to take the magazine.

'You betcha! I know it's not going to change the world,' Lexie said, ' but I just hope to be able to make a little difference to someone's life.'

'You've made more than a little difference to my life—you saved it! I don't even want to begin to think about...'

'No need to go there, Bean,' Carmel put her arm around her sister's shoulder. 'Look to the future now. Only what is ahead, not where you've been. Do I have to buy my own copy?'

'No,' Lexie laughed, and produced another copy of the magazine from her bag. 'If you're anything like my sister and me, I thought you'd want your own copy.'

'Excellent!'

CHAPTER THIRTY-TWO

'Hey there, Dad,' Lucas' voice called out from Wil's laptop.

Wil transferred the wok from the stovetop to the sink, and ran into the living room.

'Hey there, yourself,' Wil parked himself at the table in front of his computer. 'I was just cooking up a storm in the kitchen.'

'Let me guess—stir-fry!' Lucas said without a touch of doubt.

'Well, yes, as a matter of fact.'

'Jeez, Dad, time to expand that culinary repertoire of yours,' Lucas laughed.

'What time is it there?'

'Eleven hundred hours, I'm thinking about lunch, and you're cooking dinner!'

'It's great to be talking to you. You know, Lucas, the first thing I do when I walk in the door at night is turn on the laptop, log-in to Skype, and then just hope you'll call. I've missed you, son, you have no idea how much.'

'Going all soft on me, hey, Dad?'

'Been through a rough couple of months.' Wil had to work hard to control his emotions. The last thing he wanted was to be blubbering like a baby in front of his son, who was on the other side of the world, dealing with God only knew what kind of turmoil. 'Have you spoken to your mother yet?'

'Yeah sorry, old man, I spoke to her first. Don't get me wrong, I'm not choosing her over you. What I thought I was doing was getting the emotional-parent-call out of the way first. Apparently, I had the two of you mixed up. Mum was in great form. Just back from Sydney with Gramps, and said that she was ready to take you back and work things out.'

'What? This is news to me!'

'Yeah, she reckons she saw you on the telly, a press conference to do with some massive case you've been on, and that you seemed like your old self.' Lucas' face came closer to the screen, trying to scrutinise Wil's more closely. 'You do seem a little different. But you don't look too excited about what I've just laid on you, though.'

'I guess I'm a little shocked.' Wil wasn't sure how much to say. 'I don't want to disappoint you, Lucas. But I don't have any plans to get back with your mother.'

'This probably isn't the best way to have this conversation,' Lucas started to smile. 'We can do it face-to-face in three months! We're coming home, Dad!'

'Lucas, that's fantastic!' Wil didn't attempt to stop the tears that sprang into his eyes.

'Not soon enough for me!' Lucas laughed. 'I'll have to have a word with Marty as soon as I get back—he's obviously been letting you go all girlie.'

'Balls-of-steel Marty! He's been asking after you,' Wil recovered himself, got himself in check. He was ecstatic with the news that his son was to leave war-torn Afghanistan. 'I love you, son...' But the connection was lost, and Lucas was gone.

As Wil finished cooking his meal, a newfound peace settled inside him. He had no intentions of ruining his evening with any thoughts of what Lucas had mentioned—Monica's plans for reconciliation didn't figure into his new life.

Wil enjoyed the luxury of watching an entire Saturday night movie - beginning to end, in the knowledge that he could enjoy a leisurely Sunday morning sleep-in. He was a satisfied man, in that moment at least.

*

'Thanks, Megan,' Lexie said. 'I'll email it to you the minute I hang up.'

'Fabulous, Lexie, I'm expecting greatness, as usual. I'll see you on Wednesday, and we'll discuss the third and final article of this series. And, yes, you can mention your ideas for the next set,' Megan's voice was cheerful. 'Bye, lovely.'

Lexie changed into her running gear and tied back her hair into a high ponytail. Giving herself a long look in the mirror, she realised how much freer she felt, and looked, without the heavy black kohl that she had come to use as a standard cover-up. Today, she saw a fresh and vital woman.

Making sure to take a house key, Lexie headed toward the beach. Once she reached the water, she had a choice of left towards Brighton, or right to St Kilda. Turning towards St Kilda felt *right*, Lexie began to jog towards the Sunday morning crowds.

The Esplanade Market would be on. Some of the people had been running the same stalls for years. About 150 local artisans offered their creations for sale. Lexie knew many to say hello to.

She jogged at a steady pace along Jacka Boulevard, past Luna Park where the rides were already running—screams of joy and terror came from the roller coaster. Past the Palace and the Palais, venues Lexie had been to on many occasions for concerts over the years. She felt a sense of contentment and belonging. She was home now. As the foot traffic was increasing, Lexie had to slow her pace. Even though the day was cold, it was sunny. Melburnians always came out in droves when the sun shone over their city.

Lexie did a quick jump over a stray dog that had run onto the footpath. She looked up as she righted herself, recognising the fellow jogger coming towards her. She saw straight away the recognition on his face.

They stopped when they reached each other.

'Here's trouble!' Wil said to her, a smile beaming across his face.

THE END

About The Author

Susan Godenzi is an Australian writer, living in country Victoria with her husband. *DEAD GUILTY* is the first in the series of Lexie Reed Mysteries.

If you want to know more details about the why Eddie murdered Sonja, or what was going on at Madame Lourdes' that had the AFP stop Wil and his team from entering the brothel - you'll have to read Book 2. Susan is busy writing *DEAD CERTAIN*.

If you want to read a sneak peak (soon to be added), or know the publication date, hop on over to her website.

www.susangodenzi.com

Check out Susan on Facebook: https://www.facebook.com/SusanGodenzi.Writer

Feel free to drop Susan an email: susangodenzi@gmail.com

And lastly, you can find & follow Susan on Twitter @susangodenzi

www.ingramcontent.com/pod-product-compliance
Lightning Source LLC
Chambersburg PA
CBHW021309250626
47155CB00002B/449